THE
SECRECY

Dr. Yang, Jwing-Ming

Cover by Axie Breen

I would like to dedicate this novel to Mr. Tony Chee, a Good Friend for a lifetime

ACKNOWLEDGMENTS

First, I would like to thank Erik Elsemans for his help with recent Russian history. I would also like to express my appreciation to Tony Chee, Pedro Rodrigues, Robert Was, Dawid Graczyk, Marek Czuppynski, and Daniel Spiridenkov in supplying crucial information related to this novel. Deep appreciation also goes to Jeff Pratt who has offered me many good suggestions.

My deepest appreciation towards, Elias Kopsiaftis, David Silver, and Joel Pittawau for their preliminary editing. They have put so much effort into editing this novel. Naturally, I would also like to thank Vitaly Pirotsky who helped me with the Russian language in the text. Finally, I would also like to thank Nancy J. Hauser and James Norman for final editing of this novel.

FORWARD
JIM O'LEARY

Dr. Yang has been my friend and teacher for more than twenty years. In that time, we have shared the goodness of truth and learning, and the harsh realities of struggle for identity, in a world that frowns on nonconformity. Throughout all the years, Dr. Yang has shown by his example that such struggles need not devolve into self-pity, but can instead be a source of energy and focus.

In this his first work of fiction, Dr. Yang has provided a modern story of friendship, desire, loyalty, shame, and finally liberation. It is both revealing and challenging in parts. Many who are familiar with Dr. Yang's other works will no doubt share my sense of surprise at some of the elements of the story. But the overall message is one of tolerance, respect and compassion. It is laced through with a subtle message of self-conquest, and the small, day-to-day things that we can do for ourselves to help us master our inner conflicts.

Those who are close to Dr. Yang sometimes joke that it is like being friends with Beethoven, or Darwin - deeply rewarding and profoundly enriching, but not for the lazy, and not for those who want all their answers to be easy, neat and tidy. As Keats said, the true measure of a person is their ability to exist *between* certainties. This is the example, and the summons, that Dr. Yang has given to us all.

PREFACE

I have always wanted to write a story that could touch and inspire the readers' hearts and help them to open their minds. I feel that such a story must discuss an extraordinary, unexpected event and, yet, reflect the true cruelty of the real world.

Often, we forget or ignore our true selves, our deep and truthful inner self-feeling, and we surrender to the bondage of blindly following tradition and religious doctrines. In this emotional human world, or matrix, we are constantly brainwashed by traditional beliefs and taught to deny our true identity. Very few dare to challenge these old traditions and doctrines, and often these few are pushed away from society.

This novel is based on true events that were happening a few years before the end of the cold war. Though the persons and story are fictionalized, it reflects the reality of the time. Through this novel, I hope to demonstrate to readers how deeply most of us are trapped "in the matrix," blindly following what we are told. I hope this book helps the readers to open their minds and to become more aware and respectful of their own true nature.

Since the last century, we have gradually broken free of the bondage and political abuse of our government, dictators, and spiritual leaders. However, we are still in the trap of spiritual bondage that continues to lead us into constant conflicts and wars worldwide, now and in the future.

In this world, even truthful, righteous persons can be compromised by allowing themselves to stay within this matrix, and by playing along with the scene around them even when they disagree with the actions or morals of those they encounter. **I believe the 21st century is the century of spiritual freedom.** We should face and confront this spiritual bondage which has enslaved us, and which keeps us from deeper self-knowledge and realization. The main goal of this century should be the freedom of spiritual development through the open expression of true inner feelings. If we are unable to achieve this goal, then human mutual conflicts and wars will not have an end.

Dr. Yang, Jwing-Ming
September 28, 2006
Liverpool, England

1
EDUCATION

As he sat on his British Airways flight from London to Moscow, Andrew's feelings were a confusing mixture of excitement and loss. He was excited to start his new job in Moscow, a job in a country that he had been hoping almost his entire life to someday be able to explore. At the same time, he was miserable to be leaving behind Judy, the girl he had fallen in love with, as well as his father and brother with whom he was very close. As Andrew's thoughts turned to his father and brother, he remembered the day of his high school graduation. It had been a glorious day of basking in achievements and honors that had made his family proud to claim him as their own. His father's shining face still hung in his mind....

Glorious Day

The morning of Saturday, June 19, 1976, was sunny and hot. In the town of Richmond, Virginia, people had gathered to participate in Andrew's high school's graduation ceremony. Andrew's school, the Governor's School for the Gifted, was a relatively new school, established by Governor Linwood Holton in 1973. It was a school designed to provide the most academically and artistically challenging programs to some of the state's most talented students, offering courses that were advanced well beyond anything offered in the public schools. Many of the graduates that day had been raised by military parents, in families with a legacy of patriotic service to their country. Graduates were often recruited into the government's special training programs and many of them would go on to serve in the American intelligence services, or in the military's high technology research group for weaponry. Those not recruited would most likely enter military schools and continue the family tradition of service in that way or attend universities to further their education. It was a high honor to be chosen for recruitment, one that brought glory to the family and to the student himself.

Commencement was carried out on the school lawn. Though the day was a bit too hot, the enthusiasm of the crowd remained high. Parents proudly wore their military uniforms, identifying the units they served in, their ranking, and awards received in the past. They were proud of their service to their country, and even more proud to witness their son's or daughter's graduation. Most of them had traveled considerable distances to be there. Most of them were from out of state. The Governor's School was a boarding school, and all of the students were required to live in a dormitory on campus.

Andrew P. Steinberg had just turned 18 years old a few days ago. He had grown to be a very good-looking young man, nearly six feet tall with unusual, attractive eyes of a mixed green-blue color. He was a confident young man who always trusted himself, the kind of person that believed he could accomplish anything he wished to as long as he applied himself.

Andrew came by his self-confidence and proactive approach to life honestly. His grandfather, Ramel S. Steinberg, was a Russian Jew who had led his wife and two children to escape from Moscow at the beginning of WWII in 1939. At that time, Andrew's father was only 17 years old and his father's sister only 14. His grandfather had been afraid that if they didn't leave Russia, his son would be drafted into a war against Germany within a year. He seriously believed that sooner or later the war would come to Russia and cause problems for their

Jewish community. Ramel had never liked Communist society, especially the dictatorship of Joseph Stalin. He spent a fortune bribing a high-ranking Communist officer to arrange safe passage for his family to Italy and then later to immigrate to America. When he did it, Andrew's grandmother was very upset and was against his grandfather's decision since she loved Russia so much. However, during the middle of the war when the Nazi Party in Germany began to imprison and kill Jews, she became convinced that her husband had been right. Her husband's actions most likely saved the lives of the entire family. Due to his family's history, Andrew was acquainted with the Russian language and also the culture. When they were small, he and his brother always loved his grandmother's Russian folk stories and tales of Russian history. Andrew's grandfather died in 1965 due to a heart attack and his grandmother passed away three years ago at the age of 78.

When Andrew was in primary school, he was already demonstrating an extraordinary IQ. He could learn faster than most of the students and had a nearly photographic memory. Whenever he read or saw something, he was able to remember it instantly and accurately, and it would stay in his memory for a long time. Though he was encouraged to skip grades by his schoolteachers several times, his father insisted that he should stay with his classmates so that he would have the benefit of their companionship, and not have the feeling of being isolated from them.

It was exhilarating for Andrew to enter the Governor's School for the Gifted, where he was challenged and encouraged to learn by the in-depth curriculum. He had been excited to be learning and competing with other talented students. Even so, he still always stayed at the top of his class. Andrew's father, like his father before him, had raised his sons in the traditional military family way: with good discipline and a strong sense of patriotism.

Also, just like his father when he was young, Andrew loved swimming, climbing mountains, scuba diving, parachuting, and all challenging and stimulating sports. For this reason, he had a perfectly tuned physique that made most of his male classmates jealous. He had represented his school and won two gold medals in the national high school swimming championship. Many a girl believed that if she were able to attract his attention and become his girlfriend, she would be the luckiest one in the whole school.

When Andrew was 17, a few weeks after his mother's funeral, he became acquainted with Cindy F. Brown, a girl who had just transferred from a high school in California. Cindy was a great comfort to him at that sorrowful time and they fell in love very quickly. They went out for movies, swimming, and camping and hiking in the mountains.

Cindy Brown, the only daughter of a retired army general, was a beautiful girl. Though she was only 15 years old and had just started her first year of high school, she was very mature for her age, both mentally and physically. She had a beautiful and compassionate face with a pair of deep blue eyes and brown hair. Andrew first noticed her when he was swimming in the campus pool. Actually, Andrew's good looks and well-developed body had also attracted Cindy's attention her first time swimming in the pool. Their mutual admiration drew them together, and they got acquainted very fast. Though at the time of Andrew's graduation they had known each other only one year, and despite their young age, they both believed they were well and truly in love.

During the graduation ceremony, Andrew's father, brother, and Cindy were sitting in the first row, the seating area reserved for families and friends of the top ten students out of the 378 graduates. Andrew was, of course, in the honored Top Ten. Though the ceremony was short, everyone's emotions ran very high. After the ceremony, they went to the reception area for refreshments and photographs.

"Andrew, I am so very, very proud of you. You made it into the training program! I knew you would. One of only three in your class that have been selected," Andrew's father, Richard, pronounced with great satisfaction.

Richard T. Steinberg was standing next to his son wearing his navy commander's uniform. Though he was already retired, he saw this as an entirely appropriate occasion for him to wear his uniform. He had been visited by a government recruiting agent just three weeks ago and asked for his opinion about Andrew joining the government's special training program. Naturally, he had been delighted and had encouraged Andrew to accept the offer. This would be an exceptional opportunity that would ultimately lead to an exciting and challenging job in the future. Andrew personally believed that he would not be happy if he worked at some other job, doing anything aside from serving his country as his father had.

Andrew's father had joined the U.S. Navy at the age of 19. He had remained in the service until his wife passed away a year ago. When Nancy, his wife, passed away from cancer, he retired from the service and concentrated his efforts on taking care of and educating his two sons. His younger son, Peter, was 14 years old.

Peter had just finished his first year of middle high school. He was mature for his age, although shy and somewhat naïve. He also was a very good-looking young man. Though he did not have as much confidence as Andrew, he had already demonstrated his talent and potential. He was a little bit shorter than Andrew, but both Andrew and his father believed he would be the tallest person in the family in just a couple more years. He loved to play basketball and was very good at it. To him, his father and Andrew were his role models. He looked up to them and wanted to follow in their footsteps.

"Mom, I wish you were still alive and here with us today," thought Andrew. He missed his mother very much. Especially today, when he could stand with honor and pride as all of his efforts and accomplishments at school were publicly acknowledged.

"Hey, Andrew. Richard. Congratulations!" A family friend, Steve Hickly said. Mr. Hickly was there with his wife, Katherine, to participate in his only son's graduation as well. Andrew could see their son, Brian, over talking to his friends.

"Steve, Katherine," Richard nodded to them with a smile. "It's great to see you here. Congratulations to you, too. Our kids are not kids anymore. They've grown up. We're getting old, Steve."

Steve was also a military man. Richard and Steve had gotten acquainted during a school parents meeting and discovered that their families lived in the same town, Winchester, Virginia. They hit it off immediately since both of them were soldiers, and the two families had been friends since their sons' freshman year. They often went on picnics together, especially before Richard's wife, Nancy, passed away. After that, Richard lost the desire to be involved in social activities.

"Do you know what Brian will do after his graduation?" Richard asked.

"He was accepted to the University of California, Berkeley. He's been headed for computer science since he was ten years old," Steve responded.

While they were talking, Brian walked up. "Hi everyone," he smiled at the group.

"We were just talking about you, Brian," Richard said.

"Hope it's about the good side of me instead of the bad side," Brian laughed and said.

"We were talking about your future in computer engineering," Steve said. He felt very proud of his son.

"What has Andrew decided? Which university will he be in?" Mrs. Hickly asked.

"Actually, Mom, Andrew is going into the special training program to be a spy or something," Brian said.

"Well, he must be even more exceptional than he seems," Mrs. Hickly said.

"Mom, he's Superman. He learns fast and knows everything," Brian replied. "And, he's always right. Everyone in school knows Andrew. He's got all the good looks and he's brilliant." To himself

Brian thought, with some envy, "and he has the body of every girl's dreams." Brian was a skinny boy, only 5 feet 6, who wore glasses. Compared to Andrew, he had no chance of competing with him, especially to earn the hearts of the girls. He remembered whenever Andrew went to swim, dozens of girls would suddenly decide to go swim as well.

"What do you think, Andrew? Are you happy to have been chosen?" Steve Hickly asked.

"I believe that if a life has no challenges, then it is a meaningless life. I can serve America better doing this than if I go to a regular university," Andrew answered.

Andrew thought about how his father always told him and his brother to be loyal to their country, and to stand up for democratic ideals for the whole world.

"Be brave and be strong. Never show others that you are a coward," his father's voice was continually ringing in his and his brother's ears.

After they chatted for a while, Mr. Hickly's family went to greet other friends.

"Dad, what if they choose me to become an FBI or CIA agent?" Andrew asked. He looked at his dad and then at Cindy. He knew that once he accepted the offer, then his life would be very different from normal lives.

"Andrew, you're a grown man now. You must make these decisions by yourself. I respect your judgment. It's time now to learn how to take care of yourself."

Special Program Training Center

Andrew soon discovered that the training subjects and goals of the special training center were very different from the usual college or university curriculum. It was a professional military academy that specialized in training students to be government workers and military scientific researchers. In the first two years, almost everyone had the same required courses except music, arts, sports, language, horseback riding, and other elective topics that were considered not-crucial for a future in service to the country. The required courses were mathematics, physics, mechanics, electrical engineering, world history and American history, etc. In the third and the fourth year, students were divided according to their expertise and interest. While in a fashion you were allowed to choose your own path, at the same time you were often required to conform to whatever the government's needs were at that time. In the first two years, other than the required courses, Andrew also chose Russian language since he had some knowledge of it from the time he spent with his grandmother. In addition, he was hoping to gain a better understanding of Russian culture. He had inherited a love of the Russian performing arts, ballet and opera, from his grandmother and also from his father.

The training center demanded a high level of patriotic dedication and discipline. Each student was closely monitored for his or her talent and potential for future development. From observing the students over the first two years, school officials were able see how each student would fit in and serve their country most effectively.

Since Andrew's IQ was very high and his body strong and fit, one morning near the end of his second year he received a message that the school principal, General Morgan, would like to see him. Andrew made his way to the school office, where the general's secretary showed him to the general's office. Andrew knocked on the door and, when he heard a response from inside, entered.

"Good morning, General Morgan, I received a message that you wanted to talk to me," Andrew said.

"Yes, Mr. Steinberg. Please sit down."

Andrew sat on the chair in front of General Morgan's desk. He looked at the general with curious eyes.

"From your school records, I can see your performance in the last two years here has been excellent. The government really needs people like you. I wonder if you've decided what you want to do with your future."

"No, sir, I am still thinking about it. I would like to have a future which would offer me an opportunity to understand my life better and that also gives me a challenge."

"You know you have a very high IQ and are obviously very physically fit. I would like to recommend you to be accepted into some special intelligence training for the next two years. What would you think of that? After two years, you would serve your country as an intelligence agent."

"That would be a great opportunity for me, but... please allow me to think about it for a couple of days. I should be able to give you an answer then."

"Okay. Please report to me in two days."

When Andrew left General Morgan's office he had a strange feeling that, in one way he would like to be chosen as a secret agent since it would be a great honor and his life would be very challenging and exciting. But in another way, he was very concerned about how it would impact the personal side of his life. It would be a secret life, and different from others, and he would not be able to confide in those he was close to.

That evening, Andrew called his father at home.

"Dad, I talked to General Morgan this morning. He recommended that I enter the intelligence training program for the next two years. I'm just wondering what you think? You've always given me good advice."

"Well son, first you must understand that your life will follow a path that will be very dissimilar from anyone else you know. You will be in unique situations and you will not be able to share those experiences with anyone. Second, you must realize that your freedom will be greatly restricted by the nature of your job, and out of necessity for the security of our nation. Having said that, it is a very great honor to be able to serve your country," Andrew's father counseled.

"What happens if I don't like it in the future?"

"I believe that the government will allow you to switch to other government jobs," his father reassured him.

It seemed to Andrew that his father was encouraging him to accept the general's recommendation.

Andrew mulled it over during the night. He had been flattered to receive the offer - after all, there were not too many people who were qualified to accept it. Also, his eventual career as an intelligence agent would not only be a challenge, but it would also be the patriotic thing to do. Having made this decision, he finally went to sleep.

The next morning Andrew went back to the general's office. "Good morning, General Morgan," he greeted him. "After I talked to my father and thought it over myself, I have decided to accept your recommendation."

The general was delighted to hear this. "My secretary will arrange everything for you. The training center is not here. It is in a secret location that is unknown to most people. You'll receive a package within the next few days that will tell you what to do. Please keep everything confidential from now on, including your choice in this special training."

"Yes, sir. I understand."

A couple of days later Andrew received a phone call from Cindy. He was very excited to hear from her. "Cindy, I haven't seen you in such a long time. I miss you so much," he told her.

There was a pause for a few seconds before Cindy replied, "I miss you too. I was calling to let you know that I've been accepted at the University of Maryland."

"Wow, that's great! We should celebrate!"

There was another pause. Finally, Cindy said, "Well, actually, the real reason I called is to tell you that I have a new boyfriend. I hope you aren't too upset."

"What? How did that happen? Please tell me." Andrew was

stunned and disappointed.

"Well, I went to Maryland for orientation at the University two weeks ago. While I was there I met a sophomore student who was one of the volunteers who were helping us. I like him very much and he really likes me. But I also don't want to hurt your feelings."

Though the news was somewhat shocking to Andrew, he slowly realized that he wasn't really all that upset. Actually, he thought, when they were in love in high school, they were still pretty young. They didn't even know what love was yet. The more he thought about it, the more he came to feel happy for Cindy. As a matter of fact, he decided, he didn't mind that much at all. They were different people now and had different dreams about what to do with their lives. Plus, now that he had been accepted into the special intelligence training program he knew his life would be taking a very unusual turn. He was not sure his secret life would bring them happiness. Besides, for the last couple of years he had treated Cindy more like a sister than like a girlfriend. Going to school in places that were so far apart, they had seldom seen each other. Yes, this would be all right. Cindy would have her new boyfriend, and he would be free to pursue this new path.

Intelligence Training

In September of 1978, Andrew reported to an intelligence-training center that was unknown to outside people. The identities of all of the students were locked in a computer file. Anyone who wanted to access this file had to be authorized. Without a special access code, this file couldn't be opened. The system was set up to protect the identities of all possible future intelligence agents.

During the next two years, all participants would undergo six months of very strict military training and disciplines. After that, they would train at a variety of other skills such as skiing, shooting, quick memorization, swimming, parachuting, surviving in the wild, and self-defense mixed with Karate, Kung Fu, kick-boxing and wrestling.

They would also undergo training designed to finely hone their alertness and awareness. All of these special skills could be needed in the future, and the students applied themselves knowing it might mean the difference between the success or failure of a mission.

Now life was exciting and fun. Andrew was 20 years old, was benefiting from the most expensive training and most incredible experience one could ever receive, and he didn't have to pay a penny for it. He enjoyed the training very much.

The students were given two months of summer vacation each year to spend with their families and friends. When summer time came, Andrew went to Virginia Beach with his three best friends, Paul Rosen, Jeff Willis, and Michael Graczyk. They had gotten to know each other when they were all attending the special program training center. Among the four of them, only Andrew and Michael had been chosen for the intelligence agent training. In fact, Michael was being trained in a completely different location from Andrew. Though they each knew the other was in training, due to the strictures of secrecy placed on them they seldom talked about it.

The four friends loved swimming in the ocean, and during their outings to the beach their companionship and friendship grew. They went to the beach as many times as they could during the two summers. When they were there, they often competed with each other to see who was able to swim farthest from the shore. Andrew won most of the time since he began his swim training when he was very young. Aside from Michael, who managed to win three out of eight times, there was no match from Paul and Jeff.

One of the times Andrew lost to Michael was due to a leg cramp. To keep themselves safe, they always brought two life-saving tubes with them in case of an injury or cramping when they were far from the shore. They took turns carrying the lifesavers, but most of the time Paul and Jeff kept them since their endurance was not as good as Andrew and Michael.

Two years passed quickly, and Andrew soon completed his

training. At 22 years of age, he had already learned many survival and defensive skills that most people his age would never learn. He was a grown man, handsome and with an ever more powerful and agile body. Now he knew he must face the real challenge of being an active intelligence agent. He was excited, and somewhat nervous.

There would be no graduation ceremony or big celebration from this training center as there had been from his high school four years ago. Since this was a secret training center, and their identities must be protected, there was only one short speech given by General Morgan about patriotism and loyalty to the country. There were just 16 who graduated in Andrew's group.

After graduation, everyone was given a three-month vacation before they would receive their first formal assignment, although their vacation could be interrupted if an emergency mission arose. Usually, these missions were short and would not take too much of the vacation time.

Andrew was happy and excited that he might soon be called to take part in a real action and challenge, while at the same time he wanted to be with his brother and father as much as possible. He also wanted more time with his old friends, talking about life and going to the beach. His brother Peter had grown into a good-looking young man, with a naïve and innocent face, although he was still slightly shorter than Andrew. Peter had been accepted by Purdue University to study physics, a passionate interest of his.

After six weeks of vacation, Andrew received a call from CIA authority,

"Number 11, you have been activated for a short mission. You will report to CIA headquarters, room 135, for details this coming Wednesday morning at 9 o'clock."

"Yes, sir, I will do so," Andrew replied.

Andrew was a little bit disappointed since he already had plans to meet his friends on Wednesday. But along with the disappointment he was exhilarated at the thought of going on his first mission. This was a chance to prove his skills and to do what he had trained for.

The First Mission

"Gentlemen, I am Colonel Anderson. I will be your leader for this mission," the colonel introduced himself, surveying the four agents who had just reported for duty. Surprisingly, the four had never met each other before though they had all come from the special training centers and were all young men around the same age: 22 to 24 years old.

"Remember, everything we talk about and do is to be kept secret from this moment on. You can never tell anyone about this." Colonel Anderson looked each of them intently in the face. When he was certain they understood, he handed each a large envelope.

"After the briefing, study the information in the envelope very carefully. When you are finished, burn the envelope and its contents completely."

Colonel Anderson moved to a slide projector on a table and turned it on. The room light was turned off. On the screen, three faces appeared.

"Here is the situation. If you have never paid attention or you don't know, please be aware that there is a new powerful Mexican drug organization, Cártel de Guadalajara, established by Rafael Caro Quintero, Miguel Ángel Félix Gallardo, and Ernesto Fonseca Carrillo. This organization has developed and enlarged their territories amazingly fast in just a few months. A close follower of these three drug lords, named Jose Rodríguez Hernández, contacted us about cooperating with the CIA to break this new organization down. However, before we were able to get him out of Mexico safely, he was discovered and made a prisoner. He is now being held in some specific location waiting to stand trial for his betrayal. We have two or three days at the most to rescue him before he will be killed if we still want to break down this new organization." The colonel paused to pick up a glass of water and take a sip.

"The location is in the northern mountain area near Chihuahua." Colonel Anderson moved to the next slide, a map of northern Mexico. He used a pointer to show the location on the map.

"As we know from the intelligence that we've received, Hernández was being held in a big building on the hill near Chihuahua. Our mission is to mount a surprise attack on the building and bring Hernández back to United States. Any questions so far?" the colonel asked.

"Do we have a photo of Hernández? How will we recognize him?" one of the agents asked.

"No, we don't have his photo. However, as we know he was the only one held in this building, we should be able to identify him easily," Colonel Anderson answered.

"How much chance do we have of being successful, Colonel Anderson?" another agent asked, showing some nervous tension, concern, and excitement.

"Well, we don't think they expect our visit. I believe they will not have heavy guards. With five of us, if we do it right, we should be able to accomplish this mission smoothly." The colonel smiled with confidence and tried to ease the tension in the room.

"A small helicopter will take us to a nearby area. After that, we have to walk at least an hour to reach the hill. Once we have accomplished our mission, we will contact the pilot of the helicopter and he will pick us up directly on the building. We have to get in quietly and get out quickly," the colonel continued.

Though they still had some questions and didn't know the situation clearly, the four new agents did not ask very much. They just waited for the opportunity to read the information in their envelopes.

"You should not reveal each other's identity. Just use the numbers you are assigned." He pointed at himself, "I am number 21. You will be numbers 22, and then 23, 24, and 25. Just call each other by number. See you tonight at Langley Air Force Base. Report to General Smith's secretary punctually at 1900 hours."

Andrew was the last one, number 25. He knew the number designation was necessary just in case they were caught. He knew it was essential they not reveal each other's personal information.

A Surprise

It would take nearly six hours from Langley Air Force Base to reach their final destination in Chihuahua. In the helicopter, Colonel Anderson distributed a machine gun, a pistol and ammunition to each person. All of them recognized that this was a real situation and not just a practice drill. They were quiet, not knowing what would happen to them in the next ten hours. When Andrew thought of the whole thing, his imagination ran ahead of him. "Will I be injured or killed? Will they leave me behind if I am injured? What might happen if I get caught? Can I face death without fear?" As he thought of this, a cold sweat broke out with goose bumps on his skin. He believed the others, except possibly the colonel, probably had the same feeling.

"It might be better if I take a nap. It will be a long night," Andrew thought and tried to get some sleep. It took him at least two hours of struggling but finally he was so tired that he did fall asleep.

To avoid being spotted by Mexican security, the helicopter flew only a couple hundred feet above the ground, the pilot skillfully manipulating the aircraft in the darkness. When the pilot's voice came over the intercom to announce they were only 15 minutes from the landing site, Andrew woke up. His tension immediately resumed.

As soon as the helicopter had landed the pilot turned the engine off and kept quiet. Everyone got out quickly and turned on the lights they wore on their heads.

"It will be about one-hour walking from here. Please keep as quiet as possible," Colonel Anderson said.

With the aid of his military GPS, the colonel knew exactly where they were and where they should go. They all kept quiet and kept walking with their backpacks of emergency equipment and their weapons. After a half hour of constant quick walking, they stopped for five minutes to eat something and have a drink of water.

"Gentlemen, turn off your lights," said the colonel. "Our target will be only about 20 minutes from here. You will be able to see the building on the hill in ten minutes. When we are within about 100 yards you must keep a lookout for cameras. I believe there will be cameras everywhere. Numbers 22, 23, and 24, once we get into the building, immediately check every room to see if anyone is inside. To protect ourselves don't hesitate to kill anyone you encounter. Number 25, once we are in, your job is to find the video monitoring room and kill everyone inside. To avoid the sound of gunfire and alarm others, make sure you use your silencer. We must be as quiet as possible. Now black your faces and any other areas where your skin is exposed." The colonel put some black dye on his face as well as on his hands. When everyone was ready, they continued walking with a faster pace. Everyone's heartbeat picked up.

Soon they came in sight of the building on the hill. They slowed down and spread out from each other, keeping about 20 yards apart. When the colonel spotted the first video camera up in a tree, he signaled to everyone to avoid the area the camera covered. It was a slow process since they had to be careful not to be spotted by cameras that they could barely see, especially in the darkness with only a very weak light from the moon and stars.

Everything was going smoothly when they reached the main door. Surprisingly, they did not find any guards around. It was nearly 3 a.m. and they supposed everyone inside must be in a deep sleep. As Colonel Anderson had said, the enemies were not expecting any attack from the outside world in this remote place.

The colonel opened the door carefully and crept in. Seeing his signal that it was okay to proceed, the rest of the agents followed him. There were about five rooms on the first floor. The most important thing was to remove the guards monitoring the video screen. But where was that room? Based on his experience and intuition, the colonel pointed out a corner room to Andrew. He knew a room for monitoring the cameras should be a room that could also see outside through windows.

Following his instruction, Andrew opened the door quietly and peered into the room. He was amazed to find that the colonel was right. But after all, the colonel did have more experience than any of them. As Andrew looked in, he saw one guy falling asleep on a chair, while another was listening to some music with earphones on and paying only occasional attention to the screen in front of him.

Andrew knew he was supposed to kill the sleeping man and his partner, but after hesitating just a bit, he instead struck the guy wearing earphones with the stock of his machine gun, knocking him out. Then he quickly spun around and used the edge of his hand to deliver a chop to the back of the sleeper's neck to make sure he would not wake up any time soon.

Andrew left the monitor room and rejoined the team, which was just finishing checking the upstairs. The team did not find Hernandez or anyone else. The only place left to look was the basement. They entered the basement quietly and, coming from the last room at the end of the hallway, they heard a moaning sound. Upon hearing the sound they believed they had found where Hernandez was being held. Excited and anticipating the successful end of their mission, the team walked toward the room quickly. When they entered, however, there was another room beyond it and the moaning sound was coming from that room. This time, though, when they all stepped into the next room a loud clanging sound stunned everyone as strong metal bars dropped down, sealing all of the doors. They had entered a trap. Some spot lights were turned on, aimed right into their eyes. The lights almost blinded all of them.

"Ha-ha-ha! What do you know? We have caught five rabbits," a laughing voice called from the corner of the room. Without hesitation, Colonel Anderson fired his machine gun toward the sound, but just as quickly he was hit by a few shots from an opponent. The colonel was killed instantly, his body falling to the floor and his blood pooling around him.

The rest of the team froze in panic and shock. They did not know what to do next. It seemed the opponents had been expecting them. They had walked right into a trap.

"If you want to live, put down your guns, take your clothes off, and lie down on the floor with your hands behind your back. There are at least ten guns aimed at your heads," the voice said.

With the colonel lying dead in front of them, the team knew this was not a joke. These enemies meant to kill them if they did not do as they were told. And perhaps even if they did. It was well known that Mexican drug lords were cruel and cold blooded. Without options, the team followed the order. They put their guns on the floor, took off all of their clothes except their underwear, and one by one lay down on the floor.

"What are they going to do with us? How can this happen? I am only 22 years old," Andrew thought in a panic, his goose bumps breaking out with cold sweat.

One of the doors opened, admitting four guys who came and put handcuffs on the team.

"What are you going to do with us?" Number 23, the shortest one in the team, cried out with fear. He received no answer.

They were each taken away to different rooms. Andrew did not know what was happening to the others. However, he was bound with both wrists drawn tightly up above his head while his ankles were secured to two posts spaced widely apart. He could not go anywhere now. His captors left him hanging there for the rest of the night.

"I can't believe this is the end of my life, the end of the world." When he thought of this, Andrew's tears streamed down his face. He did not know what would happen to him next and was afraid to think about it.

Sometime during what Andrew thought must be the next morning, two Mexican guys came into his cell.

"Will you answer all my questions willingly or should I force you to talk?" the taller of the two said while smiling. Andrew could feel the guy was a sadist who would enjoy torturing him.

Though he was terrified, Andrew replied with silence.

When he did not get an answer, the tall Mexican took a knife out from his pocket and slowly cut off Andrew's T-shirt and underwear. In moments, Andrew was standing completely naked in front of them.

"What a pity! You have such a beautiful body. Unfortunately, it doesn't belong to you anymore. It's all mine. Understand? All mine," the tall Mexican taunted Andrew, showing his partner how he intended to manage the interrogation. "Again, will you tell me willingly or should I encourage you further?" he asked.

"I am an American citizen and my ID number is 223099. That's all I will tell you. Nothing else." Andrew looked at him with a flat expression. He knew if he begged, it would only provide his tormentors with more entertainment.

"Well, if that's what you want! Let me tell you what I will do to you. I am going to use this ping-pong paddle to spank you until bruises cover your entire body. I won't cut you open just yet. It would be less fun to fuck an imperfect body," the tall man laughed.

The tall Mexican gave the ping-pong paddle to his partner and instructed him to slap Andrew's body hard from his butt, down his thighs, and then his calves. Then he sat down on a chair in front of Andrew to watch the show.

At the first slap, Andrew did not make a sound. He felt that if he did, he would show them that he was a coward. By about the 30th hard blow, however, the pain had become unendurable. He could not help emitting a low moan at each slap. This made the tall guy very happy. He did enjoy the show. About a half hour later, he instructed the other guy to stop.

"We will take our time to torture him. Time is our friend, amigo."

The two Mexicans left the room. Andrew sighed with relief but, once again, he had been left in his hanging stance, this time with serious pain in his butt and legs. He did not know what had happened to the other three. Did they talk? Or did they continue to resist? He did not want to think about it. All he needed now was to rest after his beating. He was beginning to get weak with hunger and loss of sleep.

The next day, around what Andrew thought might be noontime, a man came in and fed him a couple pieces of bread. The man then gave him a drink of water and left. Both sadists from the previous day came back in the afternoon.

"Do you want to cooperate with us now, or should we torture you more?" the tall guy asked.

"I have nothing to tell you," Andrew answered with a weak voice. His body tensed up. He knew the consequences of refusing to talk. More torture was coming.

The men again used the ping-pong paddle to beat on Andrew's butt and legs. This brought back and enhanced the serious pain that had only partially receded from his body. After that, they cut into his body using horse spurs that were run along his torso, thighs, and calves. They alternated these two tortures for nearly 45 minutes.

Andrew continued to hold his tears, but the pain was so severe that he could not help his moaning and shouting. He could see the lower part of his body covered with marks and bruises.

"Will you cooperate now, or would you like to be tortured more tomorrow? If you don't cooperate by tomorrow, we will extend the torturing to your back and chest," the tall guy asked and laughed.

"Another day like this and I will be dead, especially without sleep," Andrew thought. "I don't know how long I will be able to hang on." Andrew was despondent and felt hopeless. However, he persisted in trying to remain stoic and not show his fear or distress to the enemies.

Next day saw the same routines repeated and, due to the old bruises and wounds, the pain was so intense as to bring Andrew to the edge of consciousness. As his torturers had said, they widened the areas they were beating to his back and upper chest. The pain was unendurable. Andrew felt so weak and tired that he thought he'd rather die now than bear any more. He regretted that he had accepted the CIA job. Now, he thought, it is time to die for my patriotism. But he was only 22 years old. He was too young to die.

After the two men had tortured him for nearly an hour, they left Andrew. Not only was his entire body aching, but his arms and legs were numb from being left too long hanging and tied up. He felt the situation was hopeless. His mind wandered, and he began to recall the good times he had had growing up. In his semi-conscious state, he did not know what was real and what was his imagination.

Rescue

Evening came again. Andrew was exhausted from his ordeal. Sleep deprivation and pain from his injuries had left him nearly comatose. He wished that he had never been born. He was barely aware when a series of gunshots sounded in the early morning, or, 20 minutes or so later, when he was untied from his hanging position and covered by a blanket. Two people carried him out of the building and put him into a helicopter. Through bleary, half-open eyes, he could see there were three others there as well. He did not care; all he wanted was to sleep.

Quite some time later Andrew was awakened by the familiar sounds of birds. He thought he was in a dream. When he opened his eyes, he saw he was lying in a hospital bed.

"What a nightmare I had! It was a dream. But it was so real. Where am I?" As he thought about this, he tried to get up and discovered that his entire body was in pain. When he took a look at the bruises that covered his legs and chest, he realized that it had not been a dream. It was real. "But how did I end up here?" he wondered in confusion.

Blurrily, he recalled hearing an extended period of shooting, then being wrapped in a blanket by a couple of people and carried out to a helicopter. After that, he could not remember anymore since he had passed out.

Looking up, Andrew saw a photo of President Ronald Reagan on the wall and realized that he was in U.S. military hospital. "We must have been rescued," he mused. "I thought we were dead for sure."

A slow smile emerged on Andrew's face. Looking at the clock on the wall, he saw it was 8:25 in the morning. He closed his eyes and began to trace back through everything that had happened during the last three days. He felt the fullness of how precious life is sink into him. He had been so close to the edge of death. After a while, his exhaustion overtook him once again, and he went back to sleep.

Around 10 a.m., a CIA officer came to visit him while he was eating breakfast. "Good morning, Lieutenant Steinberg. You look much better now than when you first arrived. How do you feel? I am Colonel Jones from the CIA office," the man introduced himself.

"Thank you, sir. I feel much better," Andrew answered.

"I know you must have many questions. I am here to answer them as best I can," the colonel said.

"How were we rescued? I thought we were dead for sure."

"When the helicopter pilot did not receive any request for picking you up, he knew the mission had failed. He contacted CIA headquarters and returned to the states. When the top authority heard of it, they realized they would have three days at most to rescue you guys before you might be killed. A rescue mission was planned, and a special unit ordered for this action."

"Everyone was saved?" Andrew asked.

"Except for Colonel Anderson, all four were saved. The other three encountered a similar fate as you. Luckily, they also survived."

"How about Jose Rodrìguez Hernández? Was he rescued?"

"No. He was removed from that location an hour before your attack. He was tortured to death the next day in front of other cartel members."

Andrew felt so sorry for Hernandez and the failure of the mission. "What was wrong? How could we enter that trap without any warning? We should not underestimate this Cártel de Guadalajara," he thought.

"What will happen to me next, sir?" Andrew asked aloud.

"You will finish your remaining vacation. Then you will receive an assignment for a steadier job. For the time being rest, get yourself recovered, and enjoy your vacation. You should know your assignment next week." With that, Colonel Jones left.

Andrew absorbed this information. "I believe I am to report for my new duty on October 1st, so I still have five weeks of vacation left."

A few days later, Andrew was released from the hospital and went home. Aside from some still fading bruises, he had almost completely recovered. Due to the secrecy of the mission, when his father and brother asked him about his bruises he explained them away as being from sparring training with friends. After a couple of weeks, even the bruises had disappeared. Due to the rigors of his experience on the mission, though his body had not changed much, mentally he had matured.

Andrew was assigned to work at the CIA headquarters in Langley, Virginia and was expected to report for duty on September 30th. A part of him was happy to be working so close to home – this way he could visit his father and brother easily. But another part of him was disappointed since working in Moscow was still his dream.

Andrew spent two days finding a nice comfortable apartment near CIA headquarters before September 30th, the day his new career, and new life, would start.

Job Assignment

Due to his high IQ and his enormous capacity for memorization, Andrew was assigned to be one of five key people responsible for international information data processing in the CIA. His main task was collecting information from CIA intelligence around the world. The information then had to be compiled, sorted, classified, and finally distributed to the relevant departments. This was a job crucial to the effective and efficient operation of the CIA. Though the job was very important to the entire CIA organization, it was not what Andrew looked for. The job was not as exciting as the field agent position he had hoped to have. He spent almost entire days sitting in the office. He missed outside activities and actions very much, though his experience in Mexico still made him feel uneasy and would occasionally trigger a cold sweat. After only one month at his new position, he was already familiar with all of the routines. Other than working, his only other activity was to go home to spend time with his father and brother.

Two weeks before Christmas, an exciting and joyful holiday atmosphere had already filled up the air. Though it was not a Jewish holiday, Andrew's spirit was lifted to see other people's happy faces.

One day during the lunch break, Andrew was sitting in the cafeteria having lunch with his officemate, Scott, who asked him, "What will you do for Christmas?"

"You know, I'm Jewish and we don't celebrate Christmas. We celebrate Hanukkah instead. I will probably just go home to see my family for the holiday," Andrew replied.

"Oh yes! I forgot you don't celebrate Christmas. But, if you're interested, I'm having a party at my house on Christmas evening and I'd like you to come. You'll have fun and it will be a chance for you to meet a lot of people." Scott looked at him sincerely.

"Well! I do need some break from the heavy work here. Okay. What time is the party and what's your address?"

"Seven p.m. Of course, you can come earlier. Actually, a few people will be coming early to help me set up."

"Great! How about if I come at six? Is that enough time? Should I bring anything?" Andrew laughed.

"Just bring beautiful girls. We always have more guys than girls. Here's the address." Scott tore a piece of paper from his notebook and wrote his address on it.

"But I don't even have a girlfriend myself! Scott, don't be kidding."

"Well, then it will be a good chance for you to find someone at the party. You're good looking. You're strong, you're smart. You should have no problem!" Scott joked with him.

"We'll see how my luck runs at the party," Andrew said with a wry smile.

Judy

It was around 6 p.m. on Christmas day when Andrew stood in front of the door for the address he had been given. He rang the bell, and, after just a moment, the door opened.

"Welcome, Andrew! Excellent timing! We were just in need of a strong guy like you to move furniture around. You know, all we have at the moment are mostly ladies," Scott joked.

"Here you are." Andrew gave Scott two bottles of a good red wine that he had spent some time picking out.

"Okay. Let's get drunk tonight," Scott replied, leading Andrew into the house.

When Andrew entered the kitchen, he discovered four ladies there preparing food. Among them was a young lady who looked to be in her mid-twenties. She was wearing a red dress and immediately caught Andrew's attention with her ice-blue eyes and blond hair. She was beautiful and, frankly, she was hot. When she noticed Andrew staring at her, she favored him with a wide grin.

"Hey there big guy. My name is Judy. What's yours?"

"Andrew. Ma'am," Andrew replied with a smile and extended his hand to shake hers.

"Wow!" he thought, "How soft her hands are!" He also noticed that she had all her nails colored a deep red. Andrew was just trying to think of something to say to get to know her better, when there was a shout from the living room.

"Andrew! I need you in here," Scott cried.

While Andrew was rearranging furniture with Scott, he could not stop thinking of the Judy he had just met. "What a beautiful lady! I wonder if she already has a boyfriend. Compared to Cindy, she is a red rose, hot and spicy, while Cindy was like a Calla Lily, pure and simple."

Andrew found an opportunity to chat again with Judy once the set-up was finished. Soon, guests would fill up the room and he wanted to take full advantage of this time alone with her. While they were talking, Andrew had the sensation that Judy was like a wild predator – and he was the prey. The idea left Andrew feeling challenged and a bit excited.

By 9 o'clock, the room was packed with people. The smell of smoke filled the home and a few guests were already drunk. Andrew and Judy were so interested in each other, they were together talking almost the entire time. By now, Judy had learned a lot about Andrew's background and Andrew thought he also had gotten a good idea about her.

Judy was about 5'7", a relatively tall girl compared with others. She knew she was attractive and was very proud of her beauty. She also enjoyed material luxury. To her, without money, there could be no love. Though she had a very good figure, the most attractive part of her was her ice-blue eyes... eyes that were like a pair of beautiful crystal swords that would prick deeply into your heart.

"Why don't we get out of here?" Judy suggested. "Too much smoke. I don't like the smell of smoke that sticks in your clothes for days."

"I'm thinking the same thing, but where can we go?" Andrew looked at her with a smile. He was thinking about taking her to his apartment so they could be alone.

"How about going to my place. It's only a few blocks away. As a matter of fact, I walked here, and it only took me 20 minutes," Judy said.

"Okay, but I have my car in front and I don't want to leave it here. Let's drive to your place," Andrew suggested.

They quickly said good-bye to Scott and left. Scott, who knew Judy well, understood the situation instantly. She had just broken up with her old boyfriend two months ago, but it seemed she had already caught her new victim tonight.

With Judy giving him directions, within five minutes Andrew's car was parked on the street in front of a beautiful, upscale apartment building. "The rent must be pretty expensive here. From her job as a secretary, how can she afford it?" Andrew wondered. "She must get a better pay check than I thought."

Judy removed a key from her purse and opened the main door of the building. As they entered the foyer and Judy led him up to the second floor, Andrew noticed marble floors covered with thick carpets and gilt mirrors tastefully set in amongst elaborate floral arrangements. It was a well-built and lavishly decorated building.

Judy used another key to open the door of her apartment, which also was beautifully designed, clean and luxurious. Andrew started wondering if he could afford her as a girlfriend. In front of Judy, Andrew felt small and conservative. Maybe even stingy.

"Would you mind sitting by yourself for a few minutes? I want to take a shower first. You know, I feel smelly after the party," Judy said.

"You go right ahead, I will enjoy myself. No problem!"

As Judy left to take her shower, Andrew wondered if this was a hint that Judy would like to have sex with him. The thought of it made him both excited and anxious. He waited and waited until nearly 50 minutes passed. Finally, Judy came into the living room wearing a revealing negligee. Now, everything was clear.

Judy handed a towel to Andrew saying, "You should take a shower too. You will feel better."

Andrew nodded his head, somewhat revealing his hidden emotion. This was obviously what Judy expected and wanted. She was sure of herself and pretty sure that she had snared a high-quality prey. When Andrew finished his shower, he came out again to the living room wearing a pair of men's pajama bottoms that he had found hanging in the bathroom. He didn't know to whom the pajamas belonged, or how they had come to be there. But he knew he was a bit jealous of whoever had worn them before.

"I found these in the bathroom. Is it okay that I'm wearing them?" Andrew asked as he entered the room. Judy was sitting on the couch. A bottle of champagne sat on the table in front of her.

"No, it's no problem! They're yours now. They belonged to my old boyfriend. They fit you perfectly, right? Both of you have the same height and a similar body type." Judy tossed her remarks off without a hint of emotion. Andrew chose to not ask any more about it. He did not want her thinking of her old boyfriend right now. He wanted her focused on the two of them tonight.

Judy poured a glass of champagne for Andrew and then one for herself. "Let's celebrate our acquaintance tonight!" she said and lifted up her glass.

"To our acquaintance and our future," Andrew said when his glass touched hers lightly.

The champagne went down easily. As they sat on the couch, Andrew appreciated the view of Judy's semi-exposed body, so beautiful and well taken care of. He could not help pulling her against his chest and gently kissing her. Judy had been waiting for him to make a move. She believed that she had conquered him.

After only 15 minutes of kisses, caresses and gentle biting they had shed their clothes and were looking at each other's bodies with building excitement. Judy now had an unhindered view of Andrew's entire perfectly tuned, mouth-watering physique.

"I wish I had found him before, such a rare specimen, yummy and juicy," Judy thought.

Judy took Andrew's hand and led him to her bedroom. Andrew allowed himself to be led as a slave might follow his master. This dynamic held as it quickly became apparent that Judy had had much more experience, and was much more skilled, in sex. Andrew felt like a student learning advanced sexual techniques. Judy played with him like he was a new toy.

An hour later, Andrew felt like he was in heaven. He thought he could live this way, every day, forever. Exhausted and satisfied, they fell asleep. When they woke up, it was already 9 in the morning. Fortunately, they did not have to get up early since it was Sunday.

After breakfast they went to a nearby park, walking and talking like a couple of young lovers. Gradually Andrew discovered that Judy's tastes and preferences were very different from his. He liked classic music while Judy liked loud rock music. He liked sports, especially swimming and basketball, while Judy liked to watch fashion shows with half naked women and men. Furthermore, Andrew was conservative financially while Judy liked to spend money. He had a lot of questions, but for the moment he did not care. He was in heaven.

As Andrew and Judy became acquainted, Andrew began spending less and less time going home to see his father and brother. They knew that he had a new girlfriend and they were happy for him. But still, they missed him. Soon, in addition to weekends, Andrew was also spending a couple nights during the week at Judy's place. He felt uncomfortable inviting Judy to his apartment, which was poor and awkward compared to hers.

Sometimes during their sex play, Judy would tie Andrew naked to the bed and then whip him with a short whip. After that, Judy would have sex with Andrew while he was completely helpless. Although this heightened the level of sensation for Andrew, it seemed the bondage excited and satisfied Judy more than it did him. For Judy, she was a master who dominated her slave. But for Andrew, whenever he was tied up and whipped it reminded him of his capture and torture just a few months ago in Mexico.

Andrew sometimes missed his old friends and their swimming outings, but he knew those days were in the past. Their lives were different now. Michael, after graduating from the special training center, had found a girl who had just immigrated to the U.S. from Russia. After dating for a year, they had fallen in love and married. Now Michael was working at the American Consulate in Leningrad,

Russia. Jeff and Paul also left Virginia and had their own lives now. Time seemed to just fly by. Before he knew it, five months had passed since Andrew had met Judy.

Memorial Day

On Sunday, May 17th of 1981, when they woke up in the morning Andrew said, "Judy, I need to go home next weekend for Memorial Day. You know, Monday, May 25th. It's a long holiday weekend. My family wants to see me, and I miss them too. Actually, it has been our tradition to visit my family's tomb on Memorial Day each year."

"I was hoping we could be together next weekend." Judy looked at Andrew with a disappointed expression.

"Well, why don't you come with me? I would like you to meet my family, and I believe they would also like to meet you. You know, we've known each other for nearly six months. My dad and my brother will be very happy to get to know you."

"Well, it's not quite what I expected." However, Judy knew that if she insisted on having her way it would lead to a fight where Andrew would feel he had to choose between his family and her, and she didn't think she could win that fight. She paused for a moment, then agreed, "Okay, I'll go with you. But remember, you owe me one."

Andrew was happy that Judy wanted to go with him. When he went back to his apartment he called his father right away to tell him he would be bringing his girlfriend home for Memorial Day.

Friday afternoon, Andrew came to Judy's office to pick her up, then drove her back to her apartment to pack a few things.

"I'm sorry to take you away from your family on this holiday weekend, Judy."

"Don't be silly," Judy replied. "I seldom visit my family anyway. I like to have my freedom. You know, family is a trap and bondage. Family controls you too much."

Andrew didn't continue the conversation. That was not how he experienced his family, but he could sense that Judy simply did not get along with hers.

It took them less than two hours to drive from Langley to Winchester. Andrew was happy to be back in his hometown. He felt sorry that since he had started dating Judy, he seldom found time to come back to visit his father and brother.

When they arrived, Andrew was excited to introduce Judy to his family. That evening, Judy stayed in a guest room. Andrew's father was a little old fashioned and believed in doing things the traditional way. He felt it more appropriate for Judy to sleep in the guest room. Besides, there was only a single bed in Andrew's old room. The house was not big, and the rooms were small. Andrew could sense that Judy had a hard time getting used to this new environment and he tried his best to make her happy. Saturday morning, Andrew took Judy out to show her the town and also some old civil war battlefields. He explained the history of the area to her. But she was not very enthusiastic and seemed to not be listening.

The family had a cook out party Saturday afternoon and a few neighbors were invited over. Andrew's father noticed that Judy stayed close to Andrew as much as possible the entire time. She only spent time speaking with others when it was absolutely necessary. It seemed like she wasn't able to mix easily with these good people. Actually, it seemed like she didn't really care to try. The party finished around 9 that evening with a home movie.

Sunday morning Andrew told his father that he would like to take Judy to see the famous Luray Caverns, Shenandoah Caverns, and Endless Caverns. These caverns were only about 30 miles from Winchester. Judy had a good time that day since she was able to keep Andrew almost all to herself. As they drove back to Winchester, she said, "I didn't realize that it could be so beautiful underground."

"Yes. I was very surprised too when my dad brought my family there when I was in primary school. You should have seen my grandma's face. She was so happy and surprised. My family loves nature very much." Andrew could see that Judy was in a better mood today. She smiled the way Andrew was used to seeing her smile. That evening, Andrew took Judy to a movie. On Monday morning, Andrew slept until almost 9 when his brother, Peter, came to his room to wake him up.

"Andrew, wake up. You have to get ready. Dad is taking us to the cemetery to visit grandpa's, grandma's, and mom's graves. You know he always brings us there on Memorial Day. You know Dad. He is very serious about this."

Andrew woke up quickly and went to Judy's room to wake her up. He asked her if she wanted to go with them.

"If you don't mind, I would prefer to stay here. Besides, that should really be just your family's reunion," Judy told him.

When the group left Judy was still in the guest room. In the car on the way to the cemetery, Andrew's father spoke up. "Do you like Judy, Andrew?"

"Well, I like her a lot, you know. We've been going out for nearly six months now. What do you think of her, Dad?"

"If you want my honest opinion, I don't think that your personalities fit each other very well. I also get the impression that Judy is the type of woman who likes to dominate in any relationship."

Andrew was disappointed to hear that his father didn't fully approve of his relationship with Judy. His father continued, "Andrew, please keep your mind open. As they say, there are plenty of fish in the sea. You know, some day you may find someone who will match your personality better."

"What do you think, Peter? You're 18 years old now. You should be able to offer me some opinion," Andrew asked.

"Actually, I had been hoping our family could spend more time together this weekend. I miss our family gatherings a lot, you know. But I'm young. I guess I just feel like Judy has built a big wall around herself that you can't get through easily. She's very defensive."

After they had pointed these traits out, Andrew could see what his father and brother were talking about. Their conversation had offered him a new perspective from which to ponder his relationship with Judy.

Judy and Andrew left to return to Langley as soon as lunch was over. On the way, Andrew gently raised the topic, "Judy, what do you think about my family?"

"Well, it seems like they have the same problem as my family. They have that traditional family tightness and emotional trap that makes you feel guilty if you don't spend time with them and fills you with obligation towards them." She implied that Andrew's family was an old-fashioned Jewish family.

Though Andrew didn't feel like arguing with her, he began to see his father and brother's point of view. Judy did have a way of seeing things negatively. From that moment on, Andrew began to build his own defensive wall to protect himself from her. He needed time to ponder and analyze his entire relationship with her. But deep in his heart, he was very conflicted. The rational part of him knew he should keep his distance from her, but in his heart, he felt that he was still in love with her.

As time passed, it did not ease Andrew's questions and the emotions that conflicted with each other deep in his heart. After a while he felt that he was just a soulless sex machine, like his only purpose in their relationship was to be Judy's sex slave and satisfy her demands.

More time passed. Andrew had now been in the same position at the CIA for three years and had been with Judy for two and a half years. He was depressed about being trapped in his boring job and was deeply conflicted about his relationship with Judy. He still believed he loved her very much, and he especially enjoyed the satisfying physical and sexual part of their relationship. But something important was missing spiritually between them. It also seemed that Judy did not want to get too deep in her relationship with Andrew. They often just met and had sex.

The Secrecy

When Andrew received notification from his boss that there was an opening in Moscow and asked him if he would like to take it, Andrew was elated. The job would be similar to the one he was doing now at CIA Headquarters. Because working in Moscow had been his original dream, he had put in repeated requests to go there since the beginning of this job. Without hesitation, he accepted the offer. He was told to report to the American Embassy in Moscow on December 12th.

When Andrew told Judy about his new job offer and decision, Judy was very disappointed and somewhat angry as he had expected.

"I will come back to see you every December around Hanukkah. And you can come to visit me and stay with me from time to time. That would make me very happy," Andrew said placatingly. He tried to comfort her, but Judy's face was frozen in a blank expression.

On Friday, December 9th of 1983, right after Hanukkah, Andrew was on his way to Moscow.

2
MOSCOW

Andrew was deep in his thoughts when a sudden hundred-foot drop of the airplane snapped him back into the present. He looked outside his window and realized that the plane was descending. The ground and some buildings that were covered with white snow came into view and he was filled with a sense of excitement. "Finally, I will be in the land where many generations of my ancestors resided," he thought.

Arriving Moscow

Andrew stepped into the arrivals hall after passing through customs and immigration. He surveyed the scene for a moment, then noticed a gentleman walking toward him.

"Andrew Steinberg? I am John from the U.S. Embassy. I've come to pick you up," the man said.

It was obvious that John recognized Andrew from photos and videos that would have been sent from CIA headquarters to the embassy. Andrew believed all his detailed personal information was probably also in the embassy's file by now. In addition, he had been notified before he left that someone from the embassy would pick him up when he arrived, so he was not surprised.

"Thank you very much for picking me up, John," Andrew greeted him.

"You're welcome. I hope you had a nice trip?" John asked.

Andrew nodded his head with smile.

As they stepped out of the airport to go to the parking lot, Andrew felt a sharp, cold wind blowing in his face. It was bitterly cold in Moscow, especially this December. On the way to the embassy, John and Andrew did not talk much. They especially stayed away from anything related to CIA business since in Moscow there was always the possibility that they were being watched or listened to. They just chatted a little bit about the weather and about life in general in Russia.

After nearly an hour of driving, they drove by a nice park. Andrew noticed that, other than a couple of people, it was almost empty, and he asked John about that.

"This is a well-known park next to the Moscow River, Andrew. The embassy is on the west side of the park and your apartment is on the north side. When the weather is good, there are a lot of people skating on a pond in the park during weekends. It is almost empty during weekdays, you know, because it can be very cold in winter. But it will be full of people in summer time," John explained.

"Will we go to the embassy first or to the apartment?" Andrew asked next.

"It's late now. There won't be many people still at the embassy because today is Friday and many workers will have left early. Mr. Buckley gave instructions that I am to take you directly to your apartment. He will meet with you Monday morning at 8:30."

"How far is it from the apartment to the embassy?" Andrew asked, concerned.

"Not far. It's only about a 20-minute walk. Actually, you will see a lot of embassies in this area, especially those from western European countries," John replied.

"In that case, could we swing by the embassy first and then go to the apartment? I would like to know how to get there on Monday morning," Andrew said.

"No problem. Actually, there will be many taxis around your apartment area that know the way and can take you to the embassy."

Within about eight minutes they came to a ten-story building with an American flag fluttering outside on a post.

"Okay, as you see, this is the embassy. Now remember the road from here to your apartment. Simply follow this street, Konyushkovskaya Ulitsa, and go straight for half a mile or so and then turn left. Your apartment is next to the Moscow River," John said.

It was true that the distance was not far. It took them about five minutes of driving to arrive at the apartment. John parked the car in front of the building.

"Everything should be all set. Your apartment is on the third floor, Suite #4. Here's the key. Do you need my help with your bags?" John asked as he handed the key to Andrew.

"Thank you, John, I have only two pieces of luggage. I should be able to handle them. See you Monday." Andrew took his bags and entered the building.

When he emerged from the elevator onto the third floor, Andrew could see there were only two suites on the floor, #3 and #4. The first thing he saw when he opened the door of #4 was a big window in a nice living room. From the window he had a wonderful view when he looked out.

Andrew placed his luggage on the floor and took a quick tour of the place. There was a medium sized kitchen next to the living room. From the living room, a short hallway gave access to the bedroom on the left side and a bathroom on the other side. It was obvious that the apartment was designed for a single person or, at most, a couple.

The bedroom was almost the same size as the living room and had a queen size bed. It also had another big picture window with a great view outside.

Andrew shivered with the cold and went in search of how to turn up the heat. After finding and resetting the thermostat, he thought,

"This is my home now for the next few years."

Andrew unpacked, then took a nice hot shower while the apartment warmed up. After his shower, he put on some comfortable clothes and moved into the living room to enjoy a moment of peace and calmness. There was a television and a stereo system in the living room. He did not know if these belonged to the person who occupied this room before, or if they were provided by the U.S. Embassy.

"Wow! The American government really takes care of its people," he thought. An appreciation for his country emerged from deep in his heart.

Settle Down

Andrew was tired after his long trip, and especially from the jetlag he had now. He found some juice, fruits, and enough foodstuffs in the refrigerator to last a couple of days. Then, even though it was only 8 p.m. he went to bed. But once he was in bed, he tossed around and did not fall asleep until almost midnight. He was excited to be starting this new chapter in his life, but in another way, he was uncertain about the future.

"Anyway, I will just use this opportunity to get to know Russia better. It is a rare chance," he thought.

After his restless night, Andrew slept until nearly 10 o'clock the next morning. He ate a quick breakfast, then, figuring it should be around 6 in the evening in Virginia, he called his father. It was Peter who picked up the phone.

"Hey! Peter, this is Andrew. Just letting you know that I have arrived in Moscow safely," Andrew said.

"Andrew! Dad and I were hoping you would call. Have you settled down okay?" Peter asked.

"Everything is good. The American Embassy had everything ready for me. I start work next Monday. Where's Dad?"

"You may have to wait for a while. He just got into the shower five minutes ago," Peter replied.

"No problem. Just tell him I called. I'll call again soon."

They chatted a little bit and then hung up since the long-distance call was expensive.

Now Andrew was ready to get out and explore the area. Since it was only Saturday he would have almost two days for his exploration. Moscow was much colder compared to Virginia in the wintertime. He bundled up with the best winter clothes he had packed, along with a scarf that Judy had given him the night before he left. He felt warm with it wrapped around his neck, and he could still smell on the scarf Judy's perfume and that body scent that was unique to her. It reminded him of both the good and the bad times with her. He remembered that Judy had worn this scarf almost all the time when they were together.

Using his apartment building as the center, Andrew began to walk around the neighborhood. He discovered most buildings were nice, high-class apartments. "I believe most of the customers for these apartments must be employees working in different embassies," he thought.

In his more than two hours of walking, Andrew discovered two small convenience stores, three liquor stores, three bars, and a couple of cafeterias. He could see all of these shops were targeting residents who had higher incomes than average Russians. He began to realize that if he wanted to buy a greater quantity of food or supplies, he would need to get out of this area.

Andrew walked in the cold windy weather for quite a while before deciding to return to his apartment. When he arrived at a corner about two blocks from his building, he discovered a nice old-fashioned Russian restaurant and decided to try his first Russian meal. With the 3,000 rubles (approximately $100) he had exchanged before he left, he should be able to survive for a few days. Before he left the states, he had been told that he could also change his American dollars to rubles at the American Embassy.

While talking to a waiter, Andrew discovered his Russian was somewhat rusty. He also found that the Russian dialect the people in Moscow spoke was slightly different from what he had learned from his grandma. But he was not worried. He believed once he got used to the way the locals talked, he would be able to understand them easily.

Andrew had a nice native Russian meat dish made from lamb. It was delicious, but he suspected the price, at almost $10, would be too expensive for the average Russian. From what he knew, that would be a significant amount for most Russians to spend on a meal. Naturally, compared to Virginia, it was cheap.

After his meal, Andrew went into a convenience store that was right next to the restaurant and looked at what they had for sale. Then he went to a liquor store to purchase a good bottle of vodka. By the time he returned to his apartment he was feeling sleepy.

"It must be because of jetlag," he thought. Usually, he could walk for hours without a problem, even in heavy snow.

Andrew had a glass of his newly purchased vodka, then took a short nap. He needed to recover from the side effects of his travel and jetlag before Monday. He was surprised to discover that it was 4 o'clock in the morning when he woke up. He took a shower and sat in the living room, for the first time since his arrival feeling a little bit lonely. He already missed his father and brother. And Judy. Especially Judy.

Andrew put some Chopin on the stereo system and closed his eyes. With deep breathing, he started to relax.

"Is this meditation or is it just relaxation?" he wondered. Once he paid attention to the music, his mind went deeper and deeper into a semi-sleeping state. Slowly, he allowed his feelings to take over instead of his conscious thinking. Once his mind was calm, he began to think about his past, present, and possible future. Then he opened his eyes and took out his computer to begin to record some of his experiences since yesterday. He also wanted to write a letter to Judy.

By the time the sun rose around 8:30 that morning, Andrew was surprised to find that it was a sunny day with a temperature a few degrees higher than yesterday. He made himself a breakfast of eggs and toast, and decided to take advantage of such rare, nice weather in wintertime to have another day of exploration.

Andrew walked toward the park and saw a few families with kids skating on the frozen pond. All around him he heard talking and joyful laughing. He indulged in people watching for a while before walking toward the Moscow River. He missed swimming very much. Swimming was the sport that he would never be tired or bored of. "It will be great to see people swimming in the Moscow River in summertime," he thought.

Andrew walked along the river and finally came to a nice modern building. He was intrigued to see that the writing on the entrance had been translated into several languages, including English, French, German, Spanish and Italian. As he read it, he realized that this was a special club that offered services to the various embassies' employees, high ranking Communist officers, and some rich Russian families.

"Wow! I did not expect there would be such a facility in this area. It must be expensive. This club must have a good business, targeting those upper-class people who can afford it," he thought.

Out of curiosity, Andrew stepped into the club but saw only a couple of people who were cleaning and preparing the place. Since they did not seem to be bothered by him, he walked in further. He wanted to see what amenities the club had to offer. He was impressed to see there was a nice sized indoor swimming pool next to which was a restaurant. Behind the restaurant was a large sized entertainment room with a nice fireplace, a couple ping-pong tables, and two pool tables. In the corner, there was a tiny bar serving drinks. He wondered if he could join the club. There were a couple more employees working inside the entertainment room. It appeared that the place would be opening soon.

"It would be great if I could come here to swim during weekends, especially since it is not too far from my apartment and the embassy," Andrew thought. He decided to go out and see what there was to see of the neighborhood, then return when the club was open in the afternoon.

In his wanderings Andrew saw many more expensive apartments and houses next to rivers. From the cars parked on the streets, he could tell that this was a high-class area for the rich.

Andrew returned to the club around 3 p.m. to find it open and went in to ask for information at the counter. He learned that it would be very easy for him to join with his American passport. The cost of the annual fee was not expensive, 1,500 rubles or about $50, based on his American income. So, Andrew went ahead and registered as a member, then entered and saw at least 50 people inside already. In the pool area, there were only about ten people swimming. He was somewhat disappointed that he did not have his swim trunks with him, but he couldn't have known he would find this place.

"I will come next weekend." When he thought of this, he smiled.

Andrew wandered into the entertainment room, where it was warm and felt cozy with the heat from the fireplace. He found a comfortable place to sit and watched some people playing ping-pong and pool. It was very relaxing. In a corner of the room there was a large TV set, tuned to a Russian program.

As it got dark outside, more and more people came in. Andrew ate his dinner in the club. The food was very good but was also somewhat more expensive than outside the club. His meal cost almost as much as it would have in the United States. After paying for dinner he had only a few rubles left in his pocket. He would need to change more money tomorrow when he went to work.

It was around 9 in the evening by the time Andrew went home. After a nice warm shower, he felt pretty relaxed. He was feeling satisfied with what he had accomplished in his exploration over the past two days. During the next months, it would be the whole of the city of Moscow that he would be exploring, he thought, especially those attractive tourist places. Now, he was excited again.

New Work

Following the directions he had memorized, Andrew found the U.S. Embassy easily on Monday morning. It was still early when he arrived, and most employees were not there yet. After showing his passport to the security guards and explaining his new position to them, they took him to a waiting room. It would be another 20 minutes or so before the rest of the employees would arrive. Andrew took a seat and patiently waited to report to his new boss, Mr. Buckley.

About 15 minutes later Mr. Buckley entered the waiting room, the security guards having told him about Andrew as soon as he arrived.

"Mr. Steinberg, Andrew Steinberg, right? I am Mr. Buckley," he greeted Andrew.

"Yes, sir. Nice to meet you, sir," Andrew replied as he stood up from the couch to shake hands with Mr. Buckley.

"Did you have a nice trip to Moscow? Have you settled down yet?"

"Yes, sir. The apartment I have been assigned is very comfortable and I am ready to get to work," Andrew replied.

"Excellent. Let me show you your office."

Mr. Buckley took Andrew up to the fourth floor where there was a nice office for him to work in. Andrew's job was to process the information reported or collected from field agents. After he had compiled, filtered, and classified the information, he would send it to the U.S. information center. Andrew knew the process pretty well since he had done similar work at CIA Headquarters for three years.

"You have a meeting with our security director, Colonel Powell, at 9 a.m. He will come to get you. If you have any questions or problems, please let me know. Anytime!" With that, Mr. Buckley left Andrew alone in his new office.

It wasn't long before a few employees on the same floor came to introduce themselves. They had been expecting Andrew to arrive a week ago. He was made to feel comfortable and welcome by the embassy staff. Everyone seemed so nice to him. He decided to step out of his office to look around and get to know the embassy's facilities. He thought he could also introduce himself to those he had not met yet. To his chagrin, he soon discovered that there were at least 200 people or more working in this building. It would take quite a while to get to know all of them. After his self-led tour, he returned to his office and started arranging his work station. About two minutes before 9 there was a knock on his door.

"Mr. Steinberg, I am Colonel Powell. I am in charge of security for the embassy," Colonel Powell introduced himself.

"Nice to meet you, sir." Andrew abruptly stood at attention to salute Colonel Powell.

"Please come with me."

Colonel Powell took him to an area of the basement that was tucked into the corner of the building. There, a room was kept secured from any eavesdropping, video or audio surveillance, or unauthorized entry. Once they had entered, Colonel Powell closed the door and locked it.

"Mr. Steinberg, this room is the most secure room in the entire building. It is very difficult for an enemy to penetrate our security in this room. Therefore, if there is any secret you need to speak about in the future, this is the place to have that conversation. You should not talk about any embassy secrets outside of this room," Colonel Powell explained to him.

"Are you sure, sir? It is not safe to talk anywhere outside of this room?" Andrew looked at Colonel Powell curiously.

"Yes. We don't know how many bugs could be hidden in this building. We also don't know if we are able to trust all of the employees who are working here. Furthermore, we are watched by the enemy at all times," emphasized Colonel Powell.

Andrew had not had a strong sense of 'enemy' until Colonel Powell's speech. Now, he began to realize that the environment he was living and working in Russia would be very different from working in the U.S. At home, he could be somewhat trusting and generally give people the benefit of the doubt. In Russia, it seemed he would have to assume that the people he met and situations he would find himself in could be hostile.

"You have to be in a condition of high alertness and awareness all the time. You will never know or even feel the full scope of the enemy's penetration into our affairs," Colonel Powell warned Andrew.

Colonel Powell proceeded to ask Andrew many questions about security and Andrew's responsibilities. It was necessary that he know Andrew better. Andrew could feel that Colonel Powell did not really trust anyone. But, Andrew realized, "Of course, this is his job."

"All you should do is do as you are instructed. Try not to get involved in other people's jobs unless you are asked to. You must also be careful of what you say when you meet people from other embassies. Do not talk about your job or duties working here; the less they know, the better. Also, do not get into deep relationships with others. Emotional relationships, especially, can be a trap. In fact, it is best if you just don't trust anyone, period," Colonel Powell stated with a solemn expression on his face.

To Andrew, it felt like he would need to build an invisible prison around himself. Now, he truly understood that the working environment in Russia would not be the same as his work environment in the U.S. "Russia is a dangerous country. Here, we treat each other as the enemy," he thought.

Andrew left his briefing with Colonel Powell feeling somewhat uncomfortable. He could foresee that life here with its strictures on making friends would severely limit his ability to participate in the competitive sports and other activities he usually enjoyed. In short, it would be boring. He foresaw that the office work, especially, would be boring.

Exploring Moscow

Before leaving the embassy for the day, Andrew collected some tourist information. As soon as he arrived home, he dove into the pamphlets to see what the area had to offer.

"Wow, what a city!" Andrew thought. "Filled with culture and the arts! This will be something I can enjoy - taking my time to explore this old culture that my grandma had always talked about."

Since he had a lot of working experience as an information and data processor at CIA Headquarters, Andrew did not feel pressured by his work at the embassy. In his down time, he started to plan an exciting future of exploration in this mysterious city on the weekends. He also hoped to go to the club often to swim.

Originally, Andrew planned to walk to the club and spend the afternoon there the following Saturday. However, due to a snowstorm on Thursday, when Saturday arrived it was still too cold to go out and the streets were covered with deep snow. According to the weather report, Sunday would be sunny. But in the meantime, wind-chill brought the outside temperature down to 20 below zero centigrade. Andrew hired a taxi to take him to the club around 2 o'clock Saturday afternoon. The taxi was cheap and fast and, most importantly, warm.

When he first entered the club, Andrew spent about 20 minutes just looking around before going to the changing room to change out of his street clothes and into swimming trunks. The swimming pool, he soon discovered, was kept at a nice, warm and comfortable temperature. It was a luxury entertainment for him in this high-class facility, especially in wintertime. From a big window, he could see the snow-covered trees, roof, and lawn while he swam in the pleasantly warm water. It was beautiful and enjoyable. There were about 20 swimmers in the pool today. Most of them, including 12 kids, were there just to play around, but Andrew was there to get a good workout. He did a few warm ups first, then began his old routine, swimming 2,000 meters without stop. To him, this was easy, especially in an indoor swimming pool.

Satisfied with his workout, Andrew climbed out of the pool,

covered his body with a towel and sat on one of the many chairs set out around small round tables next to the pool. A waiter came to ask him if he wished to order something, so Andrew ordered a glass of vodka named Purity. Then he sat there and pondered life while watching people playing in the pool. He could not help watching the young swimmers with their strong, athletic bodies. Once his drink was finished he ate dinner in the club's restaurant and went home.

Satisfied with this day, Andrew thought about the next, "Luckily, I exchanged some dollars into rubles with the embassy secretary, otherwise, I would not have enough cash to spend. I will go to Red Square tomorrow, the most famous place in Russia. They said it would be sunny tomorrow." He contemplated Sunday with excitement.

However, when Andrew arrived at Red Square Sunday in a taxi, though it was sunny, it was still very cold and windy and hard for him to walk outside for more than a couple of hours. He ended up spending most of his time inside a building near Red Square. "It would be very nice and beautiful to visit this place during summer time," he thought, and decided to come back when the weather was warmer.

Andrew finished his tour and went back home. He felt he had missed something, but he did not know what.

"Maybe I had expected too much from the beginning, but this tour today has left me feeling empty." From today's experience, Andrew realized that the best places to visit during the wintertime were museums or department stores, or possibly going to watch operas or ballets.

After four months of visiting, among other sites, the State Historical Museum, GUM (a famous department store), Tretyakov Gallery, and also watching a few opera and ballet performances at the Bolshoi Theatre and Moscow Operetta Theatre, Andrew's excitement about exploring Moscow had all but vanished. Now, he understood what was missing.

"I need to share this joy with others, especially those I love. I wish Judy were here to share these attractions with me. I believe my dad and Peter would also enjoy them."

When Andrew thought about it, he felt sad and depressed. He wondered particularly about Judy, who had not written to him or initiated a call to him since he arrived. When he first came to Moscow, he had called her almost every other day. This was the best comfort he could get when he felt lonely. However, only two months after his arrival, he couldn't reach her anymore. She just didn't answer her phone. He began to leave messages on her machine, but she never called back. He was at first concerned for her safety and called his friends in the area. Several of them said that they had seen her around and she seemed fine, though they didn't know her well enough to speak to her. When he talked to his father about this, his dad told Andrew that he had never had any communication with Judy. Andrew didn't want to believe that Judy might be abandoning him.

After nearly five months of taking in the sites in Moscow city, Andrew began to tire of his exploration. His enthusiasm for visiting museums or going to the opera or watching ballet had significantly decreased. This was simply because he was alone and there was no one to share the joy with him.

Birthday

On June 14, a Thursday a little more than six months after his arrival in Moscow, Andrew turned 26 years old. He finished his regularly scheduled meeting with Mr. Buckley, then went back to his apartment. The telephone rang just as he was fixing dinner.

"Hi Andrew, it's Dad. I just wanted to wish you a happy birthday!" There is an eight-hour time difference between Moscow and the east coast of America. So, while it was dinnertime in Moscow, it was 11:30 in the morning in Washington, DC.

"Thanks, Dad. How are you doing? I'm sorry that I haven't called you in almost a month."

"Don't worry about that. I know you must be very busy. How is

Moscow? Have you gotten used to it yet?"

"Actually, yes. It's easier now than when I first got here. You know, it's a very different environment. Dad, I'm just wondering if you've had any contact with Judy or have heard anything about her. It's strange that I haven't been able to get in touch with her the last few months."

"Have you still been calling her?"

"Yes. I leave messages all the time, but she doesn't call me back."

"I'm sorry but I don't have any idea about her at all. She's never called me," Andrew's father said. "Anyway, here's Peter. He wants to talk to you too." On the other end of the line, Richard handed the phone over to Peter.

"Hi Andrew, I hope you had a happy birthday. Thank you for the photos you sent. Moscow looks very beautiful. I wish I could be there too," Peter said.

"Wow, Peter, what a surprise! Aren't you supposed to be in college? Today is Thursday. How did you get home?"

"No, school's out. The semester ended last week. I have been home almost five days now."

They talked for a while and then Andrew asked to talk to his dad again. After everyone had said goodbye and hung up the phone, Peter asked his father, "Why didn't you tell him the truth about Judy?"

"I believe that the situation with Judy is something he should find out for himself. He knows that I don't like her too much. Let him find out by himself when he comes home for Hanukkah," Richard said.

Except for receiving a phone call from his father and brother, nobody knew about or paid any attention to Andrew's birthday. He was disappointed that Judy seemed to have forgotten his birthday as well. He just could not figure out what had happened to her. After dinner, he poured himself a glass of vodka and sat down on the couch in his living room. In the last few months, he had learned to enjoy Russian vodka, especially the good and expensive kind. But sitting there alone on his couch with his glass of vodka on his birthday was utterly depressing. This was the first time that he had felt this down since his arrival. During the first few months, he was kept busy learning his new responsibilities and environment. Now that things had become familiar and settled, he realized that living in this communist Russian society could be very lonely. He began to miss America, his father and brother, and especially his girlfriend, Judy.

Andrew began to think back on the times he had spent with Judy more nostalgically. "Maybe she wasn't that bad after all," he thought. "Plus, she also is from a Jewish family. Dad has always wanted me to eventually settle down with a nice Jewish girl."

Andrew believed that if they got married someday, even though his father didn't like her that much, in time his father would come around and accept them. He knew his father would like him to keep with tradition and marry a Jewish girl. Gradually, he fell asleep on the couch.

When Andrew awoke it was midnight. He took a shower, changed into his pajamas and went to bed but, no matter what, he could not sleep anymore. He recalled the times when he and his three friends would go to Virginia Beach almost every other week in the summer time. They had had such a good time. It felt like they were brothers. They could talk to each other openly without hiding their thoughts from each other or having to pretend to be someone else. He also recalled his times with Judy. Though he enjoyed being with her and having sex, somehow, he felt like a different person when he was with her. He and Judy didn't have that same open communication, and both kept their emotions masked from one another. With her, he had to pretend many things, and edit his speaking and actions. If he was not careful, the slightest misstep could trigger a fight with her.

When Andrew went to work the next morning, he was very tired. Lack of sleep had made his depression worse. Fortunately, work kept him very busy this Friday and time passed quickly. After he finished his meeting with Mr. Buckley and went home, he fixed a simple sandwich for dinner. Then he went straight to bed and passed out, exhausted.

3
ACQUAINTANCE

Accident

Saturday morning Andrew woke early at 6:35. Today felt like it was going to be a better day. He glanced at the calendar on the wall and saw that it was June 16th.

"It will be six more months before I get any vacation days. I promised my family and Judy that I would be home for Hanukkah," Andrew thought. "I have also promised my boss that I would stay here for at least two years. I must make it. I can make it. I am not a person who surrenders easily. I will keep myself busy and find more to interest me in Russian culture so that I won't be so restless and lonely."

Once Andrew had decided this, the depression that had bothered him for the last couple days started to fade away. With a mind that was much calmer and more peaceful, he set about fixing and eating a nice breakfast, after which he poured himself a cup of coffee and went to sit down in his living room. His thoughts took him back to about a year ago when he had had a big fight with Judy. While still recovering from the fight he had gone out with his old swimming buddy Paul, who noticed that Andrew was very upset and stressed out.

Paul had said, "Hey Andrew, you know, meditation can help you calm down your emotional mind, and make it easier to cope with stuff like this, especially Chinese meditation. There's a book called '*Qigong Meditation - Embryonic Breathing.*' It's the best I have found. After you meditate for a few minutes, and your mind is calm, then your thinking is more clear and neutral."

On this recommendation, right before leaving for Moscow Andrew had purchased this book on meditation from Barnes & Noble. He had yet to look at it, however, as he was never in the right mood to read it since meditation had sounded dull and never really caught his interest. After the last few days, though, he realized that his emotional mind was very disturbed again and this reminded him of the meditation book.

Andrew put on some Chopin. He had always loved the classics, especially compositions by Chopin and Beethoven. When he was in high school, whenever he needed to calm down, he always played the classics. He believed that listening to this music helped him to concentrate better. Andrew then retrieved the meditation book, opened to the first page, and began to read. Amazingly, the more he read, the more interested he became. There was a lot of detailed explanation in this book about traditional Chinese meditation methods, especially in the first part of the book that explained the scientific foundation of Chinese Qigong. By noon, he had finished nearly 80 pages of the basic theoretical foundation of Chinese Qigong.

"I need to stop and digest what I've read before I go any further. I must ponder every sentence until it becomes clear," Andrew decided and put the book down for now.

That afternoon, as had become his habit, Andrew decided to go to the club. It was a cloudy day in Moscow. Usually it would take him 20 minutes to walk to the club, but today he felt better and decided to stop off at a park on the way and sit there for a while.

During his walk, Andrew began to contemplate his relationship with Judy again. "Maybe I should find a girlfriend here," he thought. "I left Judy another message last night, and again there is no answer from her. Her lack of any kind of response is cold and cruel."

The Secrecy

When Andrew sat down on the bench in the park, there were only a handful of people around. He could see a few families who had brought their children to the park so they could play there. Summertime was short in Moscow and it rained often. Therefore, people appreciated any day as long as it was not raining. From their looks and dress, he could easily see some of them might be families of employees of different embassies in the area. Seeing them reminded him of his own family. Again, he thought of his high school graduation day, four days after his 18th birthday. It seemed like it was only yesterday. Graduation day had been the proudest day of his life. He received so many awards and had felt that he had a great future in front of him, like the whole world was open to him. He still remembered his father's smile and the pride that had radiated from him. He also remembered Cindy's cute face. The thought of her made Andrew smile.

"Time goes so fast, what should I do with my future? Is the career I have the one I really want?" Andrew again questioned himself and began to doubt the path he was on. It seemed like every step he had taken to date had been prearranged and heavily influenced by his family's traditions and by society. "Have I controlled my life or has my life controlled me?" he wondered. "What do I really want for my life? Do I really want to be a CIA agent?" He searched for the answer deep in his heart in vain. He was still confused about his life.

Andrew arrived at the club around 1:30 in the afternoon, just in time for a late lunch. He ordered a turkey sandwich and a glass of apple juice as he didn't like to have a heavy lunch before going swimming. When he looked around, he saw some people from other embassies with whom he had become acquainted over the last six months, though his relationships with them had stayed on the surface. He remembered what Colonel Powell said about keeping a shallow relationship with other embassies' employees, the policy of all embassies. This was to prevent any government secrets or policies being revealed to other countries among them. Although he was invited occasionally to other American Embassy employees' homes for dinner, when he attended these events they only increased his feelings of homesickness.

"I need a good, real friend here," Andrew thought.

After lunch, Andrew went into the dressing room and changed. He swam for about an hour, then went to sit on one of two lounge chairs set beside a round table. Again, he ordered a small glass of vodka to keep him warm while sitting there and thinking and watching other people swim, especially the ones with fit physiques. There were not very many people swimming today, only a dozen or so, and five of them were children. Actually, there wasn't much to watch. He was a little bit bored.

Andrew took a couple sips of vodka, then closed his eyes and relaxed. He began to ponder the ideas that he had read that morning in the qigong book. He also tried to practice the abdominal breathing techniques described in the book.

"Inhale deeply, gently push your abdomen out and perineum downward. Exhale slowly and gradually and allow the air out naturally while gently pulling the abdomen in and holding the perineum upward."

Andrew repeated the instruction in his mind and practiced accordingly. In a few minutes, he was more relaxed and felt the beginnings of a nice sensation in his groin area. "Amazing, only a few minutes, and my mind is calm and peaceful," he thought and kept practicing.

Moments later Andrew's concentration was broken when he heard some fast steps and laughter bearing down on him. He snapped open his eyes in time to see a young man in a swimsuit with a towel in his hand looking backwards toward the entrance of the swimming pool while moving rapidly in Andrew's direction.

"Watch out!" Andrew shouted.

It was too late. The young man crashed into Andrew's table and fell. The glass of vodka that had been sitting on the table slipped to the ground and shattered. One of the young man's slippers had been thrown a few yards away. The young man's friend, who was standing next to the entrance of the swimming pool, laughed loud and hard. The young man got up and surveyed the damage he had caused.

"Прошу прощения за мою неаккуратность. (I am sorry, sir. How rude I was,)" he said.

"Нет никакой проблемы. Только будьте осторожны. (There is no problem. Just be careful,)" Andrew replied.

Andrew looked at the young man more closely. He guessed him to be about 20 years old. Now he could see him clearly, he was amazed by the young man's eyes - eyes that looked so familiar, ice-blue and beautiful. He suddenly remembered that Judy had those same ice-blue eyes. That was where the similarity ended, however, as the young man's eyes held something different, something more. It seemed they had the capability of communicating with you. When the young man looked at Andrew and asked for forgiveness, the apology in his eyes was even stronger than his words.

"What a beautiful pair of eyes," Andrew thought.

While Andrew pondered this, the young man spoke to a waiter who had come to clean up the mess. Then the young man bowed to Andrew with a smile in a sincere and polite manner and left to go talk to his friend again. As the young man walked away, Andrew watched his body and how he moved.

"I know I'm a handsome guy and have a pretty good-looking body, but compared to this guy I am almost nothing," Andrew thought. He had never seen a guy with such a good-looking face matched with such a perfectly developed physique. Andrew wondered if he was an employee from another embassy or a member of a rich Russian family. From the way he had spoken, in perfect Russian and with a well-educated demeanor, Andrew was convinced the young man was Russian, not a foreigner.

"Why have I never seen him here in the last six months?" Andrew wondered.

The waiter brought Andrew another glass of vodka and informed him, in English with a Russian accent, "Your drink has already been paid for."

"Thank you."

Andrew knew the drink had been ordered by the young man to replace the one he had knocked over. It was not surprising to hear the waiter speaking English since there were so many foreigners in this club. Actually, almost all of the waiters were capable of speaking French as well. This was because before revolutionary Russia, France was considered the epitome of elegant, high level culture. This had influenced many aspects of Russian life including music, cuisine, and also language.

Andrew began to think about the young man and tried to compare him with all of his friends. "Is there anyone who was as handsome and attractive as this guy?" The answer was "no."

When Andrew thought of the young man's eyes, it reminded him of Judy again.

"How much do I miss her? Why didn't she call me for my birthday? If the situation were reversed and I forgot her birthday, she would be furious with me."

Feeling depressed once again, Andrew went home. He began to wonder how long he would end up being in Moscow. Again, he thought about his next vacation that would be near the end of December.

Andrew did not feel like going anywhere for sightseeing the next day. After a light breakfast, he went to the bank of the Moscow River that was only half a mile from his apartment, walking along the river for a couple of miles and then sitting down on a bench. In his personal solitude, he watched people and families playing along the river. Around 11 o'clock, it began to drizzle. The weather made Andrew's depression feel heavier, like a weight sitting on his shoulders. By the time he returned to his apartment, his clothes were thoroughly soaked. He took a shower and fixed some tea to warm himself up. Then he sat down on the sofa and listened to classical music while continuing to read his meditation book.

"This was a pretty depressing weekend," he thought.

Acquaintance

Andrew felt much better on Monday morning after having had a good, long night's sleep. He said to himself, "I must get up and try again to adapt to this new environment. Like Grandma used to say, 'Andrew, in America they have a saying, 'If you smile, the whole world smiles with you, but when you cry, you cry alone.'"

Monday was very busy. A lot of events had happened during the last weekend. Andrew's daily work continued to keep him distracted from feeling depressed again, and after a few days he had completely forgotten the young man whom he had encountered at the club.

On Saturday morning, Andrew again fixed a nice breakfast for himself. He put some Beethoven on this time and returned to reading the meditation book. "It's amazing. The more I read, the more I wish to know," he thought. Before he knew it, it was lunchtime.

Once again Andrew decided to go swimming in the afternoon. When he thought of it, it reminded him of the young man who had caused the accident the week before. "Will I see him again this afternoon?" he wondered.

It was strange that Andrew felt more anxious now about going to the club than before. He knew that this was partly because he was searching for a friend and thought there might be a chance of getting better acquainted with the young man. He arrived at the club with mixed feelings of expectation and hope. Again, he ordered a light lunch and a drink. When he was finished, he went swimming.

After swimming, Andrew ordered his usual glass of vodka and sat down to think about what he had read that morning in the meditation book. However today, strangely, he could not concentrate. "Why isn't my mind calm and steady today?" he asked himself, even though he knew that it was because of his hope and anxiety over the possibility of meeting the young man again.

Andrew sat for about another hour, then swam for another half hour before deciding to quit. He changed into his clothes and went to the club's restaurant. It was almost 6:30 in the evening and Andrew felt disappointed with the day. He decided to eat at the club instead of going home and cooking. This was also starting to become a habit, since there was no fun in cooking just for himself and eating alone.

The waiter came and took his order as soon as Andrew sat down. While he was waiting for his meal and listening to some music playing in the club, a voice came from behind him, "Hi, Mister. How are you doing?"

Andrew turned his head to see the young man who had caused the accident last week. He was dressed in a nice neat suit and was standing with his friend.

"How did you know I speak English?" Andrew asked with a smile when he saw the young man and his friend.

"You shouted, 'Watch out!' remember?" the young man said. "And, almost everyone here speaks English," he continued.

All three laughed.

"Again, I would like to apologize for my rudeness last week," the young man said.

"As I said, there is no problem," Andrew replied with a smile. "Would you and your friend like to join me for dinner?"

"We can sit for a while," the young man said, and they both sat down in front of Andrew. "My name is Alexandr Ivanov and this is Viktor Bunin," Alexandr said, indicating his friend.

"I am Andrew Steinburg. It is nice to meet you." Andrew extended his right arm to shake their hands over the dinner table.

The waiter came while they were introducing themselves. Alexandr, speaking in Russian, ordered something for himself, but didn't order anything for his friend, Viktor. Since Andrew could understand some Russian, he was wondering why Viktor did not order anything for him. In the next moment, Viktor answered Andrew's unspoken question.

"Here she is. I am sorry, I must leave. My girlfriend is here," Viktor said, getting up and bowing to Andrew. Viktor quickly walked toward the entrance where he greeted a nice-looking girl, leaving Andrew and Alexandr to have their dinner.

Andrew turned to his new dinner companion. "Why haven't I seen you here before?" he asked with curiosity.

"I'm an actor," Alexandr replied. "I do some stage performances such as drama or sometimes ballet. My group just completed a country tour a couple weeks ago and returned to Moscow to rehearse for the next show. We will be here for at least six months and then begin to tour again."

"Ah. You look like you keep yourself in really good shape. I know Russian stage training is very rigorous and produces excellent performers," Andrew said.

"Yes, it is true. There is a lot of spanking, so we are literally whipped into shape. That is the reason that the quality is so high," Alexandr said laughing.

"Where did you learn your English? It is very good."

"Actually, we occasionally perform English-language versions of Russian classics. English and French are required for almost all actors and actresses. I also studied English when I was in high school," Alexandr said. He paused for a second, then continued, "Okay, tell me how you learned your Russian. Your Russian is not bad either."

"I work for the American Embassy as a computer engineer," Andrew said.

"You are a diplomatic officer? I thought you were a businessman." The young man looked at Andrew in surprise.

"In order to work here, I had to learn Russian," Andrew told him. "But aside from that, my ancestors lived here in Moscow for many generations before 1940. Russian used to be one of my family's languages when I was small."

Alexandr looked at Andrew with a curious and friendly smile. "I am always interested in knowing more about America. Now if I have any questions, I can ask you. You know, one of my dreams is to be able to have a performance tour in America. I have heard a lot about your country."

"As a matter of fact, I was going to ask you about Russian tradition and culture. You know, I heard a lot of Russian stories from my grandma when I was younger. I have always been fascinated by this old culture. Now, if I have any questions, I can ask you." Andrew looked into Alexandr's eyes and laughed.

"You must have joined the club only in the last couple weeks then?" Andrew asked, even though he already knew Alexandr had just joined the club. He was hoping to learn more about Alexandr's background, remembering that he must be careful since he was working for the CIA and he should get to know as much as possible about everyone he became acquainted with.

"Is he from a rich Russian family or from a high-ranking Communist officer's family?" Andrew wondered.

"Actually, Viktor's father has a connection and through this I was able to receive permission to enter this club. Viktor's father is an important Communist officer. Last week was my first time here and I already caused trouble." Alexandr looked at Andrew and laughed. He went on, "Now, it is the rehearsal period again. I will be busy on weekdays only, very busy. But I have a lot of free time on the weekend. If you have time, I can show you around town. I know almost everything about Moscow." He looked at Andrew with sincerity.

"Were you born in Moscow?"

"No. Actually, my family is living in a small town called Vladimir, which is about 183 km east of Moscow. That is, approximately 115 miles away. I was recruited by a well-known actor, Ivan Jarcev, when I was 18 years old and came here for acting training. Actually, only two years ago I began to get involved in acting."

"How old are you now, may I ask?"

"I am 22 and have just passed my birthday."

"Really! I have just had my birthday too, nine days ago. When was your birthday?" Andrew asked.

"June 20. You must be June 14, right? That was nine days ago. How old are you now?"

"I am 26 now. Time has passed so quickly in the last five years." Andrew looked at Alexandr with a downturned face.

The waiter came with their dinners and drinks, and Alexandr asked the waiter to bring two glasses of vodka.

"I'm hungry. Do you mind if we eat and talk at the same time?" Andrew asked.

Andrew felt happy and excited over this new acquaintance. He could not help paying close attention to Alexandr's elegant manner and movement. "No wonder his movements are so supple and lithe - he is an actor and a dancer," Andrew thought.

Alexandr looked Andrew in the eye and asked, "What are you doing tomorrow? As I said, I don't have anything to do. If you like, I can show you some museums."

"That would be great. I don't have anything to do either. Actually, only last week I was beginning to feel bored about taking this job in Moscow. Obviously, it's not like in America. Plus, all my friends and family are there, not here."

The waiter arrived at that moment with their vodka.

"Let's celebrate the beginning of our friendship," Alexandr said and raised his glass.

"It's nice to have met you," Andrew said, also raising his glass to toast. After the toast, he asked, "By the way, how do you know Viktor?"

"Actually, Victor's girlfriend was one of the actresses in my team. Viktor came to watch her rehearse often. We had dinners and went to parties together sometimes," Alexandr answered before pausing for a second. He looked at Andrew with a curious smile. "How about you? Do you have a girlfriend?" Alexandr asked.

"Yes. Well, I did. I've had a couple of girlfriends before."

"What do you mean 'I did'? Don't you have one now?"

"Before I came here I had a girlfriend named Judy. But I haven't been able to reach her in the last four months."

Alexandr felt it would be impolite to inquire further and didn't ask any more about it.

Andrew said, "How about you? Do you have one?"

"Well, to tell the truth, I don't. I have been very busy with rehearsals and performances. I have never tried to build a deep relationship with any girl."

"That's a pity. You know, there are plenty of girls pursuing a performing career who are beautiful and young, especially those who practice ballet." Andrew looked at Alexandr with a joking laugh.

"Well, after you have worked together with them for some time, they are more like sisters than lovers," Alexandr joked back.

"Yes. Feelings can be very strange things. You get excited at the beginning when you are first getting to know someone, and once you get used to it, the excitement begins to wane."

"I have the same view," Alexandr responded. "You know, in my opinion, each individual emotional feeling is an invisible fingerprint. Each one is different. The most amazing part of this is that feelings change from time to time and also from environment to environment. No one can be guaranteed that his or her emotion will not change. For this reason, only the real and true deep feelings should be the guideline for any individual. I also believe there is no one who can or should use his or her own feeling to judge others."

"Wow. How old did you say you are? For your age, you seem to already have a deep understanding of the emotional mind. I happen to be spending quite a bit of time thinking about the subject myself recently. It's amazing how often we can be fooled by false feelings," Andrew looked at Alexandr with surprise.

"You know, I'm a stage performer. I know exactly what each feeling is. On the stage, I have to enact each emotion seamlessly so the audience can't see through the mask of my portrayal. Otherwise, the performance will not be touching. However, almost all people hide their real feelings inside to avoid embarrassment and criticism from others. In reality, all of us are actors going through the designated motions of a living play that was written by the human matrix. If anyone dares to jump out of this matrix or challenge this established doctrine, he or she will be considered as a sinner."

"What do you mean human matrix?" Andrew asked.

"You know, through thousands of years of development, humans have defined their emotional feelings and created traditions and doctrines. Since then, we have been trapped inside of this creation and blindly believed in it. I call it emotional bondage or the human emotional matrix. The worst part of it is, we have been killing each other in the name of these beliefs for thousands of years. I also think that because of this matrix the human spirit has been restricted from continuous development."

When Andrew heard what Alexandr said, he felt a deep respect for this young performer. He couldn't believe that at his young age, he had already comprehended so much about life. "But after all, he is a stage performer. Feeling is the key to a successful performance," Andrew thought.

As a matter of fact, what Alexandr said resonated deeply within Andrew. Whenever he had been with Judy and many others in the past, he had always felt that he needed to wear a heavy, thick mask on his face – presenting to them the self they expected to see while protecting his true self. He also often felt the pressure from his family's sense of tradition and from society's expectation that he be and act a certain way.

"How truthful you are! We are all living on a stage. It seems that life controls us instead of us controlling our own lives," Andrew said with a sigh.

"The question is, do we dare to challenge the traditional doctrines and bondage? If not, then we must hide our real emotions and become victims of this bondage of tradition. But if we do, we make ourselves outsiders. We are forever a stranger to everyone we meet," Alexandr said.

Andrew began to believe that this young man in front of him must have had a difficult past. He spoke with maturity and a great depth of understanding, especially with regard to emotional feeling. It seemed that his comprehension of the emotional mind was at least one level higher than Andrew's own. He believed that Alexandr might become more than a normal regular friend but could also be a spiritual friend who would be able to help him understand the meaning of life. Andrew decided to test Alexandr a little bit further.

"Well, since you are such a great philosopher tell me now, what is love? How do you define it?" Andrew looked at Alexandr with a challenging expression on his face.

"I don't actually have any real experience with being in love. However, I have read many of the famous scripts - almost all of them cannot be separated from love. To me, real love is a deep appreciation of another person and a willingness to sacrifice for that other person. Without this firm foundation, then love is shallow or non-truthful. Real love is always concerned with the other person's feelings and needs first instead of your own. Many stories explain this feeling, but it seems few people live this way. Since I have to perform these love stories, I often put myself into this character, and express this kind of love described in the story. But I'm sorry that I don't have any real experience."

"It is amazing to me," Andrew replied, "that you are able to learn so much about life through performing. My girlfriend Judy always expected me to do this or do that for her. As a matter of fact, she never told me exactly what she wanted. She would just give a hint and if I didn't catch on and figure out exactly what she wanted, she would get angry and start a huge fight. I'm a pretty intuitive person, and have a fairly high level of awareness, but I wasn't able to keep up with this mental game. I guess in the end I really didn't want to. When you do that, you spend all your mental energies in a relationship trying to guess at the hoops they want you to jump through instead of in an honest exchange of needs and desires, you compromise your true self."

"From my understanding, expectations or anxiety is always an obstacle to true love. People in real love shouldn't have any expectation or anxiety from each other. There should only be appreciation without demand," Alexandr said.

Andrew understood better now and could see that Judy had always been expecting and demanding him to be what she thought he should be or wanted him to be instead of who he was. He knew that in order to make her happy and fulfill her expectations, gradually he had become little more than her emotional slave.

They kept talking and laughing and, in only a few hours, they had become good friends. Andrew felt like he could talk to Alexandr without needing to mask his true self. He believed that he had found a real friend in Russia. Andrew's depression and boredom were gone. They talked until nearly 11 o'clock, when the waiter came to remind them that closing time was at 11.

"Wow. The time passed very fast. We've been talking for nearly four hours," Andrew said.

"Well, how about tomorrow? Do we have an appointment or not? I have time to show you around," Alexandr asked.

"That's great, I can't wait. Where should we meet, and what time?"

"How about 10 tomorrow morning at the main entrance of the metro train station, Chekhovskaya, which is on Strastnoy bul. From there, we can go anywhere by subway. You know, Moscow's subway system is very convenient and can take you any place in Moscow. That particular station is near my apartment."

"That sounds good. I believe I can find it easily. I will see you then."

There were two taxis at the curb when they walked out of the club.

"Good night, Andrew," Alexandr said as he got into a taxi.

"Good night, Alexandr. Again, it was great to meet you. See you tomorrow."

Since the club was not too far away, Andrew walked back to his apartment. On the way back, he felt great that he had a friend now. He kept thinking about all the things they had talked about. This was the best evening he'd had since he arrived in Moscow.

When he got home, he was still pondering the conversation they'd had. "How could he understand so much for his age?" Andrew wondered.

This also reminded Andrew what the security director, Colonel Powell, had said about awareness and alertness. After all, Russia was a country that was hostile toward America. With that, Andrew figured he'd best investigate Alexandr's background further and study his lifestyle. He also decided not to report his new relationship with Alexandr to his boss, Mr. Buckley. It could be embarrassing if he told his boss that he had a Russian friend.

"Besides, this is my personal and private business. They don't have to know it. I have accepted strict training before. I know how to handle the situation. I have confidence that I will not do anything harmful to America in anyway," Andrew thought.

Companionship

The next morning, Sunday, Andrew arrived at the metro train station, Chekhovskaya, in a taxi. When he arrived, Alexandr was already there waiting for him. The weather was still cloudy and occasionally drizzly like yesterday, typical Moscow summer weather with the temperature at a humid 72°F (22°C). As Andrew's taxi pulled up, Alexandr spotted it right away.

When Andrew stepped out of the taxi, Alexandr said, "Oh, that's how you planned to find the station. By taxi. I was worried that you wouldn't find it."

"Taxi service in Moscow is very convenient and cheap," Andrew pointed out. "I have never taken the subway. I don't like it. There are too many people and the worst part is, people smoke. I hate the smell of smoke."

"You mean that you have never taken the subway in Moscow? Then, you've missed one of the most attractive tourist sights, which is located underground in the subway."

"Really? I had heard something about that, but I thought they were only joking."

"No, it's true! Okay, how about your first lesson is becoming acquainted with the Moscow subway system today."

"Are you sure? Won't that be boring?"

"No problem. I guarantee you will enjoy it."

"How long have you been waiting? You must have gotten here early. When I arrived, it was still five minutes before 10," Andrew said.

"I am just excited. I woke up early this morning and could not get back to sleep. I thought I was very lucky to have met you."

"Same here. Have you eaten anything yet this morning? I'm really hungry," Andrew asked.

"No. I'm hungry too. Let's go have something to eat before we start the tour."

Alexandr led Andrew to a cafeteria near the train station where they went in and sat down. They each ordered some breakfast and coffee.

"Tell me more about this subway sight-seeing program. I've become curious now," Andrew said.

"The Moscow metro is one of the most marvelous urban designs in the world. As I understand, it is estimated that 9 million people travel by metro each day."

"Really? That's probably more than that of New York and London combined."

"That's what people say. I don't actually know." Alexandr looked into Andrew's eyes in wonder and continued, "A large portion of Moscow's subway system is actually part of an 'Underground

Odyssey,' an underground art museum. There are about nine stations which are worth seeing."

"Nine stations? What are they?"

"1. Komsomolskaya; 2. Prospekt Mira; 3. Novoslobodskaya; 4. Belorusskaya; 5. Krasnopresnenskaya; 6. Kievskaya; 7. Ploshchad Revolyutsii; 8. Teatralnaya; and 9. Mayakovskaya. As I know, this subway was the grand prize winner at the 1938 World's Fair in New York, the *piece de resistance*."

Suddenly Andrew felt foolish since he could not remember all of the names of the nine stations even though he had a photographic memory. Andrew decided it was because the names of the stations were not in English. He smiled at Alexandr and said, "I can't remember all of these. You will just have to show me."

After breakfast, Alexandr took him to all nine stations to see this underground museum. To Andrew, this was one of the most impressive and amazing things he had ever seen, especially since it was in the subway. When they finished, they took the train back to the Ploshchad Revolyutsii Station that was next to Red Square. It was 3:15 in the afternoon.

"Thank you, Alexandr. I had a very good time," Andrew said.

"We still have some time. Do you want to visit some museums in Red Square?"

"I've already seen most of them. You know I've been here for six months. However, we could walk around in Red Square. I am very impressed with the architecture of all the buildings there."

Unfortunately, when they stepped out of the station they discovered the rain was getting heavier. They found a cafeteria near the station and sat down to get some food since they had not eaten anything since breakfast that morning.

"Where do you rehearse? Do you think I could come to watch your rehearsal some time?" Andrew asked.

"Of course. We rehearse at Chekhov Moscow Art Theatre, commonly known as MKhT by Russians. It is located on Kamergersky per 3. Only weekdays, remember. The theater does the shows during the weekend and of course the director is very busy. On weekdays though, you are welcome to come anytime. Sometimes, we rehearse until midnight," Alexandr said. "When you come, just tell the doorkeeper that you are my friend and he will let you in," he continued with a nice smile.

"I've heard of this theater and also read about it," Andrew commented. "I read that it was founded nearly 100 years ago. It's very famous for method acting."

"Yes, method acting was founded by the actor-director Konstantin Stainislavsky, and by playwrite-director Vladimir Nemirovich-Danchenko, in 1898. This theater includes the theater itself, an acting studio-school, and also a small museum about the theater's history."

While they were talking, the food and drink they had ordered arrived. Andrew looked at Alexandr's face and kept smiling.

"What are you smiling about? Is there something funny on my face?" Alexandr asked.

"No, I am just thinking about the subjects we talked about last night, especially about the emotional matrix."

"I hope you are not laughing at me because of my shallow opinion," Alexandr said, suddenly become guarded.

"No, no. Not at all. I thought what you said was pretty profound. I'm happy to finally find someone to discuss this sort of thing with, someone who has already developed such an understanding. And there are other things I'd like to discuss with you, like, how do you define spirit? What is the difference between the spirit and the mind?"

Alexandr relaxed again. "The truth is I don't know. It is something that you can feel but cannot see or touch. All I know is that the spirit is more truthful and the mind is not."

"I'm reading a book about Chinese meditation called *Qigong Meditation - Embryonic Breathing*. It says that spirit is related to the subconscious mind while thinking is related to the conscious mind.

The subconscious mind is more truthful while the conscious mind has a mask which lies and plays tricks."

"Really. I sort of agree with this opinion. You know, I think we've been brainwashed since we were born, through our upbringing and education. As I said last night, humans have created all the emotions: jealousy, glory, honor, dignity, and hate. We are taught to act out of these emotions; they are like something we are stuck in and cannot help or change. Instead, we should be trying to attain spiritual advancement, to feel emotions but not get consumed and overwhelmed by them. I believe since humans got stuck in this pattern, we have been living in emotional bondage, trying to control and kill each other."

Andrew agreed with what Alexandr said, but since he had grown up in a traditional Jewish and military family, he didn't know how to answer him. If he agreed, then he would deny the values of his own traditions and doctrines. If he didn't agree, then he would be lying. He took a bite of his food and a sip of his tea before responding. Thoughtfully he said, "It seems that mankind is in a period of emotional conflict. To advance, we need to escape the matrix and bondage we live in. But it is so difficult to escape because we are living in and indoctrinated into the matrix which then structures our perceptions and thoughts."

"That was what I meant last night. We are just actors acting on a stage. Our lives are just like a cruel and realistic show. We have to perform what people expect of us, but some of us wish we could jump off the stage and find our real selves and set our spirits free. What did you say that breathing was called? It sounds very interesting."

"Embryonic breathing."

"What is Qigong? And what does 'embryonic breathing' mean?"

"I have just begun to read the book, so I don't quite know yet. I know that Qigong means the study or the practice of Qi. In Qigong practice, you learn to work with the energy in your body. According to the Chinese, Qi is any type of energy existing in the universe. It is called embryonic breathing because through this breathing technique, you are able to trace back to your original truthful feeling, just like a baby before it is born, with its mind free of any human matrix. It is believed that through this breathing you will be able to reconnect your spirit with nature, or the Dao."

"It sounds like a book that would interest me very much. Can I borrow it after you finish your reading?"

"Of course, it'll take me a few more weeks though."

"No problem, I can wait. I'm patient. You have to be patient in acting, especially when you're rehearsing for the show. Without patience, the quality of your performance suffers."

They talked and exchanged their ideas for a long time. Andrew remembered that whenever he wanted to talk about the spiritual side of life with Judy, she would shut him down. Judy didn't want to talk about it at all. All she cared about was material goods and her life of luxury.

Andrew and Alexandr had a very good time together that day. Andrew was pretty sure now that Alexandr would be a good and truthful friend. When Andrew wanted to pay the bill, Alexandr insisted that it was his treat this time. They said goodbye and made an appointment to see each other again the next Saturday at the club.

New Spirit

Back at work Andrew's boss, Mr. Buckley, was surprised to see Andrew's enthusiasm rise suddenly.

"He is a valuable agent to America," Mr. Buckley thought. He believed that this change was because Andrew was finally getting accustomed to his new environment. Usually, it took about six months for anyone to get used to the routines of living in Moscow and working at the embassy. He told Andrew how much he appreciated his good performance.

That Thursday after work, as Andrew walked home, he began to think about Alexandr and the good time they had had together the weekend before. Since it was still early, he decided to go to the theater to give Alexandr a surprise visit. Actually, deep in his mind, he also wanted to check to see if what Alexandr said was true or not. He grabbed a taxi and asked to be taken to Chekhov Moscow Art Theatre.

When he arrived, Andrew told the doorkeeper that he was Alexandr Ivanov's friend and that he would like to watch Alexandr's rehearsal tonight. The doorkeeper showed him the way to the performance hall. When Andrew entered the entire hall was dark. The only bright place was on stage. He saw a group of actors and actresses up there along with a male in his 40s who was giving them direction and explaining the scene.

"That must be the director, Ivan Jarcev," Andrew thought.

Andrew chose a seat in the last row and sat down quietly as he did not want to disturb anyone. He watched the rehearsal patiently. It was a historical drama and looked like some story occurring 200 years ago. Alexandr was acting the role of a privileged young officer. When he stood up among the war prisoners and shouted, "Long live the queen! Long live the queen!" the rebels took him by force to an execution area where many officers had already been hung. In his role as the young officer, Alexandr's eyes filled with tears as he faced death. An old family servant of the officer then came running through the crowd which was laughing and enjoying the spectacle of seeing the queen's officer being hung. The servant knelt down crying in front of the rebel leader and begged for his young master's life. Suddenly, the servant realized that this leader was the man they saved in the snowstorm...

Before he knew it, Andrew's eyes were wet. He was touched by the performance. It looked so real.

"Why am I so touched? Because of the story or because of the excellent performance?" he pondered for a while.

Later, he began to realize that it was because Alexandr was the actor. It was because of this that he had gotten emotional watching the show.

It was almost 9:30 in the evening before the director was satisfied with this part of the production. As the rehearsal ended, the lights of the entire hall were turned on allowing Alexandr to notice Andrew sitting in the last row of seats. Alexandr waved excitedly at him. Actually, Alexandr had been hoping Andrew would come to see his rehearsal ever since he had told him about it last weekend. Though he hoped it would happen, he also knew that Andrew was a busy man and might not be able to make it. When he saw Andrew, he was filled with expectation and surprise.

Alexandr came down from the stage and he and Andrew walked quickly toward each other. When they were close, Alexandr could not help himself and hugged Andrew into his chest. Andrew was shocked but warmed by this surprise. He returned Alexandr's hug tightly. Their breathing and heartbeats sped up. He had never had such a sensational feeling in hugging a guy before. He felt warm and emotionally touched.

Andrew could smell the sweat on Alexandr's body from the exertions of his performance. "His smell is so good and earthy," Andrew thought. He wanted to just stand there for a while breathing in Alexandr's scent. He had never had the smell of another man's body evoke this feeling before.

They hugged for a while and when they finally separated, Andrew could see that Alexandr's eyes were red. It was very obvious that Alexandr was really happy to see him there for his rehearsal.

"How long have you been here? Did you get to see a lot of the rehearsal?" Alexandr asked.

"About two hours. You did very well. I was very touched."

"Wait for a few minutes. I'll change quickly and then let's go get something to eat. We have not eaten since noon. This director is a tyrant. But a very effective and accomplished tyrant," Alexandr said with a big smile.

Since strangers were not allowed in the actors' dressing room, Andrew waited in the foyer of the performance hall. About 15 minutes later, Alexandr appeared.

"Was that fast enough? I needed a quick shower too," Alexandr said. "We've been sweating all day. Everyone is very tired."

Andrew and Alexandr walked to a restaurant near the theater and were promptly seated. Alexandr kept sneaking looks at Andrew. He could not believe Andrew had actually come to see his rehearsal. "I am so happy to see you tonight," he said.

"What's the story in your show? It looks very familiar, but I don't recall where I've seen it before."

"I know, you've probably seen the movie called 'Tempest,' by director Alberto Lattada in 1959."

"Yes, now I remember! I saw that old movie on TV when I was about 13 years old with my grandma. She loved it so much. I remember the movie made her cry almost from the beginning till the end. You know, she missed Russia very much."

The waiter came to take their order. Actually, Andrew hadn't eaten dinner yet either since he had come to the theater directly from the embassy. They ordered their food, then turned their attention back to each other as the waiter left.

Alexandr continued, "The show was based on the two novels, 'The Captain's Daughter' and 'The Revolt of Pugachev' written by Alexander Pushkin."

"I have read about him but haven't read any of his work. I seem to remember he had a short life."

"Yes. He was born in 1799 and died in 1837 in St. Petersburg. You know, he was only 38 years old when he died. But his novels are very touching and much loved by the Russians."

"Wow. How did you remember so much detail about the background?"

"It is required for everyone in the show to learn about the author. The director always tells us that if you don't know the author and his personality, how will you know the feeling of the story he created? Also, if we don't know, we will be punished," Alexandr tossed of his last remark as a simple matter of fact.

"What will the name of your play be? Tempest?" Andrew asked.

"I don't know. Maybe Tempest, but maybe not. Mr. Jarcev will make the decision, usually half way during the rehearsal period."

"Could you refresh my memory about the story? It's been a long time."

"It talks about a privileged officer of Catherine the Great's Russian Army during the 1700s. The officer was sent to a distant fort for disciplinary reasons. On the way there, he and his old servant saved a half-frozen man from death in a snowstorm. This man had gotten lost and was buried in snow. At the new garrison, against orders, the officer fights a duel with his foe. Then he falls in love with the Captain's daughter, who stood by him when he was accused of being a traitor. His foe is also in love with her. During all this time the man whose life he and his servant saved was calling himself Czar Peter III, but he was really Pugachev, a Cossack. Actually, the real Czar had already been dead for ten years at that time. He, I mean Pugachev, was the leader of a revolt in an attempt to overthrow Catherine. He had amassed a huge army of supporters from the downtrodden Cossacks. He was a clever leader but proved no match for Catherine's soldiers. Finally, he was caught and executed."

"Now, I remember it very well. Actually, this officer was not a traitor. He was loyal to the queen, right?"

"Yes. When Pugachev's followers were going to hang the officer, his old servant came forward to beg for his life. Suddenly, Pugachev recognized this old man and realized that the young man they were going to hang was actually the one who saved his life. So, he spared the officer's life."

"That's right. And that was the scene you were rehearsing today?" Andrew asked.

"Yes. Actually, we have been practicing this section for nearly two weeks."

"How did you get started with your performance career?" Andrew asked curiously.

"My family has four boys and I am the youngest one. My father is a major in the Russian special unit, a very loyal officer to the Communist party. Two of my brothers, actually, are also soldiers. One serves in the air force, while the other one is in the army."

This alerted Andrew that Alexandr was from a Communist military family. However, he kept himself calm. "How about your third brother?" he inquired further.

Alexandr laughed and said, "He is very different from my father and brothers. He is a graduate engineer student at Moscow University."

"You are different too. You are not following the same path as your father and two elder brothers."

"When my mother was pregnant with me, since my family had already had three boys she was hoping I would be a girl."

"She must have been very disappointed."

"Not only her. My whole family, my father, and also my brothers were disappointed."

"Were you treated badly because of this?"

"No. My mom told me that I have always been cute and lovable since I was born. In just a couple days, I was accepted and loved more than the others." He looked at Andrew with a funny and joking smile.

"How about your father? Are you afraid of him? You know, my father is also a soldier. My brother and I were afraid of him, but of course we loved and respected him as well."

"Same here. My father seldom smiles. Only if something really makes him happy. My family, all of them have been brainwashed from birth and educated severely to be loyal to the country and Communist party. My father always tells us not to be afraid to die for the country."

The waiter brought their food and drink and they dug in ravenously since both of them were very hungry. But after only a few bites, Alexandr paused and said, "When I was 17, in the third year of high school, due to my ability in acting and dancing I was chosen to play one of the main roles in the school show. Actually, we represented the school to participate in the national high school stage performance competition. We won second place from among 15 teams."

"What was the name of the show?"

"'The Seagull,' written by Chekhov in 1896." Alexandr opened his mouth wide and could not help yawning.

Andrew could clearly see that Alexandr was very tired after a long day of rehearsal and decided not to continue asking questions. But, Alexandr continued talking.

"In the competition, I was spotted by a well-known actor and director, Ivan Jarcev. The one you saw tonight. The next day after the show was over, I was called to the principal's office in school. When I went in, I saw Mr. Jarcev sitting there as well. He told me that I had strong potential to become one of the best actors in the future. He asked me if I would like to continue my acting training and become a professional. I told him that I was not sure. He left his name and address and asked me to think about it and talk to my parents about it. If I was interested, I could come to Moscow to see him after my graduation."

Alexandr drank some tea before continuing.

"When I went home, I discussed it with my parents. Because Mr. Jarcev was so well-known and respected, they believed it to be a rare opportunity. My father and mother encouraged me to go and pursue this for my life and future. Therefore, after my graduation from high school when I was 18, I went to see Mr. Jarcev in Moscow. Eventually, I moved in and stayed with him temporarily."

Alexandr yawned again. Andrew saw it and said, "Why don't we end our talking for tonight? You're tired. You need a nice rest."

Alexandr really was tired. He had been excited by Andrew's visit, but when he began to relax, he felt thoroughly exhausted. When he heard Andrew's suggestion, he thought, "Here is a good man. He's concerned with my needs more than his own desire. It is rare to see this in today's society."

Alexandr nodded his head with an expression of appreciation, "Okay. See you Saturday morning at the club."

Andrew called for a taxi and left while Alexandr walked back to his apartment since it was only a few blocks away.

Planning a Trip

Andrew arrived at the club on Saturday morning at about 10 o'clock. He came earlier than usual, hoping that Alexandr would also be there. But when he arrived, he didn't see Alexandr. He wondered if Alexandr would arrive later and then wondered if he'd even come at all. After all, they had known each other only one week. Although he saw a couple of employees from the American Embassy there with their families, Andrew didn't feel like joining them. To be polite, he said hello to them and then went into the social room and sat down on a couch in the corner. He ordered some breakfast because he had not eaten yet and was really hungry. As he dined, he occasionally took a look towards the entrance of the club. Andrew was eager to see Alexandr and get to know more about his new friend. In his heart, he could not deny that he already liked him quite a lot.

The waiter brought a glass of juice, a cup of coffee, a plate with two eggs and ham, and a couple of pieces of toast – a typical American breakfast that you could not get outside of the club easily. As Andrew began to eat, he saw Alexandr come in. He was very excited and waved to him. Unfortunately, Alexandr didn't see him and kept walking straight toward the swimming pool area. Andrew wondered if he should go after him or not. He didn't know how seriously Alexandr viewed their friendship. After all, again, they had met only a week ago. It would be embarrassing if he ran after him and found out that he was not as serious about their relationship as Andrew was. He had stood up to follow, but after reconsideration, sat back down.

In a few minutes, Andrew saw Alexandr come in to the social room and scan its occupants, obviously looking around for someone. Andrew waved his hand at him and Alexandr came toward him.

"Are you looking for someone?" Andrew asked.

"I am looking for you. I was beginning to think you had not come yet," Alexandr replied.

Andrew was very happy to hear that Alexandr had looked for him immediately after he came in. It reassured him that Alexandr appreciated their friendship as much as he did.

"I just arrived about 20 minutes ago. Are you hungry? I was just having breakfast," Andrew said, looking at Alexandr expectantly.

"I was busy reading the script again this morning. You know, if I don't have it memorized by next Monday I will be in trouble with my director. I forgot to have breakfast while I was working on that. And after I memorized the script, I rushed right over here."

"Can't you read your script tonight?"

"No. If I put it off, my mind will be preoccupied with thinking of it all day and that will get in the way of my fun. Now that I have memorized it, I don't have to worry about it and I can spend as much time as possible with you."

Andrew was surprised that Alexandr would talk so openly about how much he appreciated being with Andrew, without masking his emotions or feelings.

"Let's share this breakfast. We can have our lunch early today," Andrew said with a smile. He turned to face the waiter and asked for another set of silverware.

"No, no. I shouldn't eat your breakfast," Alexandr protested.

"Don't be silly. Yours is mine and mine is mine. Right?" Andrew laughed and looked at Alexandr with a funny face.

When the waiter brought an extra spoon and fork, Andrew asked, "Alexandr, do you like coffee or tea?"

"Tea. Please."

Andrew ordered another glass of juice and a cup of British black tea. He then divided everything in half. "Okay. That side is yours.

Don't be shy."

"Thank you. You are very kind." Alexandr looked at Andrew and laughed, then he picked up a fork and began to eat.

In only a few short minutes the plate was clean. The waiter brought another glass of juice and a pot of tea along with a cup.

"To our friendship," Andrew said and brought up his glass of juice.

"To our friendship," Alexandr repeated, looking at Andrew sincerely.

"What should we do today? I don't want to swim now. I prefer swimming later in the day."

"How about playing ping-pong? There are a couple of ping-pong tables in the corner. Do you play?" Alexandr asked.

"Okay, let's go. But I have to tell you that I am not very good at it."

"Me neither. Let's just have fun," Alexandr said and led the way to the ping-pong area.

As they approached the tables, some other players were just leaving. Another table was occupied by two teens.

"See how lucky we are," Alexandr indicated the available table.

After a few rounds, Andrew recognized that Alexandr was actually pretty good. He had no chance of defeating him. "Where did you learn this?" he said. "You are pretty good."

"I used to play with my brothers on the holidays when I was in high school. There were many ping-pong tables in my high school. Ping-pong was one of the common school sport competitions. You know, ping-pong is very popular in Russia. It is fun and doesn't cost too much."

"To tell the truth, I have played it only a few times."

"My coach in high school always taught us that you could improve your alertness, awareness, and concentration through playing ping-pong. I believe he was right. I believe that I was able to concentrate better than many of my classmates in the school because of playing ping-pong. I found that my speed and reaction time in general also improved," Alexandr said.

The Secrecy

"You play like you're a professional. Now show me some tricks."

Alexandr smiled at Andrew and began to show him some of the basic skills of playing. They had a good time. After they had played for about two hours, Andrew believed that he had improved a lot. He had always been able to catch on to things quickly, especially in sports. Alexandr was surprised at how fast Andrew picked up on the tricks and tactics of the game. By the end of the morning, Andrew had almost beaten Alexandr once.

"Let's take a break and have some lunch. Someone ate half my breakfast and now I'm hungry again already," Andrew joked.

"Okay. Let's go to the dining room and find something to eat."

In the dining room they sat down at a table in the far corner. They chose the spot as a place where they would be able to talk freely. "What else do you like?" Andrew asked when they had ordered. "I like to listen to classical music a lot, especially Chopin and Beethoven."

"Really? I also like Chopin and Beethoven! As matter of fact, I love almost all classical music. We use them a lot in the show. I also like nature, climbing mountains, swimming, and running. You know, I must keep in good shape for my performances."

Andrew was delighted to hear that almost everything Alexandr liked were also his favorite activities. "We have a lot of the same favorites," he said. "We should have fun together."

The waiter brought lunch and they dug in with gusto. When the waiter brought the bill, Andrew said, "Just put it on my account."

"No, no. I should pay for it," Alexandr interjected.

"Look, I don't want to offend you, but I think I can afford it more than you can. Besides, when I work outside of the U.S., I get a higher rate of pay. Really, I am happy to pay for it."

"That's very nice of you. I just feel like I am taking advantage of you."

"Nonsense. Let's rest for thirty minutes and then go swim. They say it is not healthy to go swimming immediately after eating. We might sink."

They both laughed. Andrew ordered a couple of glasses of red wine which they brought with them to the swimming pool area. No one was sitting at the table that Alexandr had fallen into a couple weeks ago. They took seats at the table and Andrew looked at Alexandr and then at the table before starting to laugh.

"You know, I want to thank this table. Without this table, we wouldn't know each other. I am so glad about what happened here."

"Me too. I really feel like I have finally found a sincere friend. You know, you may know many friends but to find one that matches your personality and spiritual feeling is not easy."

"What do you mean spiritual feeling?"

"You know, like we've been talking about. The kind of feeling that can stimulate and inspire your thinking to help you find what you really want in life. The feeling that your life has been enlightened. I don't know how to explain it in words. It is that deep feeling inside here," Alexandr said using his right index and middle fingers to point at his heart.

Actually, Andrew knew precisely what Alexandr meant. But he could not describe or explain it either. It was a natural, instinctive sensation that made him feel like he had known Alexandr for a long time, long before they actually met. It was something that made you feel that life was fulfilling and joyful. It was a feeling that they didn't have any false masks between them.

"I wish the feeling I had with Judy was like this. Unfortunately, it was not. Absolutely not," he thought.

"Wake up. Are you dreaming?" Alexandr lightly broke into Andrew's thoughts.

"No. The meaning of this spiritual feeling is so profound, I need to ponder it. It's a feeling of your true nature, without pretending or wearing a mask. You feel spiritually free with yourself and others."

Alexandr looked down and felt a little bit uneasy when Andrew said this. The truth was, Alexandr was experiencing this very feeling they were talking about for the first time in his life. However, deep inside, he was still locked in the bondage of his reality. He was relieved that it seemed that Andrew hadn't noticed his discomfort and confusion. They continued talking until the prescribed wait period between eating and swimming had passed.

"Let's go swim now. I need to think about this before we can discuss it further. You know, we're talking about something that's so intangible - it cannot be seen, it can only be felt with an honest and sincere heart," Andrew said seriously, then shook his head. "Anyway, let's get changed and swim," he concluded with a chuckle and stood.

"You go first. I must say hi to some friends who just came in. I'll meet you later."

Andrew looked toward the social room that was next to the swimming pool. He saw that Alexandr's friend, Viktor, with his girlfriend, Alena, had just arrived and were talking to the waiter.

"Okay. See you later."

Andrew went into the dressing room, changed, and came back to the swimming pool area. He jumped in the water to wait for Alexandr, however 15 minutes passed, and he was still waiting. He was beginning to wonder if Alexandr would join him after all, or if he had gotten tied up with his friends. While he wondered about this, he saw Alexandr come into the pool area wearing his swimming trunks and carrying a towel in his right hand. Alexandr put his towel on the chair and walked over to the swimming pool.

"There you are. I was starting to wonder if you might have left with your friends," Andrew said.

"No, of course not. My friends were telling me that they are going to get married in six months. After that, they plan to move to a small town called Kolpino near Leningrad. You know, his job."

"I see. How old is he? He looked so young."

"He is 24 years old and his fiancée is 22. His father is a high-ranking Communist officer and they have money. Usually, when you're rich, you don't have to worry too much about your future. So, you can get married earlier."

"When do you plan to get married?"

"I don't know. I don't plan for it. You know, I'm still young. I'm only 22. I want to experience my life first. How about you?"

"I don't know either. Remember I told you that I have a girlfriend, Judy, in America? We've been out of touch for a few months. She stopped calling me back."

"I hope she is okay."

"I am pretty sure that she's okay. Otherwise, my family would have told me already. But I could tell last time I talked to them that there was something else about her that my family didn't want to tell me."

"Well. Let's swim first and talk later."

They swam for a while. Andrew thought he might challenge Alexandr to a swimming competition since he was beaten in ping-pong. "What do you say if I ask you to have a race with me?" Andrew looked at Alexandr with a big smile.

"Well. It seems that your swimming skills are better than mine. I may not have any chance."

"Then how about endurance? Let's see who is able to swim farthest."

"Okay." Alexandr began to swim toward the other side of the swimming pool and Andrew tried to catch him.

After an hour and a half of swimming without stop, Alexandr raised up his right hand and gave a signal to Andrew. Andrew stopped doing laps and swam over to him. He could see that Alexandr was tired and puffing.

"I am too tired. I cannot continue any longer," Alexandr said looking at Andrew and seeing that Andrew was not nearly as tired.

"That means you lost. We are even now." Andrew looked at him with a triumphant smile.

"How do you have so much endurance?"

"I have always loved swimming, you know. Actually, my friends and I used to go swimming in the ocean."

"Really? I have never even seen the ocean. We have only the sea and the sea is much smaller than the ocean, you know."

"It doesn't matter if you swim in the ocean or in the sea, you feel the same. We humans are small compared with either the sea or the ocean."

"Which ocean did you go to? Atlantic or Pacific."

"Of course, the Atlantic. I'm from the east coast – Washington, DC. The Pacific is on the other end of the U.S., on the west coast. When I was in college studying computer science, my friends and I would go to Virginia Beach almost every other weekend in the summertime. We swam and competed for hours without stop to build up our endurance."

"I have never swum in the sea or the ocean. All my swimming was done in a pool or in the Moscow River. This is like a tiny, fake ocean. I hope I can swim in the ocean or sea someday."

"Is there any beach open to the public near Moscow?"

"Yes, on Moscow River. There are a few beaches in the Silver Forest (Serebryany bor). These are a series of lakes and channels on the Moscow River that is about 12.5 miles north of the city center. But there are no beaches near the sea."

"You are talking about beaches on lakes and rivers. But I was talking about a beach on the sea or ocean."

"Oh. Right. The closest one on the sea is near Leningrad on The Gulf of Finland that is connected to the Baltic Sea. I was in Leningrad once for a performance, but I was too busy to get out and explore. I don't know very much about Leningrad at all. I don't know if they have any beach that is open to the public."

"I have heard and read about Leningrad. It's a city full of Russian tradition and culture. I've been told it is the second most beautiful city other than Moscow in Russia. Hmm. It's about 440 miles from Moscow. If we took the train, it would take us at least 7 hours to get there."

"Are you crazy?" Alexandr broke in. "It sounds like you are

planning to go there."

"Yes, I am. Why not? Why don't we go next Friday night and stay there until Sunday? I am very interested in seeing the city and I would like to swim in the sea. This would also give you a chance to experience the beach and the sea. It's very different from swimming in a pool, you know. The water is salty. When you swallow it, it makes you thirsty and if you get salt water in your nose, it's very uncomfortable. Because of the salt content, you can float on top of the water easily. And there's an undertow, which is a current that flows toward or away from the shore. If you don't know the current, you can be carried away into the deep ocean without even feeling it. Many people die swimming in the ocean each year because of this."

"Really! If it's so dangerous, why are there so many people who like to swim in the ocean?"

"Because it's fun! It's more challenging and exciting! Once you know how to deal with the current and waves, then it is much more fun than swimming in a pool."

"It sounds fun. It's hot in July. You know, the summer in Russia is very short. If we miss this month and the first two weeks of August, it will be too cold."

"True. You know what? Let's fly there," Andrew said.

"I would like to but, to be honest, I can't afford it." Alexandr looked at Andrew with his face downcast. He didn't want to disappoint Andrew, but he really could not afford it. It was too expensive to fly.

"Don't worry about that, this will be my treat. I have always wanted to visit this city and see the culture there. I've heard that they have many fantastic museums."

When Alexandr heard this, his face flushed, and he said, "I can't accept that! It will cost too much of your money!"

"Don't be silly. You know, I don't spend much here in Moscow. And my apartment is free," Andrew tried to reassure Alexandr. "Besides, you will be acting as my tour guide. You were there before, right? I can't ask my tour guide to pay for the trip." Andrew looked at

Alexandr's shy face and laughed.

"But I don't really know Leningrad at all. When I was there a year ago, I was only able to go in certain special areas. All I remember is that the city is very beautiful with many fine examples of Russian culture. But..."

Andrew broke in, "Alexandr, I really want you to come with me, and I won't take no for an answer. I have been enjoying our talks and our time together. We'll have a lot of fun, and we'll get to know each other better. Don't you think so?" He looked at Alexandr with affection. "Let's go this Friday right after work. How about sometime between 7 and 9 p.m.? I'll check the times and make reservations for the tickets," Andrew continued.

"I don't think I have anything to do next weekend," Alexandr said slowly, beginning to warm to the idea. "Actually, I was planning to show you around Moscow again."

"Okay then, it's settled. I'll come to see your rehearsal again this Thursday, if I may. We can talk more about it then. Let me give you my phone number. If you need to contact me at any time, call me after 6:30 p.m."

"Can I call your office?"

"No, please don't. They record and check all phone calls, you know. We won't be able to talk freely."

"Okay. Let's rest now. I'm tired," Alexandr suggested.

They climbed out of the swimming pool and went over to the table where they had left their towels on the seats. After they had dried off and sat down, Andrew looked at the waiter standing near the entrance area and gave him a signal. The waiter came and bowed to him. Andrew ordered two glasses of vodka.

"Do you love your acting career?" Andrew asked Alexandr.

"Yes and no," Alexandr replied. "I enjoyed the performing arts so much when I was a teen. However, since I became a professional, I don't enjoy it as much since there is a lot of pressure. Now, it is more for glory, pride, reputation, and money. I feel that I am a slave of these fake feelings. I enjoy the arts and performing, but I hate the trap of doing it for these reasons."

"How often have you traveled and performed?"

"Well, usually, it takes half a year or even nine months of rehearsal and preparation before we go on tour. Then, we perform the same show for the next two or three years in different cities. If the show is not popular, we might only tour for a year. After the first week, you begin to feel like a robot repeating the same thing over and over. Soon, if you're not careful you can lose the feeling of creation. It becomes a business and not an art anymore in some ways."

"How long were you traveling during the last show?"

"About 18 months. Our old show finished about a month ago. As you know, we began a new rehearsal period only three weeks ago. I don't know how long this rehearsal period will last. Once the director is satisfied with our performance, and the contract is signed, we will begin to tour again."

They talked until after 6 p.m. Time just seemed to speed by when they were talking together.

"I'm hungry again. Let's eat something. Swimming always makes me hungry," Andrew explained.

"I'm hungry too. Let's change and go eat."

They went into the dressing room to shower. For some reason they were a bit uncomfortable to see each other naked, though both of them had showered with guys before. Andrew couldn't help peeking at Alexandr as they showered. "He has such a nice body," he thought.

While he was thinking this, he noticed that Alexandr was looking at his body as well. That made him somewhat embarrassed and he felt uneasy.

"Hey, you're in great shape. It must be all the swimming," Alexandr said, trying to ease the awkwardness of the situation.

"Actually, you're in great shape yourself."

"Well you know I have to keep my body in good shape, or else. If I don't, I'll lose my job."

They finished showering and got dressed, then went to the dining room for dinner. The feeling of being embarrassed evaporated and the feeling of ease and comfort that had come to characterize their time together returned. They ordered their meals and drank some very fine vodka.

"So, what kind of workout do you have to do to be in such perfect shape? I've always been interested in fitness," Andrew asked curiously.

"You know, we rehearse six to eight hours per day, five days a week. We're conditioning our bodies all the time. You probably saw during last Thursday's visit that all of the performers have good bodies. It's required, and they're very strict about it. How about you?"

"You were right, I've done a lot of swimming over the years, and sometimes I'll go to the fitness center to lift weights and try to build some muscle."

They both felt surprisingly comfortable talking about each other's body and were happy to know someone who was as serious as themselves about taking good care of their own health and fitness. It seemed that both of them were not just attracted by each other's looks, but also each other's health.

"What are you doing tomorrow? If you're interested, I can take you to see some more museums and tourist sites," Alexandr said.

"I have no plans. That would be great. Where should we meet? When?"

"How about the same place and the same time as last week."

"Great. Oh, I almost forgot. Here is my telephone number." Andrew took a piece of paper from his pocket notebook to write down the number and gave it to Alexandr.

It was already 8:30 by the time they finished eating, so they said goodbye to each other and went home.

Contact Old Friend

Once Andrew was back in his apartment he decided to call his old buddy, Michael, who was now working at the American Consulate in Leningrad. He dialed the number he had for Michael's home.

"Кто это?" ("Who is it?") Michael's wife, Olga, answered the phone.

"Hi, Olga. This is Andrew from Moscow."

"Hi, Andrew, it's been a long time. Michael told me he's spoken to you a few times since your arrival in Moscow. He talks about you and your old swim trips all the time."

"Is he around? Can I talk to him?"

"Of course. Hold on a minute, he's playing with our son upstairs. Let me get him." Olga put the telephone on the table and went to get Michael.

Andrew flashed back to their long friendship and the history they shared.

When Michael's father was only seven years old, his grandparents had emigrated from Poland to the U.S. right before World War II. Michael is 27 years old now, one year older than Andrew. Andrew recalled how Paul Rosen, Jeff Willis, Michael Graczyk, and he used to go to Virginia Beach to swim. "What a good time we had," he thought.

Andrew also remembered how they used to compete in swimming to the farthest place from the shore to see who had the best endurance. They often took two lifesavers. If they didn't, they might drown due to fatigue. It was often a two-hour competition. Though Andrew won most of the time, he had been beaten on three occasions by Michael. Michael was the one who threatened him the most in these swim competitions. One time, Andrew had gotten an agonizing cramp in his left calf when he was out in the deep water. If there had been no lifesaver around, he would surely have drowned. When Michael had realized Andrew was far behind him, he knew something must be wrong and swam back for him. He immediately grabbed Andrew and managed to get him over to the lifesavers that Paul and Jeff were towing behind them. "The Gang of Four." He couldn't help but to smile.

Later, Michael fell in love with Olga, who was from Leningrad. Olga's family had immigrated to America in 1979. They were married one year after Michael and Andrew completed their special intelligence training. Now they had a two-year-old boy. When Andrew applied for the American Embassy job in Moscow, Michael had already applied for a job working at the American Consulate in Leningrad.

"Andrew, old pal, are you well?" Michael's voice passed through the phone.

"I am fine, Michael," Andrew answered. "Actually, I'm doing pretty good. I've been very much enjoying touring around Moscow and viewing Russian culture."

"That's great. When you called me last time you sounded depressed."

"I'm okay now. I just missed the family and old times with friends."

"I can understand that. So, what's up? Anything new?"

"Actually, I wanted to ask you a few questions."

"Okay, shoot."

"Is there any beach that's open to the public in Leningrad?"

"Andrew, are you kidding? This is not America. The summer is very short here. There are no beaches open to the public. Usually, when people want to swim, they just go and find a spot. What happened? I know, you miss the old times we had, right?"

"It's true. I miss you guys and the good times on the beach." Andrew's voice showed his disappointment.

"Tell you what. I found a spot on the beach not too far from Leningrad that is good for swimming. It's a secret spot I learned about from a local guy here working for the American Consulate."

"Really? Tell me more."

"You know, almost all the beaches around Leningrad are covered by pebbles, not sand like Virginia beaches. Also, the water tends to be very shallow. You have to walk for a long distance to reach any kind of depth for swimming. Only this spot is covered with sand and the distance from the shore to the deep water is short. And there is less pollution. But the best part is the underwater current." Michael was excited by Andrew's enthusiasm.

"You've been there to swim?"

"Yes. Twice. Once with my family, and once with that local guy. My wife doesn't like swimming, especially in the sea. Are you thinking of coming?"

"Yes, next weekend. Can you go?" Andrew asked, but hoping Michael couldn't so he could be alone with Alexandr.

"No, sorry, I can't. It's my wife's birthday. If I go, she will kill me." Michael laughed at the other end.

"I have a friend coming with me."

"A girlfriend?"

"No. Just a friend I met. You know, most girls don't like deep sea swimming."

"Okay. Say, I think I can borrow a car from the office for you. There is always a car available for use by an employee here and I believe there's no one who is going to use it this weekend. When are you going to arrive?"

"I don't know yet. I think we'll probably arrive Friday night. Then I could come to see you Saturday morning. I am sorry that you have to be there for me."

"No problem, pal."

"How about I meet you at the American Consulate at 9:00 a.m.?"

"That would be great. I could still get home for breakfast after that. We always get up late and eat late during the weekend."

"Can you also book a hotel for me? You know the city better than I do."

Michael guffawed, "You owe me now, pal. No, it's no problem. There is a nice hotel, Hotel Neva, on ul Chaikovsgkogo 17. It is one of the oldest hotels and has been in operation since 1913. And it's only three or four kilometers from the Consulate. American Consulate employees use this hotel for their visitors all the time. You can walk from the hotel to the Consulate in 20 minutes. I'll book a room for two. Friday and Saturday night, right?"

"Yes. Just tell me the address of the Consulate. Or I could find it out in the office here."

"Let me just tell you – it's on Furshtaditskaya ul, on the south of Neva River and north of Leningrad."

Andrew wrote everything down on the note pad on his desk.

"Okay. Now, tell me the location of this secret beach spot. I promise I won't reveal it to anyone" Andrew said.

"Are you kidding? You're going to take your friend there already. Okay, okay. Write this down carefully. When you leave the consulate, turn left. Next, turn right onto Liteyny pr going north. Then turn left into Pirogovskaya nab which connects to M10 or E95 in about 27 miles. When you reach the town of Bellostrov, get onto highway A123. Then drive another 37 miles or so until you reach the town called Ozerki. The beach is on the north side of that town. You cannot miss it. You are an expert ocean swimmer, you should be able to spot the place easily."

Andrew wrote down everything and repeated his notes to Michael to make sure he had them right.

"It's correct, pal," Michael confirmed.

"Oh yeah, how do I return the car?" Andrew asked.

"Simply drop it off at the consulate. After you pass the guards at the gate, drive directly to the parking lot. Then just give the key to the doorkeeper of the consulate. We always do it."

"You are great, pal. I owe you."

"No sweat. If you have more questions, call me again. It will be good to see you next Saturday. See you then."

After Andrew hung up, he immediately found his map of Leningrad and traced out the directions Michael had given him. "This looks very easy. We'll have a great time," he thought.

Second Moscow Tour

When Andrew arrived at the Moscow train station at 10 o'clock the next morning, Alexandr was once again already there waiting.

"Did you have breakfast yet?" Alexandr asked as Andrew got out of the taxi.

"No. I got up late. You know, I'm always lazier on the weekend."

"Not 'lazier.' You should say you are 'more relaxed and taking it easy' on the weekend," Alexandr looked at Andrew and laughed.

"Okay. Let's eat first and then go adventuring."

They found a cafeteria near the train station and ordered some breakfast.

"Where should we go?" Andrew asked as they sat waiting for their food.

"I think you'll like the Russian historical museums such as Moscow City History Museum or the Contemporary History Museum, and also art galleries such as 'Art Museum, Kostroma' or 'Art Museum, Sergiev Posad.' There are so many museums and galleries in Moscow. It would take you a couple weeks to see them all. If you wish to study them in detail, it could take you a few years."

"Alexandr, since today is sunny and nice out, why don't we spend time doing some outdoor sight-seeing? We can save the indoor activities for rainy days. You know, you don't always see the sun shine in Moscow during the summertime." Actually, Andrew had already visited some of the ones Alexandr mentioned in the first few months when he arrived. But he didn't want to tell Alexandr that.

"You're right," Alexandr agreed. "In that case, how about we go to the Museum of the Great Patriotic War and the Victory Park first. Then, we can go to the Alexandrovsky Garden at the city center. We'll be tired after all that."

"Yeah, that sounds good. I was in Alexandrovsky Garden before. Two months after my arrival, I went there once. However, it was a cold and snowy day. Not a good day for outdoor sight-seeing. So, I definitely need to go again."

The waiter brought their food and they began to eat. Suddenly, Alexandr raised up his head and stared at Andrew.

"Do you believe in reincarnation?" Alexandr asked, looking at Andrew with a curious look.

"Yes, I do. But sometimes.... I don't know."

"I believe our acquaintance was not an accident. I believe our meeting was pre-arranged by our destiny. Somehow, I feel that we have known each other for a long time. I even believe that we had a very close relationship in our previous life."

"Yes. It seems strange, but I have that same feeling that I have known you before."

"Actually, I have become convinced that we met in this life to fulfill our destiny of the continuation of our relationship from the last life. I don't know how to explain it."

Though Andrew did not believe this concept of pre-arranged destiny as much as Alexandr, he could not explain why he felt so very differently when he was with Alexandr. He had never experienced this feeling with anyone else. He was not only enjoying his companionship with Alexandr, but also felt excited and inspired both spiritually and physically. He had to admit to himself that he felt attracted to Alexandr.

After breakfast, they went to the Museum of the Great Patriotic War and Victory Park first. They stayed there until almost 2:30 in the afternoon.

"Should we continue to the next stop, Alexandrovsky Garden?" Alexandr asked.

"Sure, but let's find something to eat first."

They found a nice restaurant and went in. Once they were sitting down, Andrew looked at Alexandr and said, "Oh yeah, I almost forgot the most important thing."

"What?" Alexandr looked at Andrew with a curious expression.

"I talked to my friend in Leningrad and he told me of a secret beach spot where we can go swimming in the sea."

"Really? I thought it was hopeless. There are not supposed to be any open beaches near the sea in Russia."

"I'll tell you more about it this Thursday. I'll make reservations for the plane tickets tomorrow."

Alexandr was very excited to know that they would go to Leningrad next weekend for some sight-seeing and swimming at a beach. In a few minutes, the waiter had brought their food and drinks. They ate their meal, then went on to Alexandrovsky Garden where the flowers were blooming, and it was very beautiful and relaxing. There were also very many people there. They found a bench and sat down.

"This is pretty different from what I saw and felt when I came here in February," Andrew said.

Alexandr looked at Andrew with a funny smile.

"What's so funny?"

"Nobody would come to this garden in February. Only Americans," Alexandr laughed.

Andrew suddenly felt silly for coming here at the wrong time. But today was a beautiful day, so they simply sat there and enjoyed the sunshine. In only a couple hours, the sun would be gone. Though they didn't talk very much, they felt the warmth and comfort of their friendship. They watched people walking by and enjoyed the serenity of the park. Andrew knew that this kind of silent relationship was precious and not easy to find. He could sit with Alexandr like this without talking for a long time, just enjoying the companionship. He remembered whenever he was with Cindy or Judy in the past, he felt he had to keep them entertained or engaged in talking all the time, otherwise they felt that they were being ignored and not loved.

To show his appreciation, Andrew took Alexandr to a very elegant and expensive restaurant that evening. It was so elegant and expensive that only high-ranking Communist officers and some foreigners were able to afford it. This reminded Andrew of the time he took Judy to a very elegant and expensive restaurant for her birthday. But instead of enjoying a special evening they had only ended up having a huge fight.

"Anyway, I want to forget about her. I just want to enjoy tonight with Alexandr," Andrew thought.

Dinner was splendid but they both had a little too much to drink. By the time they finished dinner, it was already 9:30. They left the restaurant and grabbed a taxi. Andrew asked Alexandr to tell the driver his address so he would be taken home first.

"When can we meet again?" Andrew asked.

"I am always very busy during rehearsal from Monday through Wednesday. I feel so tired every night and need sleep. The best day is still Thursday, right after rehearsal."

"Actually, Thursday is better for me too. Usually, I have a lot of work to do from Monday to Wednesday. You know, there are always a lot of things to take care of at the beginning of the week. As a matter of fact, I usually work late on those three days. So, Thursday is great," Andrew said with a smile.

In just 25 minutes or so, the taxi stopped in front of Alexandr's apartment.

"See you Thursday. Good night."

"Good night." Alexandr replied.

Trip Arrangement

Monday at noon, Andrew went home from the embassy. Usually he would eat lunch at the embassy, but today he felt like going back home for a while. He also had some personal business he wanted to take care of and didn't want to use the embassy phones. When he arrived home he first called around to some airlines, discovering that there were about 11 flights per day from Moscow to Leningrad.

"It's great that there are so many flights. That means there are a lot of travelers between Moscow and Leningrad each day," Andrew thought. He made two roundtrip reservations and then called Michael in Leningrad.

"Hi, Michael, I was expecting you would be home for lunch. I know your wife's fabulous cooking. Say, your home is near the U.S. Consulate, isn't it?"

"Yes, I admit I enjoy coming home to have lunch with my wife and son. I'm a family man now with two masters. I have to fulfill their wishes."

"I always knew you were a family man. Anyway, sorry to interrupt your lunch."

"We haven't started eating yet. Olga is just getting the table ready while I watch our boy."

"I just called to confirm that my friend and I are coming Friday night and leaving Sunday afternoon. How about the car? Any problem?"

"What do you think, pal? You're in good hands."

"Hotel reservation?"

"Of course. It's all set, under your name. Just tell the hotel clerk your name. I'll see you Saturday morning at 9:30, right?"

"No, 9:00 a.m., Michael. You're getting old."

"Okay, okay. I'm just in heaven. Well, lunch is ready, so I'd better go. See you Saturday."

"Thanks a lot, pal. See you."

2nd Rehearsal Visit

After having such a good time on Sunday, Andrew could not wait until Thursday and the upcoming weekend. As he sat back in his office, he just could not believe that destiny was so amazing, and always arranged things in such a strange and complex way. He knew if his grandparents and parents hadn't grown up here, he would not have had any temptation to come to Russia. If Alexandr had not accidentally bumped into his table, he would not have finally found a true friend. He began to believe what Alexandr said about destiny. His work weeks passed so quickly now since he had met Alexandr, and each day he was full of energy and happiness.

That Thursday again after work, Andrew went to the theater at 6:30 to watch Alexandr's rehearsal. He could see Alexandr up on stage and again Alexandr could not see him since he was sitting in the dark in the last row of seats. It was the same part of "Tempest" that the team had rehearsed last Thursday. As he watched Alexandr's rehearsal, he could see that each step, each body movement, and each word coming out of his mouth was an art. Alexandr had a special way of expressing the meaning of the story. It was elegant and deeply touching. It was as if Andrew was listening to a very fine piece of classical music, and each deliberate subtle aspect was expertly performed. In just a few minutes, he had become absorbed again into the show. Especially now that he had been reminded of the story. Still, he was moved even more this time while watching.

When the director clapped his hands, Andrew jumped. The rehearsal stopped, and the director gave the actors a ten-minute break. The director then turned to talk to the theater manager. Andrew woke up from his deep absorption in the story of the play. He never thought the performing arts could be so touching. Again, he wondered as he had last week, was it because Alexandr was one of the actors, or because of the story itself?

As soon as the break began, Alexandr immediately searched for Andrew's presence. From his seat in the dark, Andrew could see that Alexandr was anxious and expecting him. Alexandr came down to the last row and at last saw Andrew sitting there, smiling.

"How long have you been here watching?" Alexandr asked.

"Since 6:30, about an hour and a half," Andrew replied.

"Tonight's rehearsal was very smooth. I believe we'll be able to get out of here early."

In fact, while he was talking, the director announced that that night's rehearsal was over.

"See? What did I tell you?" Alexandr said. "We know his temper and personality. Wait in the lobby. I will change quickly and come out there to meet you."

About 15 minutes later, Alexandr emerged in his street clothes, and the two headed out of the theater.

"We have not eaten anything since noon. I told you, this director is a killer. A top-notch killer, but still a killer." Alexandr looked at Andrew with a funny smile.

"It seems like you're always hungry. But it's okay, I'm hungry too. What should we have to eat?" Andrew asked.

"Something quick. It's 8:15 already."

For the sake of expediency, they went to the same restaurant where they had eaten the previous Thursday and settled in.

"So, are we going to Leningrad?" Alexandr asked anxiously once they had ordered. It was obvious that he had put a lot of hope into going on the trip.

"Everything is set," Andrew replied. "We will leave Moscow on the 7:45 flight tomorrow night and return on the 5:10 flight Sunday night. There will be a car ready for us to use and a hotel room is already reserved."

"You are super! By the way, do you know which airport? There are five airports around Moscow, you know."

"Sheremetevo-1. That airport serves domestic flights. Do you know it?"

"Not really. It's too expensive for most Russians to fly. When we went to Leningrad for a performance a year ago, we were on a bus. It took us nearly eight hours to get there."

Their dinner was nice and relaxing. They were just happy to see one another again after going a few days without being in each other's presence.

"Let's call it a night. We'll need our rest for tomorrow," Andrew suggested.

"Okay. See you tomorrow night at the airport. I will be there at the front door at least 90 minutes before take-off."

Andrew grabbed a taxi to return to his apartment. As Alexandr walked home he was very happy and excited. He thought, "This must be what it feels like for a child who has learned he will be going to Disney World." Though he had never been to Walt Disney World, he had read about it and heard about it. All Russian kids knew about it, and it was every kid's dream to go there.

Leningrad

Sheremetevo-1 airport was located about 19 miles northwest of Moscow city. The terminal handled most of the flights to and from Leningrad, the Baltic States, Belarus, and northern European Russia. Andrew arrived at the airport by taxi around 6 p.m. It had taken the taxi about 40 minutes to get there. When he stepped into the terminal, he saw Alexandr was once again already there and waiting.

"You're here early. When did you get here?"

"Fifteen minutes ago. I'm just so excited. I didn't know how long the city bus would take to get here from the center of Moscow. It took more than an hour. I wanted to make sure that I wasn't late."

They each only had carry-ons for the two-day trip. After they checked in for their flight, they had some tea. Andrew thought about how this would be the first time he and Alexandr would be alone together for two days. He sat in happy anticipation during all of their hour and 20-minute flight. As soon as they arrived in Leningrad, they grabbed a taxi at the airport to take them to Hotel Neva, on ul Chaikovsgkogo 17. By the time they were checked in, it was nearly 9:40 in the evening.

Andrew walked into the hotel room, dropped his bag and announced, "I'm exhausted. I'm going to shower and pass out. Tomorrow will be a big day – it will be very exciting to swim in the Baltic Sea. I'm just wondering how cold the water will be."

Andrew crawled into bed right after his shower. By the time

Alexandr had finished his shower, he found Andrew was already sound asleep. Apparently, he had had a busy day. Alexandr turned off the light and went to bed as well.

The next morning when Andrew woke up around 7:30, Alexandr was still sleeping soundly. Andrew knew that weekends were the only time that Alexandr could have a nice rest, so he did not disturb him but lay there looking at him for a while. He could not help admiring Alexandr, who was sleeping in his underwear. "He is such a sleeping beauty," he thought. Then Andrew got up and went into the bathroom to get cleaned up. When he came out, Alexandr was sitting up.

"Good morning. Did you sleep well?" Andrew asked.

"Yes. I've been so excited, I couldn't sleep for a few nights. It feels good to have finally slept well."

"Tell you what, I must leave in half an hour to pick up the car at the U.S. Consulate. I should be back here by 9:30. Why don't you get ready while I'm gone? You could order some food from room service so we can have breakfast here."

"That sounds good, I'll wait here for you."

"Oh, by the way, there is a city guide in my luggage. If you get bored, why don't you take it out and see if you can find some good places to go sight-seeing tomorrow. You know we'll have the whole morning and most of the afternoon before we have to return to Moscow."

Andrew left with the map he had brought. On the map, he had made a few marks showing the important sites for this trip. It took him about 25 minutes to get to the U.S. Consulate, arriving at 8:45. He showed the guards his ID and was allowed to go in. Only five minutes later, from a consulate window, he saw Michael arrive in his tiny little square car.

When Michael stepped into the building Andrew shouted out a hearty greeting, "Michael! Hey! It's been more than two years! It's so great to see you, pal."

"Andrew, you look exactly the same, still young and fresh. Why haven't you been caught by some girl yet? Still playing the bachelor? Find any local girls?"

Andrew's face flushed. He knew that he felt an attraction to Alexandr, but Alexandr was a guy, not a girl.

"Ha ha. Okay, be serious. The car. The car," Andrew replied.

"Don't be pushy. You're always the same. So aggressive. Andrew, Andrew, I am so happy to see you again! First, give me a hug." Michael stepped forward, grabbing Andrew in a quick hug and then releasing him. "Wait here for a minute while I go get the key from my office."

Michael disappeared down a hall and a short time later reappeared with the consulate's car key. He led Andrew out to the parking lot.

"Okay, this is the one, pal. It's yours until tomorrow afternoon. Be careful. Don't damage it and don't get into any accidents," Michael warned.

"Okay, okay. Don't mother me."

Andrew took the key, opened the car door, and then also checked the trunk. This was a habit he had developed when he was attending the training center. When he opened the trunk, he saw a lifesaving tube there.

"Just in case, if you need it," Michael said. "You know, it's not easy to find a lifesaver like this in Leningrad. Not too many people use one."

"Thank you, pal."

Andrew was so grateful for Michael's consideration, he couldn't help throwing an arm around Michael's shoulder. As they looked at the tube for a moment, both of them thought back to the time Michael saved Andrew's life during their competition, swimming back for him and bringing him the lifesaver as he struggled with his leg cramp. Andrew grabbed Michael with both arms and gave him another tight hug.

"Am I missing a good old time?" Michael wondered to himself.

"Please give my regards to Olga and kiss your son for me," Andrew said. "I am sorry that I couldn't see them this time. Oh yeah, and tell

Olga happy birthday."

"All right. See you later, Andrew. Take care."

Andrew drove the car back to the hotel and parked in the hotel's parking lot. When he went in their room, Alexandr was already waiting anxiously for him. The hotel service personnel had come with their breakfast, so they sat down to eat. Even though they didn't talk much, it seemed that they communicated just as well in the silence. They felt comfortable as long as they were together. After they ate, there were some leftovers which Alexandr put into a plastic bag and placed in his luggage.

"I am not used to throwing things away, especially food," Alexandr explained.

Andrew laughed quietly to himself. He didn't like leftovers. He had never saved leftovers when he was in America. But then, he didn't have to.

When everything was ready, they went down to the car. Andrew opened the trunk to place their bags inside.

"Is that a lifesaving tube? It looks like a spare tire," Alexandr joked.

"Ha ha. My friend Michael says it isn't easy to find a good one here. Anyway, it's just in case. We probably won't need it since I'm not going to compete with you in the sea."

Andrew followed Michael's directions and after nearly two hours of driving, they finally reached Ozerki, a small town near the shore. As Michael had instructed, he passed the town and went north. After ten more minutes, he saw a spot where there was more sand than others. He stopped the car and stepped out to survey the area. From the looks of the beach, he was sure that this was the spot that Michael had talked about. He could see it had a good current and nice waves. The distance to the water was not too far. Perfect. Andrew was filled with anticipation.

"I believe we have found the secret spot my friend told me about. And it's a perfect warm sunny day. I'm just wondering how cold the water is," Andrew told Alexandr.

Andrew found a flat area with some big rocks around it and drove the car over next to the rocks. When he and Alexandr looked at the beach, other than an older couple they could see walking along the beach some distance away, there was no other person around. Andrew could see that the water in the Baltic Sea was more greenish than the ocean at Virginia Beach. "Let's change," he said.

They took their pants off then covered themselves with the towels they had brought from the hotel while they changed into swim trunks.

"I don't want to leave the car door unlocked and the keys inside. It could be stolen. We don't know this place. But I also don't want to take the keys with me as they could be lost in the sea," Andrew said.

"Let's lock our belongings inside the trunk and then hide the keys somewhere," Alexandr suggested.

So, they did. They found a small rock behind a larger one. Andrew placed a handkerchief on the ground and put the key inside. He then covered it with the smaller rock. No one would know the keys were there except them.

Andrew took Alexandr to a higher spot where they had a good view of the water. There he explained how the current worked.

"You see those two waves coming toward the shore? Between them is a nice calm place. But don't be fooled, this is the current channel. The water there will take you out from the shore very fast."

He continued to point out the current and the waves and explain the potential dangers to Alexandr.

"Wow. I had no idea that it could be so challenging to swim in the sea," Alexandr said.

"Okay, the lesson is over," Andrew announced. "Let's go swim!"

As they stepped into the water they were surprised to discover that the water was not as cold as Andrew had expected. When he saw the excitement on Alexandr's face, he was so happy that he had brought him here. It seemed to Andrew that Alexandr looked like he was reliving his childhood. And Andrew felt the same way. They played in the waves and the current like they were 15 years old again and had a really great time together. After a couple hours, Alexandr had become familiar with the aggressive environment of the sea. They forgot the time, but eventually began to feel worn out.

"I am tired and hungry. Let's go back to the car and rest for a while," Andrew suggested.

They swam back to the shore and retrieved the key to the car. Andrew took his watch out from where he had stored it in the car. "Wow, it's amazing. We've been in the water for three hours already. No wonder I'm hungry."

"Can you open the trunk, Andrew?"

When Andrew opened the trunk, Alexandr went to his luggage and took the morning leftovers out.

"Do you want some?" Alexandr asked.

"You are a lifesaver. I forgot you had hidden food. Give me some! Give me some!" Andrew laughed.

They shared what Alexandr had brought. It was not much, but it offered them some comfort.

"It's nearly 4:30 now and the sun will weaken quickly. I can already feel that it's getting colder. Do you want to continue or quit for today?" Alexandr asked.

"I think that's enough for today. Let's go into town and find something to eat. I'm still pretty hungry."

They changed and drove back to the little town. However, it was not easy to find a restaurant there.

"Let's go back to Leningrad. I don't believe that we'll find any restaurant here," Andrew said. He found a gas station that offered some snacks and bought some cookies. Then he refilled the gas tank and drove them back to Leningrad. They went straight to a restaurant in the city, their hair still messy from the beach.

"Andrew, I want to thank you for today. I had a very good time. I'll remember this day forever." Alexandr looked at Andrew with a smile.

Back at the hotel, they each took a shower and washed the salt from their bodies, then sat down to plan the next day of their holiday.

"Do you have any idea where we should go tomorrow?" Andrew asked.

"Yes, I checked your tourist guide this morning. I believe there are three places worth visiting."

"Really? Tell me," Andrew asked eagerly.

Alexandr was happy to oblige and proceeded to talk Andrew through the details of his plan.

"I think we should visit Palace Square first. There is a Winter Palace there. Across the square from the Winter Palace, there is the General Staff Building that is the first place the tourist guide suggests. After that, we can go to the Russian Museum. It used to be Mikhailovksy Palace and there's a big nice garden called Mikhailoviky Garden. If we still have time, the third spot will be Yusupov Palace. It's not far from the Russian Museum."

"Well, it seems you've studied the guide book well. I will follow your lead. See! I told you that you would be my tourist guide." Andrew laughed. Then he yawned deeply and realized how tired he was.

"It's only 10 and I'm ready to sleep. I haven't had such a good workout in a while," Andrew said, stretching his shoulders which were a bit sore from swimming.

"Why don't you lie down, and I can give you a nice massage," Alexandr offered.

"Really? That would be heaven. This is first-class tourist service." Andrew took his shirt off and lay on his bed face down with only his underwear on.

"We have a lot of experience with massage in the theater, especially from the dance performances," Alexandr explained as he began the massage with a light touch from head to feet, gentle and soft.

Andrew immediately relaxed. It seemed that his energy calmed down quickly from the top of his head to the tips of his toes. He closed his eyes and just enjoyed the moment. Alexandr moved to massage his neck, shoulders, and then gradually his back.

"He is so skillful, like a professional masseur," Andrew thought.

While Alexandr massaged Andrew, he could feel the depth of Andrew's relaxation settle into him. He thought how amazing it was that Andrew could place himself in such a deep meditative state so quickly. Alexandr knew exactly how to manipulate the tense areas. When his massage reached Andrew's hips and thighs, Alexandr realized that Andrew was asleep. He drew the covers up over Andrew's body and then he also went to bed. He was tired after so many hours of swimming. He had never before swum so much in one day.

Andrew woke up the next morning around 7:15 and saw that Alexandr was still sleeping. He remembered that he had fallen asleep while enjoying Alexandr's massage expertise. He looked at Alexandr and felt a strong emotional attachment.

"I have never met a person like him," Andrew thought, knowing that he had thought this many times already in just the last few weeks. He went to take another shower and brush his teeth. When he finished, he saw Alexandr was sitting next to the window and staring outside at the scenery.

"Good morning. Sorry I fell asleep so fast last night. I had intended to give you a massage too. Thank you for that," Andrew said with a smile.

"You're welcome. I was just thinking how much I appreciate the time we've had together," Alexandr said, returning the smile.

"We won't have as much time today. Let's go sight-seeing."

They had managed to visit just a couple of sites before it was time to leave. They returned to the hotel and quickly packed, and then went to return the car to the U.S. Consulate. Andrew asked Alexandr to wait outside while he brought the car keys to the doorkeeper. From there they took a taxi to the airport. They rushed through the check-in process and barely made it onto their flight. It was early evening by the time they arrived in Moscow. They took a taxi from the airport and went to Alexandr's apartment first.

"I'll come to see your rehearsal this coming Thursday again," Andrew promised.

"That's great. I believe we'll be starting to rehearse the next part. It won't be so great at the beginning. You know, everything is always awkward at the beginning," Alexandr replied, looking into Andrew's eyes.

"I know what you mean. See you then."

3rd Rehearsal Visit

Andrew's improved mood made it much easier for him to get through his work week, and soon enough it was Thursday again. Going to Alexandr's rehearsal had become a highlight of Andrew's week. When Andrew went into the theater that night he noticed that the stage set was very different. As Alexandr had said, apparently, they had begun rehearsing the next section of the story. The rehearsal was a kind of stop-and-go, as the director kept interrupting to instruct the cast and crew. It was discontinuous, but interesting to watch. This section showed the battle between Catherine the Great's soldiers and the rebels. As the action continued, the rebels were defeated and their leader, Pugachev, was captured. There was not too much of Alexandr in this scene. All the same, Alexandr was required to be there on the stage and Andrew could see him sitting there, listening and studying. Andrew felt that this part was not as exciting or as touching as the last part they had rehearsed in the past two weeks.

The rehearsal was very long. It was not until nearly 9:30 that the director gave the order to end for the night. Alexandr knew Andrew must be sitting in the last row, waiting. When the lights were turned on, he came down quickly.

"You're still here! Sorry to keep you waiting. It was a long and tiring day today. You know, it is much harder to coordinate the scene with so many actors on stage."

"Of course it is. I'm pretty hungry now, though, so go change quickly," Andrew replied.

"I'm hungry too. I'll be right back."

In a short while, they were sitting in their usual Thursday night cafeteria.

"What do you think about today's rehearsal? No good, right?" Alexandr asked.

"Honestly? It's not as exciting as the last two weeks. Too many interruptions and too much chaos. I almost fell asleep."

"I'm sure that after three more weeks, it will be better. You know, this was only the fourth day of rehearsal for this part of the play."

While they were eating, Andrew asked, "Would you like to get together tomorrow night? It would be nice to have some fun on a Friday night, since we don't have to get up early the next day."

"Well, I would like to get together with you, but I always go to practice my martial arts on Friday nights. The studio is very close to my apartment. There are fewer people practicing Friday nights and there is no regular class, so usually I am able to get some space for myself."

"Really? I didn't know you practice martial arts! What style?"

"It's a mixture of Russian traditional fighting and some other arts. It includes kicking, punching, Russian-style wrestling, and joint-lock techniques. It was designed for real combat, very practical and effective."

Andrew had had a lot of advanced martial arts training himself in the CIA, a mixture of boxing, Japanese Karate, and Chinese Kung Fu, and he had become a serious enthusiast of all martial art styles. He was very interested to see how effective Alexandr's Russian mixed style could be, and to learn if Alexandr could actually execute the techniques.

"How long have you practiced martial arts?"

"All my life. I think I told you my father is in the Russian special unit and two of my brothers are soldiers. My father taught me how to fight since I was six years old."

"How about let's practice together? I also started learning martial arts a few years before I came to Russia. It would be fun to see the differences between what we have each learned."

"That would be great. Why don't you meet me at the front door of the theater tomorrow night? Usually, we don't have rehearsal Friday afternoon after 3. You know, there's always some show going on and the theater is opened to the public on Friday nights. Friday afternoons are used to prepare the stage. When do you get out of work?"

"I can be there at 6 o'clock," Andrew replied.

4
THE TRAP

Injury

The next night around 6, after a very busy day at work, Andrew came to the theater to meet Alexandr, who was already waiting for him at the entrance.

"Sorry if I'm a bit late," Andrew apologized.

"Don't worry. Let's go. It'll take only ten minutes or so to walk to the studio. It's at the corner of ul Petrovka and Krapivensky per. Once you know the way there, maybe we can meet there in the future," Alexandr replied and began walking. He knew that if they were too late, the good practice areas in the studio might be taken by others.

Once they arrived they changed into their practice clothes quickly and found a nice corner for themselves. They stretched and warmed up, and each practiced by themselves for about 30 minutes. Alexandr looked pretty fast, but Andrew believed that since he had taken high level training in the Agency, he would have more advanced and practical techniques than Alexandr.

Andrew asked, "Do you want to go a few rounds with me? It will be fun to see each other's fighting skills."

"I believe that you will be too good for me. You know, since I came back to Moscow I don't practice as often as I used to. I have always been busy in the theater."

"That's all right. We can take it easy," Andrew said and assumed a posture ready to fight.

Alexandr immediately took a defensive posture as well.

In the first round, Andrew kept his attacks to just some light power and medium speed. However, he was surprised to find that he couldn't even get close to Alexandr. Alexandr knew how to keep a good distance at all times. This was not easy, especially for beginner martial arts practitioners. It seemed that Alexandr was not even trying to attack him. He began to speed up and increase the power of his attacks. However, no matter what, Alexandr could always keep a safe distance, and he used a defensive strategy only. After the first round, Andrew began to realize that he had encountered a high-level practitioner.

They took a three-minute break, then began the second round. Andrew was a little bit upset and tried all of the most effective techniques he knew to attack Alexandr aggressively. At the end of the second round, he still hadn't managed to achieve any advantage over Alexandr. He hadn't even landed a hit. Now, he had almost run out of techniques and was starting to feel very disheartened. He just could not believe that here he was, a young man in his prime, at his peak reaction-time and speed, and still he could not subdue Alexandr. He didn't know that Alexandr was taking a defensive position only because he was simply testing Andrew's skill level, particularly gauging his techniques, speed, awareness, and alertness.

On the third round, Andrew was starting to tire already due to his constant attacks. He had to win before he ran out of energy and patience. He faked an attack with his hands and initiated his most powerful roundhouse kick aggressively. But it did not matter. Alexandr maintained his defensive position. When Andrew initiated another right-leg roundhouse kick, Alexandr squatted down at very high speed and accurately swept Alexandr's left leg standing on the ground. Andrew fell quickly with a shock, seriously injuring his right ankle in the process. He stayed down on the floor in extreme pain. Immediately, Alexandr came forward and apologized.

"I am very sorry, Andrew, I didn't mean it," Alexandr said, kneeling down to take a look at Andrew's ankle.

Andrew sat on the floor, his face flushed and breathing heavily. Andrew was surprised that Alexandr's techniques were so precise and fast with extremely high levels of alertness and awareness. He realized that Alexandr must have trained pretty hard since the age of six to reach this level. It was amazing to him that he, a professional secret agent, could not take care of a layman fighter for the first time in his life. Deep in his heart, he admired Alexandr very much for this level of skill, but at the same time he was completely embarrassed. He remembered the words of Sun Zi, a well-known Chinese military strategist, from his book, *The Art of War*:

"If you know your enemy and also yourself, hundred battles, hundred wins. If you know either only your enemy or yourself, you will have half of the chance to win. If you don't know both your enemy and yourself, you will lose in every battle."

Andrew had just been too arrogant and proud of himself at the beginning of this fight and had exposed all his special techniques in the first two rounds. He had lost control of his emotions and had allowed his assumption of his own fighting superiority to cloud his judgment.

"It's not your fault. You are good, much better than I expected," Andrew said with a painful smile.

"Let's be finished for today," Alexandr replied. "My apartment is on Petrovsky per, only a couple blocks from here. Let's go to my apartment so I can take a look at your injury. I have some medical experience and I have some Russian herbs specifically for this kind of injury."

Since the next couple days were the weekend and he didn't have work in the morning, Andrew agreed. Alexandr helped Andrew to get up and limp to the dressing room to change. They walked back to Alexandr's very slowly. When they finally arrived at the building, Andrew realized that it had no elevator.

"Which floor are you on?" Andrew asked, in a great deal of pain after the agonizing walk.

"The third floor. I am sorry that there is no elevator in this building. We will walk up very slowly." Alexandr could see that Andrew was in pain and he felt embarrassed that there was no elevator.

"It's okay. Let's take it easy."

"Wait. I'm sorry. You should not be putting so much pressure on your injury."

Before Andrew knew what he was doing, Alexandr had bent and picked Andrew up, putting him over his shoulder.

"Whoa! No! It's okay, I can make it," Andrew protested.

"No," Alexandr insisted, "This is my fault." He climbed the three floors of stairs with no difficulty, even with Andrew draped over his shoulder.

"He's barely winded?" Andrew thought in amazement.

Once inside the apartment, Andrew could see that Alexandr's place was very simple and small, a typical Communist style apartment. Obviously, Alexandr had very little money. Near the entrance on the left side was a bathroom with a toilet. Next to the bathroom was a simple kitchen. There was a mirror on the right-hand side of the wall above a clothes chest. On the left side of the room was a double-size bed with a headboard on the left against the wall. The other end of the room was a small balcony. Between the balcony and the bed, there was a coffee table with two couches. Obviously, this apartment was designed for a simple couple without any children. Though the room was small and simple, it was very neat and clean. Andrew could see that Alexandr was a person with good discipline.

Alexandr said, "Why don't you take a shower, and make sure to clean the ankle area. I'll take a look at the injury afterwards." Alexandr found a clean towel for him in his closet.

"Thanks, I do feel pretty sweaty, especially after our sparring."

While Andrew was taking a shower, Alexandr cooked a simple

Russian dinner. Just as he was finishing the meal Andrew came from the bathroom, limping terribly. He had intense pain in his ankle, and it was swollen like a small balloon.

"Oh no! Please sit on the bed, Andrew," Alexandr said with a look of concern. He brought some ice wrapped in a thin cloth from the kitchen area. "Hold this ice on your ankle while I take a quick shower."

Alexandr gave the wrapped ice to Andrew with a worried expression and went into the bathroom. Ten minutes later, he came out. "Feeling any better?" he asked.

"Yeah, it's a little better now. Less pain."

"Why don't you eat something first and then I will take a look at your injury."

"Actually, I'm not feeling hungry," Andrew replied.

"Come on. You'll feel even better after getting some food in you. It's simple Russian food... potatoes, cabbage. I just warmed it up," Alexandr said encouragingly and looked at him with a smile. He helped Andrew walk to the kitchen area, seated him in a chair by a small dining table, and served him some food.

"I'll just give you a little bit first. If you like it, I have plenty of it," Alexandr said and sat down on the other side of the table. He watched Andrew carefully as he took his first bite.

"This tastes pretty good. Are you sure that you cooked it yourself?" Andrew looked at him with a joking smile.

"Of course. I used to help my Mom cook. This is the family's secret recipe."

When Alexandr saw that Andrew had begun to get his appetite back, he stood up and poured two glasses of vodka, passing one to Andrew.

"This will also help you to ease the pain," Alexandr said.

As they ate and drank together, both of them relaxed and began to feel a little inebriated.

"Okay," Alexandr said, "come sit on the edge of the bed and let me take a look at your ankle."

Andrew limped over to the bed and sat down near the headboard. He put the pillow behind his head and leaned back against the headboard. Alexandr moved a small stool next to Andrew's right leg. He knelt down and placed Andrew's leg on the stool, then he began to rub the swollen area gently. Though it generated some minor pain, the rubbing also began to circulate blood in the injured area. In order to loosen the tension at the ankle, Alexandr also massaged Andrew's calf, feet, and toes. After about 20 minutes of this, Alexandr picked up Andrew's right leg and shifted to sit on the stool, gently holding the leg in his lap while he continued his massage. Andrew felt that the pain had been significantly reduced. He closed his eyes and enjoyed this highly skilled massage. He felt incredibly comfortable and also so fortunate that he had become acquainted with Alexandr.

Suddenly, he felt Alexandr kissing his leg and knee. He opened his eyes and saw Alexandr looking at him with tears in his eyes. Andrew was shocked but also deeply touched. He was seized with an impulse of love and used his right hand to gently pull Alexandr's hair, tugging his head toward him. Alexandr allowed himself to be pulled forward and finally their faces were only a few inches apart. Alexandr's eyes were red and his face flushed. He moved his lips to Andrew's in a soft kiss. Andrew closed his eyes in response. They kissed each other, slowly moving their bodies onto the bed.

This close up, Andrew inhaled Alexandr's body's scent. Unlike the earthy after-rehearsal smell of before, this after-shower aroma was like smelling a nice flower. It made him feel happy and relaxed while at the same time excited. He had never smelled anything like it before. "Compared with Judy's perfume this is so natural and comfortable," Andrew thought.

Andrew had never kissed a man before. He would never have even considered it. But somehow, kissing Alexandr was different. It felt stimulating, sensual, and enjoyable. This was absolutely different from kissing his girlfriends. It seemed that their spirits were blended together in this moment, speechless, in a high level of sensation and feeling. Alexandr reached down to take Andrew's underwear off and Andrew then did the same to Alexandr. They used their hands to caress each other's entire bodies and their noses to smell each other. Their hearts beat faster in unison. Alexandr began to kiss Andrew's entire body slowly from his face to his feet.

Andrew enjoyed Alexandr's attentions and compassion very much. His excitement built and soon he felt his anticipation of penetrating Alexandr's body growing rapidly. While in a way he felt unnatural, he was very much aroused. Finally, after Alexandr used his teeth to gently bite Andrew's nipples and his tongue to play with them for a while, he moved his mouth down Andrew's body to play with his penis using his tongue. Andrew was elevated to a new plane of enjoyment. It was just not the same when Judy did it. His eyes filled with tears at the sensation. He couldn't help adjusting his own position so that he could use his mouth to play with Alexandr's penis as well. This was the first time he had ever sucked a guy's penis. He blushed at the thought of what he was doing, but his heartbeat got faster and faster.

Finally, Andrew turned Alexandr over to face down on the bed and gently penetrated his body. With Alexandr's skillful coordination, Andrew experienced a long and intense orgasm. Once it had subsided, he turned Alexandr over and hinted that Alexandr should penetrate his body as well. He could tell how expertly Alexandr was able to play the game, continuing to keep him excited for a long time. When Andrew reached another orgasm, Alexandr did too. As the intensity of their passion faded, they kissed and lay quietly and peacefully on the bed. They had had the most wonderful evening of their lives.

The next morning when Andrew awoke, Alexandr was already up and preparing some breakfast.

"What time is it, Alexandr?"

"It is almost 9, my sleeping beauty," Alexandr said as Andrew looked at him with a big smile.

"What a surprise," Andrew thought. "I have always been straight. I just don't understand how this whole thing happened. Have I hidden the other side of me in the closet? Or have I constantly denied the other side of me? This is such a serious sin according to my religion. But if it is a sin, why are there so many priests doing it behind closed doors? Are they hiding their real selves? Or is it because they were repressed? Did this happen only because I have been so repressed myself recently? But, I have no doubt about what happened last night. It was the most real experience of my life. Why should that be a sin? I should not be made to feel guilty for this because of my programming from religion or from society. Who am I, really?" His mind raced as he pondered the questions.

"Wake up? Still sleeping?" Alexandr asked.

Andrew smiled back. He emerged naked from the bed and went in search of his clothes so that he could get dressed.

"I am just wondering if you have done this before?" Andrew ventured, then paused for a second. "You were just so amazing and skillful at everything."

"Honestly? Yes, I have had a few experiences before," Alexandr admitted. "But I have never had the same feeling as with you last night. I felt my heart was going to jump out of my body. I don't know what it is, but I am pretty sure that I would die for you if necessary."

"This is my first time with a man. I have had many experiences with girls before, but they were never like this," Andrew said. "It was wonderful, but I have such guilt now. Did you have guilt after your first time?"

"Yes. Russia's traditions are more severe than any other culture, especially the doctrines of the church. But eventually, I realized that we feel guilt only because we're taught to feel guilty. First, I cannot change who and what I am, and second, it is my life and I don't believe any other human has the right to use his personal judgment or feeling to judge another person's true feeling. I just want my life back. I just want to be the real me instead of the me wearing a mask."

"It's true, like we were talking about...Society has this ancient matrix of behavior that we are trapped within. We're taught to be controlled by these traditional ideas of right and wrong, and to kill each other for them, instead of just being truthful and trying to truly understand one another. Humans have defined the meanings of glory, dignity, pride, jealousy, hate, joy, anger, and sadness, all of this emotional bondage. Then, once everyone is rooted in what they think they are supposed to feel, they believe that only they know how to live correctly, and that others are wrong and evil. And we kill each other for it. And the whole world is still stuck in this spiritual trap which makes us deny ourselves the natural-born right to true freedom. I wish all humans could escape this bondage and stop trying to control each other."

Alexandr could not believe that just now Andrew had almost completely agreed with what he had said a couple weeks ago. "Andrew is an open-minded guy and is very different from others," he thought.

"I thought you would be more of a traditional close-minded person since you're from a Jewish background and a military family," Alexandr said out loud with a surprised look.

"Yes. It's true. However, the deeper you get stuck into this, the more you bounce back. I think that's because I grew up in such a predetermined life that was arranged so tightly by my family that once I woke up, I could comprehend it more profoundly than others. What I need to have is the freedom of open expression for my true feelings. I don't mean only in regard to this relationship with you, either. I mean that everyone should be more free to experience their life openly without being forced into a certain path or structured life, and that we should all respect each other's differences more." Andrew sighed.

Alexandr nodded. They began to eat breakfast, but after only a few bites, Andrew looked at Alexandr with curiosity, "I don't understand how your martial arts could be so proficient. You know, there are not too many people who are as good as you. You have a high level of alertness and awareness while fighting. This is always the hardest aspect of the training in any martial arts."

"Actually, I learned most of it from my father. I've told you he is an officer serving in a Russian special fighting unit. He has been with that unit for 25 years. They practice barehanded fighting all the time. As I said, he began training my brothers and I when I was six years old. When I was 16, under my father's recommendation my two eldest brothers and I were accepted as disciples by a well-known martial arts master. In fact, this master had been employed by the Russian government to train special units in practical combat arts. I was under his severe training for two years before I came to Moscow."

Andrew began to understand that Alexandr was a person who didn't like to show off. Actually, with his fighting capability, he could be one of the best martial artists in the United States.

"How about your third brother? Did he also learn from this master?"

"Well, he did but only for six months or so. He left home to go to Moscow to attend graduate school at a university."

"This master must be amazing since your skills are so high."

"Actually, I was very slow in the beginning. However, under his very strict and severe training, I began to build up my alertness, awareness, speed, and power. My master always told us that without these fighting elements, even if you have learned tons of techniques, they would be useless since they could not be applied in a real combat situation."

Andrew nodded, agreeing with him.

Alexandr continued, "I heard that America is very beautiful. I've read a lot about the sights, like the Grand Canyon and Niagara Falls. From the pictures I have seen they look beautiful."

"Yes, they are. I wish I could show you these places the same way you show me Moscow."

"I just love nature. I wish I could afford land up in the mountains. Nature is so pure and real and open, and I think it helps you to become the same way."

Since Andrew was injured and it was inconvenient and difficult to walk, they decided to stay in at Alexandr's apartment and chat. They wanted to know each other more. After last night, everything was very different. Now they wanted to be free of any masks they had kept between them and be emotionally naked and open to each other. They felt very close to each other, and yet still didn't know very much about each other.

On the other hand, Andrew could not reveal that he was actually a CIA secret agent. A couple of times he felt the impulse to tell Alexandr this final hidden secret so they could be entirely truthful with each other, but Andrew just couldn't do it. He felt trapped by his situation, and bound to secrecy, forced to play his role in this matrix. When Alexandr asked him about his family and life, again he told Alexandr the lie that he had graduated from Maryland University with a master's degree in computer engineering. Since his family had been here in Moscow for several generations, he had applied for this embassy job for the opportunity to trace his family heritage. He had always been attracted to Russian history and culture, having first learned of the culture from Russian folk stories told by his grandma.

Andrew also asked Alexandr to tell him more about his family. He wanted to know everything about him; he was so fascinated by him.

"Why don't you come with me to Vladimir to meet my family next Saturday?" Alexandr suggested. "I have not seen them for a long time. I usually visit them once every two weeks, but I've been so busy I have missed several visits."

"That would be great, if it is not too much trouble." Andrew grew excited about the prospect of getting to learn more about Alexandr's background. Furthermore, it would also offer him an opportunity to get out of Moscow and see the countryside.

"Not at all. I believe my family will be very happy to meet you, especially my Mom. She's always dreamed that she could visit America someday," Alexandr replied.

They stayed in Alexandr's apartment all day Saturday, and then spent another night together. Alexandr tried his best to cook different dishes of Russian food for Andrew, and they cooked together. Even though there was still some discomfort for Andrew to stand and move around due to his injury, he enjoyed spending this time being so close with Alexandr.

Early on Sunday afternoon, Andrew finally took a taxi home. He knew that Alexandr would need some time to memorize his script for the next day's rehearsal. If he didn't, he could be punished Monday.

4th Rehearsal Visit

After work on Thursday, Andrew stayed late in the office making some copies. Then he went to the theater again to meet Alexandr. Actually, he was not interested in the part of the play they were rehearsing, but he was very much interested in spending time with Alexandr. Even though he would only get to be with him for an hour or so, he had looked forward to it all week. When he arrived at the theater this time, it was closer to 7:30. Andrew's ankle felt much better already. He could now walk without too much pain, although he knew that it would take another week or so to recover completely.

Only a few minutes after his arrival, the director gave the order to end the rehearsal. As usual, Alexandr came down to the stage to greet Andrew first before going back to change.

"You finished early today," Andrew greeted him.

"Yes. The director had diarrhea today. He didn't feel good all day."

"Well, I guess that's great for us. We will have more time tonight."

Again, they went to their usual cafeteria, it seemed to have become a special place for them. It was not just that they had good food there. They had also shared a lot of great time talking and being together in this place. After they sat down, Andrew took out a copy of the book, "*Qigong Meditation - Embryonic Breathing*," from a brown bag and gave it to Alexandr.

"I don't think it would be easy for you to buy this book in Russia, so I made a copy for you before I came. I hope you enjoy reading it as much as I do."

"Wow, this is a surprise. You must have spent the whole afternoon to make this copy. Isn't it illegal to make a copy in America?"

"Yeah, but this is Russia, not America. I believe the author will not mind having a reader like you. You know, not too many people like to study the deep aspects of spiritual cultivation. To most people, we are weird and spooky," Andrew said with a laugh.

"I will begin to read it whenever I have time. I'm very curious to see what it says."

"What do you want to do Saturday, I mean how do you want to meet? Remember, you talked about going to Vladimir?"

"I was hoping that we could be together tomorrow night," Alexandr said. "Why don't you come to my apartment and we can leave from there Saturday morning."

"Great idea. Remember, I still can't spar with you yet," Andrew warned.

"No sparring. I just want to be with you. I'll skip my training tomorrow."

"I'm just kidding. I'll come to your apartment directly. When will you finish rehearsal?"

"Usually we are done by about 3 or 4 p.m. on a Friday, but it could be early if the director is still sick."

"I won't be able to get out of my office until 5:30. I have a meeting with my boss at 4 o'clock every afternoon."

"Well, then I'll be expecting you around 6. Do you want to go out or eat in my apartment?"

"Come on. Your cooking is far better than any restaurant in Moscow. I prefer your cooking. And besides, that way we can have a quiet dinner without too much noise. And of course, no smoking."

"It's still early. Why don't we go to your apartment now and chat there for a while?" Andrew suggested. He just hated the smoke-filled air in the restaurant that was produced by only a few people around them.

They paid their bill, then walked to Alexandr's building. Back in the apartment Alexandr poured some vodka for Andrew and himself. Alexandr asked Andrew to take a shower again so he could rub his ankle. The swelling had gone down significantly but Andrew still felt some pain when he walked on it. Andrew showered and again sat on the edge of the bed. He was immediately reminded of their time together last weekend. Alexandr again moved the stool to the side of the bed and lifted Andrew's right leg on top of it. He gently rubbed the wounded area and then gradually increased the intensity of the massage. After 15 minutes or so, Alexandr pushed Andrew to lie on the bed, face down, and began to massage his entire body. It was so relaxing and enjoyable. Andrew felt that this intimacy and loving touch was even more pleasurable than if they had sex. It was just so good to feel so close with someone.

Friday, after his meeting with Mr. Buckley, Andrew went to Alexandr's apartment where Alexandr greeted him at the door with a big smile. He had been anxiously waiting for Andrew since 4 o'clock that afternoon. He had spent quite a bit of time preparing and cooking the best dishes he had learned from his mom. A candle had been set on the small dining table in the kitchen area and lit. Dinner was ready. Alexandr hugged Andrew tightly and kissed him. There was no shyness or embarrassment between them now. They only felt their anticipation and eagerness to touch and kiss each other. The mutual passion was sensual, and a comfort.

As he ate, Andrew praised Alexandr's skill in the kitchen. "Amazing! Your cooking is so good. I bet if you opened a Russian restaurant in America, you would be very successful and rich," Andrew said smiling.

"No," Alexandr replied. "I enjoy cooking, but if it turns into a business, I'm sure I would get sick of it. It's just like acting, you know? I enjoy the art but not to perform for business. It loses the real feeling and meaning of the art."

Alexandr and Andrew went to the shower. They washed each other's body and enjoyed the intimate time together. It was a leisurely shower that led naturally to bed, and sex. Andrew felt much more comfortable this time without experiencing the pangs of guilt, since he had psychological prepared himself. Actually, he had been waiting for this moment for a whole week.

Visiting Alexandr's Family

The next morning, Andrew and Alexandr woke early and had a light breakfast. Andrew, on his part, still felt full from the previous evening's big dinner. Then they changed and went to the train station, where Alexandr purchased two round trip tickets on the 9:10 a.m. train to Vladimir. Since it was about 115 miles away, it would be about a two-hour train ride. If there weren't so many train stops along the way, they could have arrived earlier.

Once in Vladimir, Andrew asked, "Do we need a taxi to get to your home?"

"Andrew, there are not too many taxis in this town," Alexandr pointed out. "It is not big. It will only take us about 25 minutes to walk to my home."

Alexandr's parent's house was located just outside of the town at the end of a collection of many small houses. The house marked the end of settled life; once past it, wild nature took over. Alexandr's father and his eldest brother were home when they arrived. His second brother, who was on duty with the military, could not come home this weekend, and his third brother was still in Moscow at school. When they stepped into the house, Alexandr's father was sitting on the couch smoking. His mother, who had been busy in the kitchen preparing lunch, rushed out to hug him. His eldest brother was still sleeping. Later, Andrew realized that his brother had just arrived home early that morning after a whole night of traveling.

Alexandr introduced Andrew to his father and mother. Andrew

could see from her eyes that she was very excited to meet him. She lavished attention on Alexandr, whom she had not seen for almost a month, then returned to the kitchen to prepare more food for their company. Delicious aromas wafted throughout the house.

Andrew spoke to them in Russian. Though his Russian was not that good, it was good enough to make himself understood. After a few minutes' conversation Andrew could see that Alexandr's father, very similar to his own father, was a typical soldier with serious discipline. Though he didn't smile much, Andrew could feel that he was a nice man with strong principles. All he spoke of to Andrew was Russian tradition. They tried to avoid talking about politics since it was a sensitive topic. Once lunch was ready, Alexandr went to his eldest brother's room to wake him up. He introduced Andrew to his brother.

They had a very nice lunch. Alexandr's mother had cooked her best dishes. Though Andrew could feel the warmth and friendliness in their hospitality, he felt that he had to maintain an unnatural barrier between himself and this traditional family. He was very careful of what he said and behaved as best as he could. The only person who made him feel like dropping the barrier was Alexandr's mother, who was attentive and genuine. She asked many questions about America, wanting to know what the country looked like, what the people were like and what choices there were for people to make their living. Whenever Andrew could not communicate with her clearly, Alexandr would act as an interpreter. Actually, right after lunch, Alexandr's father lit up another cigarette and went outside to take a walk as was his habit. Alexandr's brother also went out right after lunch to go visit his friends, leaving Andrew to have a very good time chatting with Alexandr's mother.

"No wonder that Alexandr loves his mom so much. She is such a sweet lady," Andrew thought.

Alexandr's father returned from his walk about an hour later and sat to talk with Andrew for a while, then went to take a nap. Andrew and Alexandr stayed until nearly 4 o'clock when they had to leave to catch their train. As they got ready to go, Alexandr gave his mother a big hug goodbye. Alexandr's mother then surprised Andrew by reaching out to also give him a hug. The gesture warmed Andrew's heart - receiving the love of a mother. It was like Alexandr's mother was treating him as her own son. This meant a lot to Andrew, whose mother had passed away when he was 17. It was so kind and loving and reminded him of how much he wished that his mother was still alive. Adding to the feeling, on their way out the door Alexandr's mother gave them a big bag of home-cooked food to take back to Moscow.

Once they were back on the train, Alexandr gave Andrew a very nice and unusual designer pen as a gift. On the top of the pen, there was a bluish sapphire-like crystal. "My father received this pen as a gift from a friend. I don't really need it, and I want you to have it. When it is in your shirt pocket, it looks very beautiful," he told him.

"But this must be very expensive, since it looks like a rare stone. It's stunning with the color so blue, just like your eyes." Andrew looked at Alexandr in surprise, since the pen seemed very precious.

"Compared with our friendship, this is nothing. I just want to give you something so you remember me and our relationship," Alexandr told him.

"I will wear it all the time. Whenever I see it or use it I'll remember you," Andrew said smiling at Alexandr.

There were so many people on the train that it was very noisy, so they didn't feel like talking. And since they had gotten up so early that morning, they were both tired and took a nap. It was almost 7 when they arrived back in Moscow.

"Alexandr, why don't you come to my apartment tonight?" Andrew suggested.

"Really? Where is your apartment?"

"A few blocks from the American Embassy. Actually, it's not too far from the club."

Since Alexandr was very curious to see where it was and how it looked, he said, "That would be great. I just hope it won't be too much trouble."

"You must be kidding. It would be wonderful to have you there to keep me company."

Alexandr and Andrew grabbed a taxi right in front of the train station and took it to Andrew's apartment. As they arrived, Alexandr noticed that the apartment was located in a relatively rich area. Almost all of the apartments here were still new.

"Wow! You have a big apartment. This is double the normal size. Everything is so elegant and modern," Alexandr said as they entered.

"Well, almost all of these apartments are new. They were built specifically to rent to embassy employees from different countries."

"It must cost a fortune to rent this place."

"I believe so, but I'm not paying for it. All of the expenses here are paid for by the American Embassy." Andrew looked at Alexandr with a funny smile.

"Do you want some wine, or some vodka?" Andrew asked as they walked into the living room.

"Red wine, if you have it. I'm beginning to like it. You know, I always drink vodka. It's cheaper and more common in Russia."

"Why don't you go take a shower first? Let me warm up some of the food your mom sent home with us."

When Alexandr came out of the shower, Andrew asked him to continue warming up the food. "There are so many different things your mom gave us. And I would also like to go take a quick shower."

Alexandr took over while Andrew went into the bathroom. By the time he came out, dinner was on the table.

"Wait a minute," Andrew said and went into his bedroom. He came back out holding something.

"I would like you to have this." He handed Alexandr a scarf made of fine wool.

The scarf was very soft in Alexandr's hands and he could tell it was expensive. Not too many people wore this kind of thing. He brought it to his face, rubbing it against his cheek and sniffing it.

"I bought it in America last December," Andrew explained, "and I used it last winter. I'm sorry that it's not brand new, but I hope you'll enjoy having it." Andrew still had the other scarf from Judy that he could use.

"Don't be sorry. I like that it has your smell. I'll never wash it. Whenever I wear it, I'll remember you." Alexandr looked at Andrew with appreciation.

Andrew and Alexandr spent a wonderful, relaxing evening in Andrew's apartment. The next morning, they took a walk over to the Moscow River. It was beautiful.

Alexandr returned to his own apartment early in the afternoon. He needed time to memorize and practice his script for Monday's rehearsal.

5
THE SECRECY

The Mission

As part of his weekly routine, Alexandr arrived at KGB Headquarters to report on his progress. He was ordered to report to KGB Headquarters every Monday morning at 8 a.m., before his 10 a.m. rehearsal. In fact, most of these routine reports were not necessary since the KGB knew the actions of every one of its agents through various means of surveillance. However, these routines would reinforce the agents' behavior and loyalty.

On the desk in front of the KGB commandant, General Damitri Kupcov, there was a large brown envelope and a videotape. Without opening it, Alexandr already knew that these were the photos and videotape of his sexual activities with Andrew in his apartment. Immediately he felt tense and uneasy. He had a strong feeling that this mission was not going to be the same as the previous two.

"Доброе утро, Генерал Капков." ("Good morning, General Kupcov.") Alexandr raised up his right hand and saluted.

"Доброе утро, номер 21." ("Good morning, Number 21.") The general looked at him with a smile. It was obvious that, from the photos and the videotape, he was delighted about the success Alexandr had had so far with Andrew. Alexandr had been assigned as Agent 21 since he was in training and his name was never spoken.

They were forbidden to call each other by name directly.

Alexandr looked down a little bit and tried to avoid direct eye contact with this KGB general. He was feeling a mixture of reticence and uneasiness. He knew his emotions were not as detached in this mission as they had been in the others. He was also afraid that the general had already seen through his uneasy feeling.

"Это Ваша самая лучшая работа. Кажется, что Вы улучшили ваши навыки. Иначе, Вы действительно выразили вашы реальные эмоции." ("This has been your best performance yet. It seems that you have improved your skills. Otherwise, you have really touched your real emotion.")

"Я полагал, что я имел больше опыта и поэтому в состоянии действовать более естественно и эмоционально." ("I believe that I have had more experience and therefore am able to act more naturally and emotionally.")

"Я только хотел напомнить Вам, что Коммунистическое будущее должно быть вашим первой задачей, не вашими личными чувствами. Понятно? Если Вы лояльны партии, Вы имеете неограниченную выгоду. Однако! Если Вы попадете в реальную эмоциональную западню - Вам конец." ("I just wanted to remind you that the Communist future should be your first concern, not your personal feelings. Understood? If you are loyal to the party, you have an unlimited benefit. However, if you fall into a real emotional trap, it will be the end of your life.")

The general looked at him with stern eyes, while speaking in threatening tones. Controlling his subordinates by using fear tactics had always worked for him. Actually, this had always been the most effective psychological control throughout the Communist party.

To avoid being suspected by General Kupcov, Alexandr raised up his head and looked directly into the general's eyes. He just hoped this would earn the general's trust.

"Я никогда не предам Коммунистическую партию. Я родился Коммунистом и умру Коммунистом. Я буду всегда верен партии." ("Sir! I will never betray the Communist party. I was born a Communist and will die a Communist. I will always be loyal to the party.") Alexandr looked at the general firmly.

"Это хорошо. Теперь слушайте внимательно." ("That's good. Now listen carefully.") The general smiled at him in an approving manner and continued, "Вы должны теперь взять эти фотографии и видеозапись, чтобы угрожать тому агенту ЦРУ и вынуждать его сотрудничать с нами немедленно. Вы имеете максимум две недели." ("You must now take these photos and the videotape and use them to threaten that CIA agent and force him to cooperate with us immediately. You have two weeks maximum to accomplish this.")

"Да. Генерал Капков." ("Yes, General Kupcov.") Alexandr saluted and took the photos and videotape, turning smartly and leaving the room.

Though the meetings had been short each time, the mission was clear and the tension extremely high. Alexandr had always known that the day he must reveal his secret to Andrew would come, but, in his heart, he had started to wish it never would. From his last two experiences, he knew it would happen in a familiar pattern.

Inner Conflict

Alexandr was in severe and painful conflict. He didn't know how to tell Andrew, or how to threaten him with the evidence. His mind could not concentrate on the rehearsal at all on Monday. He was blamed and warned seriously by the director. He was also whipped twice, once on his left arm and the other time on his right leg. Whipping punishments were common in any high-quality performance training in Russia. He had not been whipped for nearly a month now.

Walking home that evening, his eyes began to tear up as he thought of his situation. When he arrived home, he put his jacket away and lay down on his bed. He could not help but recall the joyful times he had had with Andrew. But he dare not express any emotional unsteadiness now since it was possible he was still being watched.

Now Alexandr could really feel and comprehend the pain of spiritual bondage. He began to understand why the western world was talking about freedom of thinking, behavior, and speech. This was just like being a robot that was remote-controlled or a slave who's only purpose was to satisfy the master's wish. There was no self-dignity or self-identity. He realized that he had lost his ever since he became a sexual tool of the great Communist party. He was beyond sad and depressed, and thought of committing suicide.

"Somehow I must tell Andrew the truth," he resolved.

Real Love

The following week was the longest of Alexandr's life. By the time Thursday came, he was in complete turmoil, and could barely contain his anxiety and sadness. When Andrew met him again after rehearsal Thursday night, Alexandr's mind was very conflicted. This time, his whole mission was different. He didn't want to hurt Andrew. However, if he didn't follow his orders, he would be terminated. The punishment would be especially cruel if he was caught as a betrayer of the Communist party. He would first be tortured severely until he confessed every detail of his past actions, and then if they showed mercy, he would be executed quickly. Worse, all of this made him realize that above all else, he really was in love with Andrew.

From the look on Alexandr's face when they met, Andrew could tell something was seriously wrong. Alexandr seemed to be happy to see him, but to also be suffering internally.

"Is there anything wrong? Alexandr, you look confused and very upset," Andrew asked in concern.

At hearing Andrew's words, Alexandr thought to himself that no one had ever known him so well. "It's nothing. It's just the rehearsal did not go as well as the director wanted. We all got punished,"

Alexandr replied with a painful smile.

They stopped for a light and fast dinner together, then Andrew walked Alexandr home to keep him company. He knew that this was probably the most important moment in their relationship so far, and that Alexandr needed his friendship and comfort. Alexandr appreciated Andrew's considerate attention very much, but the more kindly Andrew treated him, the more deeply he felt the pain in his heart. When they entered Alexandr's apartment, Alexandr took his shirt off and the bruise from being whipped was visible on his left arm.

"What happened here?" Andrew asked, putting his hand out to lightly touch the bruise on Alexandr's arm.

"I was punished Monday due to my lack of concentration. The rehearsal was bad, and the director was angry."

Though Andrew had heard about how hard and strict Russian actor training was, he had never believed it until now. He felt very sorry for Alexandr and wished he could share some of his pain. "Are you still hurting?" he asked.

"Not physically, but mentally, inside, very much," Alexandr said.

Andrew held Alexandr for a while to comfort him. Then, since it was late and Alexandr was obviously very tired and didn't want to talk, Andrew said goodnight.

"See you this Saturday at the club," Alexandr said.

"Take care of yourself. Have a good night's sleep. It'll be better tomorrow," Andrew said, smiling at him as he closed the door.

True Concern

Saturday morning, Andrew and Alexandr met in the club at 10. Alexandr had regained some control over his outward appearance and tried his best to act normally. While Andrew could tell that, though Alexandr seemed generally better, he was still having some uneasy feelings. But Andrew believed this was due to the pressure of his rehearsals. He was completely unaware that the pain Alexandr bore was much more severe than he could imagine. According to General Kupcov's order, Alexandr was to reveal his identity immediately, and begin to blackmail Andrew and bargain for Andrew's betrayal of his country as soon as possible. But Alexandr just did not have the heart to do it. Now that he was with Andrew, he kept quiet most of the time and his face lost its usual cheerful expression. Alexandr knew he had to do something. He knew that next Monday morning would be one of the hardest mornings of his life. He knew he would have to face General Kupcov and report his progress.

"Alexandr, I wish you would tell me what's wrong. If there is anything that I can do to help you, please let me know," Andrew said, his voice full of concern.

This was the second time Andrew had said this to Alexandr in the last two hours. When Andrew put him on the spot like this, he just couldn't help that his eyes turned red. He turned to look into Andrew's eyes with an expression that begged for mercy. He felt that his heart was about to break, and he wished he had never been born. In an attempt to ease the unhappy moment before he lost control completely, Alexandr tried to say something unimportant, and engage in distracting conversation.

They stayed in the club only for a couple of hours, and then Andrew suggested, "Why don't we go to my apartment so we can talk there more privately. Somehow, I don't feel like staying here today."

Alexandr nodded his head with an uneasy smile. Deep in his heart, he was still wondering how to tell Andrew the whole situation. He thought he might find some courage to tell Andrew when they were alone in Andrew's apartment. But he knew he must be careful. "Any wrong step could trigger a huge problem for both of us," he thought.

They walked into Andrew's apartment, hanging their jackets on hooks next to the entrance. Andrew poured some vodka for Alexandr and himself, and they sat on the couch next to each other.

"I want to help," Andrew said. "What do you usually do when you're sad like this, Alexandr? You must have had some sad experiences in the past."

Alexandr looked at Andrew with a funny smile.

"Yes, when I was a child, whenever I was sad, my grandma would sing a song for me. After my grandma passed away, whenever I was sad, I thought of her song."

"Will you sing it for me? Maybe you're not in the right mood now but maybe this would help you feel better."

Alexandr looked into Andrew's eyes for a moment. At the thought of his grandma, his own eyes turned red with tears.

"Маленький мальчик. Не делайте Вы кричите. Дождь прошел, и темнота пошла. Солнце повысилось, и радуга появилась. Маленький мальчик. Маленький мальчик. Не делайте Вы кричите. Улыбка - лучшая медицина печали. Жизнь радостна, и счастье будет с Вами. Маленький мальчик. Маленький мальчик. Не делайте Вы кричите." ("Little boy. Little boy. Don't you cry. The rain has passed, and the darkness has gone. The sun has risen, and the rainbow has appeared. Little boy. Little boy. Don't you cry. Smile is the best medicine of sadness. Life is joyful, and happiness will be with you. Little boy. Little boy. Don't you cry.) Alexandr sang with a soft voice. A tear rolled down his cheek.

"Who wrote that song?" Andrew asked.

"My grandma. She used to always sing for me and my three brothers."

Strangely, thinking about his grandma and singing her song actually did make Alexandr feel a little better. He and Andrew proceeded to get a bit drunk, then Andrew took him to the bathroom where they showered together. Afterward, Andrew asked him to lie down on the bed, and he began to give him a massage. He knew his skills might not be as good as Alexandr's but he believed this massage would help him relax and hopefully ease his depression somehow. During the course of the massage Alexandr, who hadn't had a good night's rest for many days, fell asleep. Not wanting to disturb him, Andrew pulled the covers up over him and went out to the living room.

He took another blanket from the storage closet and sat on the couch until he, too, finally fell asleep.

Alexandr woke the next morning at 7:30. He looked around and recognized that this was not his apartment. He recalled what had happened the night before and realized that he must have fallen asleep during the massage. He put Andrew's pajamas on and went into the living room where he saw Andrew sleeping on the couch. It touched him to think that Andrew had slept on the couch so that he could have an undisturbed night's rest. He stared at Andrew for a few minutes, then decided that he would not reveal his identity to Andrew, at least not this weekend. Once he made up his mind, his whole attitude changed. He wanted to enjoy his time with Andrew for as long as possible. "I have one more week," he thought.

Alexandr went to the kitchen and dug in the refrigerator until he found some eggs and ham. He got some coffee going - he knew Andrew always drank coffee in the morning – and began to fix breakfast. Andrew woke to the pleasant smell of coffee and the sounds of Alexandr's meal preparation. He came into the kitchen to the sight of Alexandr at the stove cooking two eggs.

Alexandr saw Andrew come in and said, "Good morning. I'm sorry to let you sleep on the sofa. I must have fallen asleep when you were massaging me." Alexandr looked at Andrew with a smile.

"That's all right, you needed the rest. You seem to be in a better mood this morning," Andrew replied.

"Well, after a nice sleep, I thought it over. I decided to have a good time with you while I can. Other things are not important. Let's have a good time today."

"Where shall we go then?"

"Let's go swim at the club. We didn't swim yesterday," Alexandr suggested.

"That's a good idea. I haven't tried swimming since I hurt my ankle. But it feels pretty good now, and I really miss swimming."

They went to the club and spent the entire day there, swimming, relaxing and just enjoying each other's company until, at about 8 p.m., Andrew thought it was time to go. They needed to rest for tomorrow, which would be another busy work day. Andrew found a taxi right in front of the club and gave the driver some money to take Alexandr home. He opened the taxi door for Alexandr and said good night, then strolled back through the streets to his own apartment.

Pressure

Standing directly in front of General Kupcov, Alexandr was very nervous and frightened. General Kupcov stared at Alexandr with his sharp, discerning look, and made Alexandr even more tense.

"Почему Вы не подчинились заказу и выполняли миссию в прошлый выходной, номер 21?" ("Why didn't you obey the order and carry out the mission last weekend, Number 21?")

Alexandr knew that even though General Kupcov had given him two weeks' time to complete his mission, the General of course wanted it done as soon as possible. Even though Alexandr was more terrified than he had ever been in his life, he knew he could not show this in front of General Kupcov. That would be a disaster.

Steeling himself, he called upon all of his actor's training and looked straight into the General's eyes. "Генерал. Я действительно намеревался раскрыть себя этому агенту ЦРУ несколько раз. Однако, после того, как я обдумал это, я был убежден, что это не было правильное время, чтобы сделать это." ("General, I did intend to reveal my identity to this CIA agent a few times. However, after I thought it over, I was convinced that it was not the correct time to do it the right way.")

"Почему бы нет?" ("Why not?") General Kupcov barked with an angry expression.

"Сначала, Эндрю упоминал, что, так как он работал для посольства, он иногда прослушивался или сопровождался агентом ЦРУ. Я не мог найти правильный момент и правильное место, которое было безопасно показать мою идентичность в прошлый выходной. Это - просто, потому что я не знал, прослушивался ли Эндрю или сопровождался агентом ЦРУ." ("First, Andrew mentioned that since he was working for the embassy, he was occasionally bugged or followed by a CIA agent. I could not find the right moment and right place that would be safe to reveal my identity last weekend. This is simply because I didn't know if Andrew was bugged or followed by a CIA agent.")

This was quite possible since other KGB agents had often been followed by foreign officers. In addition, the KGB had also followed their own diplomatic officers working in Russian Embassies outside of Russia. Alexandr's argument made sense and General Kupcov was somewhat convinced about his consideration. The General nodded his head. When Alexandr saw it, he knew he had begun to control the situation.

Alexandr continued, "Кроме того, так как Эндрю был агентом ЦРУ, который прошел очень строгую программу обучения прежде чем он приехал в Россию, я не полагаю, что было бы легко убедить его предавать его страну. так как он не женат и без детей, шантажировать его гомосексуальными фотографиями и видеозаписью, не работает. Он не заботиться о раскрытии гомосексуальной идентичности." ("Furthermore, since Andrew is a CIA agent who has gone through a very strict training program before he came to Russia, I don't believe that it would be easy to convince him to betray his country. Not only that, since he is not married and without any children, to blackmail him with homosexual photos and a videotape might not work. He might not care about revealing his homosexual identity.")

General Kupcov knew that public homosexual activities were increasingly common in the western world. He recalled that when KGB headquarters initiated the tactics of using homosexual activities to subdue western embassy workers around ten years ago, it had worked very effectively since homosexual activities were considered sinful in western society. However, since an enthusiastic crowd of at least 75,000 people from around America paraded through the capital on October 15 of 1979 in a homosexual rights march and urged passage of legislation to protect the rights of homosexuals, homosexuality had gained visibility and become recognized in a more positive light. In 1984, usually, this kind of blackmail would work on those who were married, who already had children and were living a heterosexual lifestyle.

The general also remembered that originally the KGB had wanted to set up the trap for Andrew using a beautiful young female agent. But they realized that since he was single and had only a girlfriend in America, he might not care about any such evidence. That was their reason for changing their strategy and using Alexandr with the intention of seducing him into homosexual activity. This had worked with other agents several times, and they suspected Andrew would surrender to them in this way. But now, Alexandr's report had convinced General Kupcov that the possibility of subduing Andrew in this way was not as great as he had thought.

When Alexandr saw the shift in General Kupcov's expression, he knew he was winning.

" я знаю, Эндрю влюбился в меня глубоко. Может быть что, если я использую любовь и угрозы, Эндрю, что, если он небудет кооперировать с нами, это будет конец наших отношений. Кроме того, наши отношения будут также показаны американскому Посольству, карьера Эндрю будет подвергнута опасности." ("I believe Andrew has fallen in love with me. It may be possible for me to use this love to threaten Andrew that if he doesn't cooperate with us, it will be the end of our relationship. In addition, our relationship will be revealed to the American Embassy. If that happens, Andrew's career will be endangered.")

General Kupcov thought about that for a moment, then looked at Alexandr, "Номер 21, Вы имеете одну неделю, чтобы убедить его. Не вздумайте завалиться. Я предупреждаю Вас. Помните о последствиях." ("Number 21, you have one week to convince him. Don't fail. I am warning you. Remember the consequence of failure.")

"Да, Генерал Капков. Я попрошу, чтобы он пошел на пляж со мной в следующий выходной и и раскрою себя." ("Yes, General Kupcov. I will ask him to go to the beach with me next weekend and find the opportunity to reveal my identity.")

The General gave him a signal to leave. That meant he approved of the suggested action. Alexandr raised up his right hand, saluted and left.

When he came out of the office, Alexandre realized that he was trembling and that a cold sweat had broken out on his forehead.

Release from Rehearsal

Alexandr left General Kupcov's office and headed directly over to see his performance director, arriving about 15 minutes before rehearsal was due to start at 10. He knocked on the door of the director's office and was greeted by the director's harsh voice.

"Войдите." ("Come in.")

"Доброе утро. Г. Джарсев. Я хочу принести извинения за свою репетицию на прошлой неделе." ("Good morning, Mr. Jarcev. I have come to apologize for my poor concentration in rehearsal last week.")

"Я только что говорил с Генералом Капковим. Вы вы свободны пока пока ваша миссия не достигнута. Я найди вам замену . Когда ваша миссия закончена, Вы должны немедленно возвратиться и возобновить вашу репетицию." ("Yes, Alexandr, I have just gotten off the phone with General Kupcov who tells me you have more important matters to take care of. You can have the time off now until your mission is accomplished. I will replace your role temporarily. When your mission is over, you should immediately return and resume your rehearsal schedule here.")

His director, Mr. Jarcev knew how much pressure Alexandr was under now because Mr. Jarcev was also a Russian secret agent. When he was younger, the director had accomplished a few important missions for the Communist party. Later, when he passed his 35th birthday, he had received an order removing him from active secret agent service. Instead, he would become responsible for recruiting new candidates for the KGB, specializing in bribery and blackmail. Alexandr was actually his fifth victim-turned-recruit. When he found Alexandr and seduced him into his trap, in one way, he felt very proud of himself that he had again contributed his talent to the great Communist party, but in another way, he knew that he was leading one more young man into a dark future without freedom. He felt particularly badly as, after three months of living together with Alexandr, he had developed a strong emotional attachment to this unusually sensitive and intelligent young man. He looked at Alexandr now with an expression of mercy and sadness.

"Удачи. Всего лучшего." ("Good luck. Wish you the best.")

"Спасибо, г. Джарсев." ("Thank you, Mr. Jarcev.")

Another Request

Monday night, Alexandr called Andrew on the phone in his apartment.

"Hello, this is Andrew."

"Andrew, it's me."

Andrew was surprised that Alexandr would call him, especially so soon, on a Monday night. "Doesn't he have rehearsal tonight?" he was wondering.

"Are you OK? This is a surprise. I thought you'd be in rehearsal," Andrew responded.

"Yes, but we got out early. The director had a dinner meeting with the program sponsors tonight. You know, about the next performance tour."

"How do you feel now? Better? I worried about you all last night."

"I'm okay, thank you. I was just wondering if it would be possible for us to go to the beach in Leningrad again next weekend? I really enjoyed the trip we had last time and miss swimming in the sea."

"Yeah, that was a good time. Amazing, it's been nearly a month already. I miss it too. You feel like going again?"

"Yes, very much. You know, summertime is almost over and if we don't go this weekend, we may not have a chance to go again this year."

"Okay, let me arrange it. I'll make a reservation for airplane tickets and also a hotel. Would you like to stay in the same hotel?"

"Of course. It was very nice and comfortable. I would like it very much. And we will have good memories inside that hotel."

"I should know by tomorrow night if the trip can be set up. Why don't you give me a call in the late evening?"

"Okay, talk with you then. Good night."

Right after hanging up, Andrew thought it over. He knew the first thing to find out was if he could again borrow the consulate's car. Booking plane tickets and the hotel would be easy. He picked up the phone again and dialed.

"Hello. Who is it?"

"Michael. It's me, Andrew. Your old pal."

"Well, Andrew, you miss me already? What's up?"

"I'm just wondering if it's possible to borrow the car this coming weekend. My friend and I would like to go to the beach again. You know, our secret spot."

"Wait a minute. Our secret spot? It was my secret spot. Now, you want to take it over." Michael laughed aloud on the other end.

"Come on, pal. Yours is mine and mine is mine! Isn't it?" Andrew joked back.

"All right, seriously, you want the same arrangement as last time, right?"

"Yes. Do you expect any problem with the car?"

"Not really. Usually the car is unavailable on weekdays, but it isn't used on weekends. It's used on the weekends only if there is a surprise intruder like you." Michael looked at the calendar on the wall and continued, "You must know that the weather will not be as warm as a month ago. It will be a bit colder now. I don't know anything about the water temperature now. I've only been there in late June and July."

"It doesn't matter. It will just be more of a challenge. Can you do it for me one more time, pal?"

"No problem. I'll call your office tomorrow afternoon and confirm the whole thing."

"Okay. Thanks a lot!"

"No sweat. Wait a minute. How are things going? Last time I talked with you it seemed that you were not very happy with your office work," Michael said.

"Yes. You knew that when we were still in America. You know, I like the outside intelligence work, not office work."

"Wake up, pal. You know neither one of us can be in action intelligence. We are too soft and emotional. We are office workers only."

"You really think so? I am very disappointed about my job."

"Okay, stop a moment and ask yourself this question: Can I pull the trigger and shoot a person in cold blood? I know you are loyal to America. But, can you just obey orders and shoot someone you have never met?"

When Andrew thought about it, he knew that he couldn't do it. He was not a cold-blooded person detached from his emotions. Especially now, after he had grown to know and love Alexandr, he recognized that he was actually a very emotional person. Suddenly, he realized that that was why he had never been considered for active duty as a field agent by the CIA. He paused for a long time before responding.

"Michael, you're right. I don't think I can," Andrew replied.

"I thought about it pretty thoroughly after I got married," Michael told him. "Now, I just want to have a peaceful and secure job. You know, I'm a family man. I have my wife and son to take care of."

"I understand. You've brought up many good points and you make me think I need to reconsider my own future. Thanks a lot, pal. You are a good and sincere friend! Talk with you tomorrow."

Andrew hung up the phone and went to his meditation couch, where he closed his eyes and tried to calm down. After a few deep breaths, he thought again about what Michael had said.

"Can you pull the trigger and shoot a person in cold blood?"

The sentence kept repeating in his head.

Andrew recalled his first mission in Mexico. He had not been able to pull the trigger then and shoot the video monitoring guys in cold blood. He started to ponder and analyze everything that had happened three years ago, then suddenly snapped is eyes open. There were too many contradictions!

How did Mexican drug lords know about the attack in time to set up a trap?

How could the building have such intricate traps set up in such a remote northern Mexican area?

How did Colonel Anderson know where the video monitoring room was?

Why had those Mexican drug dealers not done any serious harm to their captives' bodies? The injuries they had sustained were only on the surface and not at all life threatening.

Finally, Andrew concluded, "That mission was not real, it was only a test. It was a pre-arranged test. Actually, there was no danger involved. It was only a show. The colonel's killing and the blood on the floor were all fake. Now that I think about it, I believe even the ammunition distributed to us was not real."

"Now I know why they did not assign me as a field agent. I am too compassionate," he sighed.

Another Arrangement

Tuesday morning, around 11:30, Michael called Andrew's office.

"Hi Andrew. Everything is set. I'll see you this Saturday morning, same time."

"Thanks Michael. I owe you one more time. See you Saturday." Since this was a private call on their office phones, they knew they shouldn't talk too much. They knew that their conversation would be recorded.

At lunchtime, Andrew again went home to make arrangements. He made a reservation for two round-trip tickets to Leningrad, then called the hotel. But when he tried to reserve a room, he discovered that Michael had already booked it for them. As he hung up the phone, he recalled his last time at the beach. Alexandr and he had known each other for just a few weeks during their last trip. Now, a month later, their relationship was very different.

"This will be a wonderful trip," he thought.

Andrew received a call from Alexandr almost as soon as he got home from work that evening.

"Hi Andrew. How is everything?"

"I thought you wouldn't be able to call me until late. You got out of rehearsal early again tonight?"

"Yes. The negotiations between the director and sponsors continued tonight. They didn't come to an agreement last night."

"That's great. If I knew that, I would have come to meet you in the theater. How about tomorrow? Will you be early again?"

"I believe that they'll reach agreement tonight. It's always like this."

"About the trip. Everything is set - the same flight number and time as before. How about if I meet you this Thursday and we can talk more?"

Andrew didn't want to say any more over the phone and wrapped up their conversation quickly. He knew that the KGB or CIA might be listening in.

From Tuesday to Thursday, Alexandr just stayed alone in his

apartment, constantly replaying over and over again how he intended to tell Andrew about his identity as a KGB agent. His heart was in the worst pain of his life. He did not know if he should betray Andrew's friendship, or betray the great Communist party. He was very depressed, and several times, after drinking vodka in the evening, he again considered setting himself free by committing suicide. However, when he opened his drawer and saw the gun hidden underneath some clothes, he also saw his face in the mirror on the wall above the clothes chest.

Two tremendous forces were pulling him apart. He thought of his mother and how much she loved him. He again thought of Andrew and how good it felt to be with him. And then he thought of General Kupcov's ugly face and uglier threats.

"Which way do I turn?" he wondered again and again. The thoughts just kept circling around in his head.

Finally, he stared at himself in the mirror, looked deeply into his own eyes, and felt his thinking clear.

"If I kill myself, I will be dead. If I betray my country, I will also be dead. Since I don't care about my own life anymore, why should I worry about the consequences of my personal future? I must do what I think is morally right. I must tell Andrew all of the truth."

Once Alexandr had made his decision, his eyes began to shimmer with a kind of hope. He no longer felt afraid of either General Kupcov or the great Communist party.

"I don't want to live my life in darkness forever. I'd rather die," he thought.

Before Trip

Thursday, when Andrew arrived at the theater, Alexandr was already standing outside. Alexandr could not let Andrew know that he was temporarily out of rehearsals due to his secret mission. Andrew saw him waiting there as he got out of the taxi.

"You're really early today. It's only 6:30," Andrew commented.

"Yes, my director didn't feel well, so he ended rehearsal early." Alexandr looked at Andrew with a happy smile. Andrew was glad to see that whatever had made Alexandr so upset last week had apparently been resolved.

"That's great," Andrew said. "We have almost a whole evening! What should we do tonight?"

"How about having dinner first and then we can go to either your place or my place to talk," Alexandr suggested.

"Let's go to the club and have dinner there. They always have the best food and, since it's Thursday, it shouldn't be too crowded. Plus, it's not too far from my place, so afterward we can go over there to talk and listen to music."

Alexandr nodded his head with a smile as they went to find a taxi to take them to the club. Dinner was a relaxed and pleasant event with Alexandr's improved mood. After dinner, they walked to Andrew's apartment.

Andrew poured some brandy into two glasses and gave one to Alexandr.

"Try this. This is brandy. It's quite different from vodka."

"It tastes good," Alexandr said after he had a sip. He looked at Andrew and felt like saying something, but before he spoke, he hesitated.

"What do you want to tell me? It looked like you wanted to tell me something but then stopped yourself."

"I am just wondering if you could forgive me if I did something stupid that in the end harmed you?"

"What are you talking about?"

"I'm just afraid that our time together will not last long."

"Why not? Why wouldn't it?"

"You know, you're American and I am Russian. You will return to America someday and I will be stuck here. Our countries are mortal enemies. Furthermore, we must continue to hide our relationship from the Russian general public. I think that will get harder and harder to do. I am just worried about our future."

Andrew didn't know that Alexandr's worry was actually about something else much more serious. Alexandr was afraid that when Andrew knew the truth, it would be the end of their relationship entirely. Not only that, even if Andrew did cooperate with the KGB, it could still be the end of his career or even his life. And if he didn't, he would be killed. When Alexandr thought of this, his eyes teared up again. Andrew saw it and drew Alexandr into his arms and held him tightly.

2nd Trip to Leningrad

Friday night when Andrew arrived at the airport, again Alexandr was already there. Once they were on the plane, Andrew asked, "What would you like to do with your future? Continue stage performance for your whole life?"

"No. You know, the stage life is always short for everyone. When time passes, and you get older, you become not as important as when you were young. Actually, I would like to become a martial arts teacher. I like martial arts a lot and I enjoy teaching."

"Will it be easy to teach martial arts and earn a living in Russia?"

"No, it won't be at all easy. If I become famous in my performance, I may be able to become a performing teacher or director. But you know, there is a huge amount of competition in Russia. How about you? Would you like to work for your government as an engineer forever?"

"No. I applied for this job because I wanted to come here to trace back my roots and to see the places where my grandparents and parents grew up. You know, my grandma talked about it all the time when I was small."

"And have you found your roots?" Alexandr asked.

"Honestly, no. It seems nothing is the same as the way my

grandma described it. Times have changed, and I believe the people's mentality has also changed. Actually, after six months of working in Moscow, I already missed home. I felt lonely."

"Do you still feel that way?"

"No. Now, I know you and spending time with you is the best thing happening in my life. I believe this is like what you said about destiny. I mean, you and I were supposed to meet each other. I just feel very lucky about our acquaintance. I'm glad that you bumped into my table almost two months ago," Andrew laughed.

"Then what do you really want to do? Become a computer engineer again when you return to America?"

"Not really. I don't even like computer science. I like outdoor activities and more physical jobs."

"Maybe you can teach martial arts. I heard you can make a good income by teaching it in America."

"Yes, if you are good. There are many competitions and exhibitions where a teacher and his students can display their skill."

Alexandr and Andrew had an uneventful and pleasant flight, looking into the future and imagining what life could be like. The plane arrived in Leningrad on time, and they headed to the hotel.

So far everything was going just as planned, but once they checked into the hotel, Alexandr became saddened with the prospect of what he had to do. He struggled to hide it by portraying his emotions as simple affection for Andrew. Andrew was surprised that Alexandr was so emotionally expressive all night. But he believed that it was because they had had such a good time a month ago in this same place. Alexandr, for his part, suspected that this would be the last night they would be able to share their true feelings with each other. He didn't say much. After dinner, they showered together and then went to bed to be close to each other.

The next morning Andrew was awakened by the alarm on his watch. It was already 8:30 and he was supposed to meet Michael at 9 at the U.S. Consulate. He looked at Alexandr, who was still sleeping, and slipped out of bed as quietly as possible so as not to disturb him. Andrew dressed quickly and wrote a note for Alexandr before leaving the hotel room. When he entered the consulate building, he saw Michael sitting on a couch reading a newspaper.

"You're late, pal," Michael said.

Andrew stepped forward and gave Michael a hug.

"I'm sorry, I overslept. My friend and I talked too much last night."

"That's all right. Here's the key. You know what to do. I have to get going now. My wife is waiting for me at breakfast," Michael said.

"Okay. Thanks very much. Talk with you soon."

Andrew collected the car and drove it back to the hotel, where he found Alexandr awake and taking a shower.

"You don't have to take a shower this morning, you know. In just another two hours you'll be covered with salt," Andrew laughed.

Like last time, Alexandr had ordered some breakfast. This time, he had also asked the kitchen to prepare sandwiches and a few drinks. He remembered how hungry they were when they finished swimming last time and knew they would definitely need it today. They might be at the beach for a long time.

They finished breakfast and Andrew drove them to the beach in Ozerki, finding his way there by memory. He parked the car in the same place and hid the key under the same rock. It was a little bit windy today and the waves were higher than last time. The temperature was only about 65°F. Fortunately, when they went in the water, it was not as cold as they had expected.

Secret Revealed

"Andrew, let's go out deeper this time. Here is too shallow. I think I learned enough last time that I can handle it. I'm not afraid of the sea anymore," Alexandr said.

Andrew was happy to hear that, since he had been thinking about the same thing.

"Let's go," Andrew said and began to swim out toward the depths. Soon they were over a hundred yards from the shore.

"Andrew, wait. I need to talk to you."

Andrew slowed down and let Alexandr catch up with him. Alexandr's face had turned very serious. At first, he just looked at Andrew and shook his head a few times. He didn't know how to say what he needed to. He just looked at Andrew and tried to control the tears that wanted to gather in his eyes.

"What's wrong?" Andrew could sense the seriousness of Alexandr's distress. He thought perhaps Alexandr had been hurt or something. He swam even closer to him.

"Andrew, you must believe me. I love you very much. But I need to tell you the truth, no matter what. Please believe me that I do not wish to do anything to hurt you."

"What are you talking about?" Now Andrew could see that the problem was even more serious than he had thought.

"I have had serious pain in my heart during the last two weeks. If I don't tell you the truth now, I would rather die." Alexandr's voice trembled as he spoke.

"What are you talking about?" Andrew asked again, staring into Alexandr's eyes. All he could see were Alexandr's tears. Andrew's heart pounded in his chest.

Alexandr paused for a moment with his mouth open, and then said, "I am KGB, a Russian secret agent."

"What did you say? You are joking. Right? If this is a joke, it is not funny." But Andrew could sense that Alexandr was not joking.

"In the last two months, my mission has been to seduce you into a sexual relationship. The KGB needs information from you about the CIA network in Russia. They have photos and videotapes of our sex."

Andrew felt Alexandr's words hitting him like stones. For a moment, he was stunned speechless as he stared into Alexandr's teary eyes. Then he shook his head like he might be able to shake

Alexandr's words away, turned, and began swimming far out into the deep sea, as hard and fast from Alexandr as he could. He distanced himself further and further from the shore, swimming furiously and becoming completely lost. His anger and disappointment filled him, occupying all his senses so that he was blind to the waves and the current. He couldn't believe this was happening. What a fool he was to be so easily trapped by the lie of Alexandr's love! He wanted Alexandr to take back what he had said, for it to not be true! But deep in his heart, he knew that it was true, and that Alexandr's relationship with him had been a ruse.

Andrew swam for over an hour, exhausting himself until he could no longer think or feel. When he finally stopped and turned, he could barely see the shore. As his anger cooled and his mind became more rational, he thought of the position that Alexandr was in. He realized that once the KGB knew that Alexandr had revealed his identity to Andrew, if Alexandr did not follow through on his mission but instead betrayed his country, he would be terminated immediately. This was a period of very high risk for Alexandr. As Andrew looked at things from Alexandr's perspective, and contemplated the very real danger of the situation, he began to forgive Alexandr. He realized that Alexandr would have no choice but to obey his orders if he wanted to live. Suddenly, Andrew felt very foolish to have acted so impulsively and swum away. He needed to talk with Alexandr! He needed to get a better understanding of this situation so that they could plan together how to solve it. Unfortunately, by now the current had brought him to such a distance that the shore almost disappeared from his eyes. He was exhausted and wondered if he would be able to return to the shore with the strong current pulling him away. He realized that he was in a grave situation, and his life was in danger. Even with his experience, he knew he would have a hard time surviving the swim back. That thought made him worry about Alexandr too. His worry got deeper and deeper as he started back toward the shore, trying to ration his energy as much as possible.

Rescue

When Andrew swam away, Alexandr could see how badly he had been upset. Alexandr deeply regretted hurting Andrew and wished he had never become involved with the KGB. As he watched Andrew swim farther and farther away from the shore, Alexandr was frozen in indecision and helplessness. When minutes passed and Andrew did not stop, but continued going out into deeper and deeper water, Alexandr unfroze and swam immediately back to the shore. He found the car key under the rock, opened the car's trunk and removed the lifesaver, thinking, "I'm going to need this."

Running back toward the water, Alexandr could see Andrew was now far in the distance, just a tiny dot in the sea. He started to swim toward Andrew but because his head was now at the horizon of the sea, being tossed around by the waves, he could not see Andrew anymore. In just a short time, he had already lost his orientation. Doing his best to swim in a straight line, he tried to follow in the direction he had started off. After swimming as fast as he could for nearly an hour, he still could not see Andrew anywhere. He was so worried and felt so guilty, he could barely think for terror that Andrew had already drowned.

Alexandr screamed Andrew's name, but the sound of his voice was immediately swallowed by the waves. Salt burned his eyes, nose, and throat. He was exhausted and didn't know what else to do. How can you find a single person in such a huge sea? Alexandr collapsed on the tube and rested for a few minutes, panting, then again started swimming and crying out Andrew's name.

Andrew was gradually and slowly swimming toward the shore, but it seemed that it was still very far away. He believed that he might be able to last for another half hour or so, but the shore was still probably an hour's swim away. He was bone-weary and also very worried about Alexandr. Where was he? And what was he doing? Had he tried to follow? Was he still out here somewhere? Had he drowned? Andrew began to regret his irrational action. His rashness might just cost him his life.

Andrew tried to stay afloat and tread water to rest for a moment. As the waves lifted him, he saw Alexandr about a hundred yards away with the lifesaver. He raised his exhausted arm and waved toward Alexandr, who spotted him and immediately swam toward him. His spirits lifted and with them he felt his strength begin to return.

"He didn't just leave me out here to die. He risked his life and came for me," Andrew thought. The realization overwhelmed him with emotion and relief.

When Alexandr arrived with the lifesaver Andrew could finally rest for a moment, collapsing onto it in relief. Alexandr gave Andrew a few minutes to gather his strength, then encouraged him to begin to swim toward the shore holding the lifesaver, with an also exhausted Alexandr hanging on, kicking with his legs as best he could. Andrew tried to catch his breath as he looked into his dear friend's eyes. The salt of the sea mixed with the salt of his tears and he felt very grateful. He smiled at Alexandr and reached over with his right hand to hold Alexandr's left hand. Their feeling of love and friendship had never been so strong.

"I am really sorry, Andrew. I truly love you, but I am stuck between being true to you and my life under the control of the KGB. I don't know what to do, Andrew. You must help me. They have me trapped!" Alexandr yelled, crying uncontrollably.

"Alexandr, it will be all right. After I calmed down, I could see how much risk you were taking in revealing your identity to me. And I can feel in my heart that our connection is real. Now, you must tell me everything that happened from the beginning and we will figure this out together," Andrew reassured him.

Alexandr told him the complete story of his life and how he himself became entangled in the KGB's trap as they slowly made their way back to shore.

The Truth

"I had come to Moscow to learn from this well-known actor, Ivan Jarcev. Mr. Jarcev let me stay with him in his apartment temporarily, since I didn't have a place to live there," Alexandr began.

"Why didn't you stay with your brother, the student at Moscow University?" Andrew asked.

"I suppose I could have, but I didn't want to for a few reasons. First, my brother had a girlfriend and they were living together. Second, it was a great opportunity to get close to this famous actor. He was also the director of a new show that I thought I might be able to get into if I stayed close to him. As an 18-year-old, it was a rare opportunity. You know, there were hundreds of people that wanted that role. And finally, if I stayed with him, I believed I could learn from him all the time by watching him, on the stage and off."

"Then what happened?" Andrew asked anxiously as he kicked and propelled them towards the shore.

"In the first three months, he taught me the correct body movements, the way of acting and expressing the words, and also ballet. You know, I always loved ballet and dreamed of becoming one of the most famous ballet dancers in Russia. There aren't many excellent male dancers and if you're good you can earn a lot of money." He looked at Andrew with an honest and sincere expression on his face.

Alexandr continued, "In order to help my postures, he often had to adjust my body position, and move my arms, legs, or even head. One night after rehearsing a short performance, he gave me some wine, and I got a little bit drunk. He stepped forward and hugged me, and then kissed me. Though I was shocked, because of my deep appreciation for his teaching and for his taking care of me, I didn't refuse him. He then undressed me, and we went to bed. It was the first time I had sex with anyone."

"Did you enjoy it?" Andrew asked.

"Honestly? I did. I felt so close to him and had a nice warm feeling in my heart. You know, at the time I was alone in Moscow and I was only 18."

"How old was he?"

"He was in his early 40s. However, due to his acting and dancing career, he actually looked like he was in his early 30s."

"Sorry I interrupted, please go on."

"After that we had sex a few more times within a couple of weeks."

"Did you love him?" Andrew asked with just a hint of jealousy.

"Actually, I didn't know. Though I felt some physical and mental stimulation, and even excitement, spiritually it was a very shallow connection." He looked at Andrew with a bitter smile and continued.

"One day, I was visited by a Communist officer who told me that an important high-ranking officer wished to talk with me. I was taken to a big building and led to an office where I saw a Communist officer in uniform sitting at one side of the desk. Mr. Jarcev was also there. On the desk in front them were photos of sexual encounters. When they showed the photos to me, I realized that they had been taken when this director and I had sex in his apartment."

"What was your reaction then?"

"I was frozen for a long time. Speechless. I didn't know what to do. I felt like I had been tricked and my emotions betrayed by this director. Deep in my heart, everything that I had felt was good became so ugly," Alexandr replied. "This officer with a solemn face then asked me if I would like to work for the government, for the Communist party. If I accepted the job, first, I would demonstrate my loyalty to the party. Naturally, they already knew how much loyalty to the party there was in my family, with my father and two of my brothers serving in the military. Second, I could earn a very good income, three times more than any other regular salaried job. But third, if I didn't join them, all these photos would be revealed to my parents. It is considered extremely sinful and shameful to be homosexual in our conservative

Russian society. If they did this, it would not only destroy my parents' trust in me but would also hurt my mother tremendously. I simply couldn't allow that to happen. I love my mom," Alexandr exclaimed with tears running down his face.

"It must have been difficult for you. They truly had you trapped," Andrew said.

"Yes. Later, I realized that under the Communist government Mr. Jarcev also did not really have any choice, and I began to forgive him. Basically, we're all victims of the Communist party. After I thought it over for a couple of days, I accepted the job and became an agent. Even though I was unhappy and angry because I was being blackmailed, eventually my father's lessons to me about loyalty to the Communist party won out, and I gradually let the anger go. I moved out of the apartment with that director and moved in to another apartment, the one you visited. It was smaller, but it was cheaper, so I was able to send money home. You know I must help my mom. My father and brothers do not bring back too much income as soldiers, and my third brother is still in school."

"Are you really loyal to the Communist party?"

"Honestly speaking? No. I have never liked Communism. I love Russia and feel sorry that all Russia is under Communist control. You know, under the Communist system, you don't have your freedom. I accepted the job because I didn't have any choice, although I could earn more income to help my family."

"Did you still have a sexual relationship with that director after this?"

"No. I couldn't after I knew the truth. Actually, I still respect him as my performance director. But I don't love him at all and don't think I ever did."

"What was your mission once you started?" Andrew asked.

"Because of my looks, they sent me to a special training center in the suburbs of Moscow for two years of training. Whenever there was a rehearsal going on in Moscow, I'd join rehearsal in the afternoon from 2 o'clock until evening, and at the same time I underwent KGB training in the morning. If there was no rehearsal, I would be in the training center the whole day. We trained at martial arts and practiced barehand combat skills. We learned languages such as English and French, how to use guns, and other basic courses necessary to acting as a secret agent. But I was also taught the skills of seduction and sexual techniques, where and how to kiss, how to get my partner excited, and so on."

"No wonder you are so skilled at sex. I had wondered how you seemed to have so much experience when you only mentioned a couple relationships." Andrew looked at him with an uncomfortable smile.

"Together, there were about 30 young, handsome male candidates in the training center during my time there. We rehearsed seduction scenarios and practiced all of the skills with each other every week until the program instructor was satisfied. You know, all of these young candidates were chosen from the whole country to be secret agents. I heard there was also a group of 45 female candidates who were receiving similar training. We never met the other group, though."

"Then what?" Andrew asked. Although he believed the story, it was so incredible that he still had a hard time accepting it. "I wonder if the U.S. has programs like this?" he thought.

"When I was 20, I was assigned my first mission. The target was a high-ranking officer working at the British Embassy, about 42 years old, married with two children. He was an easy target since I was young and handsome and had an attractive body. In only a few weeks, he was led into the trap. This officer was then of course blackmailed and forced to reveal a lot of important secret information to the KGB. The mission lasted for nearly a year until this officer was relocated to another country. I didn't have any feeling of emotional attachment or even of feeling sorry for him. I didn't have any feelings about it at all. It was simply a job that I had done well for the Communist party. Since then, I've been treated as a very high potential and valuable agent. I received a promotion after that first assignment and a reward in cash. I remember when my mom received the money I gave her, she was so surprised that she cried. Our family really needed the money. She could not believe that I was able to support her with so much money as an actor."

Alexandr, who had been mostly keeping his eyes focused in the distance while he told his story, risked a look at Andrew as he continued, "The target of my second mission, when I was 21 years old, was a French bachelor who worked as a clerk in the French Embassy. Though he was already 48 years old, he had never married. To outside people, he was a playboy and lived a very luxurious lifestyle. People often saw him with different girls in public. However, nobody knew that he was actually more attracted to men. Whenever a beautiful female Russian agent tried to attract him and lead him into the trap, she always failed. He would never go beyond just going out for a night."

Alexandr was tired since he had been kicking his legs as he spoke this whole time. The shore was slowly getting closer.

"Let me take over the kicking. Rest for a minute. Go on," Andrew said.

"When I found the way to approach him, though he pretended that he was not interested visibly at the beginning, I could sense that I already had him. Finally, we became good friends. After nearly six months of our relationship, he was kidnapped and taken to an office in the city blindfolded. When he saw the photos and videotapes of our sex in front of him, he was so shocked that he nearly fainted. He wanted to kill himself at that moment. Nobody knew his secret. If this secret was revealed, he would not be able to keep his job or face anyone he had ever known. However, after 30 minutes, he calmed down. He realized that if he didn't obey the KGB's command, he would have only one choice, to commit suicide. So, he obeyed any command the KGB gave him. Though he didn't have too much valuable information, he helped the KGB to place three bugs in secret places in the French Embassy. About six months later, this clerk suddenly disappeared and nobody outside of the French Embassy knew what had happened to him. Some rumors said he was sent back to France, while others said he had committed suicide."

"Then, who was the next target?" Andrew asked.

"You were... are," Alexandr said bitterly. "Before you injured your ankle, everything that happened between us was planned and only part of the seduction. However, after that night, I couldn't deny that I had some special feelings for you that I've never felt before. I didn't know what that was. I began to feel that every action I took on behalf of the KGB was wrong and a betrayal to your sincere friendship. I was so touched that evening. You realize, all our actions that night were photographed and videotaped."

"How did they take photos and videotape us? There was nothing inside of your apartment."

"The mirror above the chest is different. A camera is behind it. They could see us from a room in the next apartment, but we couldn't see them. Furthermore, there are a couple bugs hidden in my apartment for recording conversations."

"Why didn't they use some KGB girl to trap me?"

"They know you're not married. They know you have this girlfriend, Judy. Usually, if you don't have any family, especially children, it is not as effective to use female sex to set a person up. However, if they can get you involved in a homosexual relationship, then most people need to protect their reputation, and they're trapped."

"Ah. I was completely blind. I trusted you with my whole heart. I became emotionally attached to you in a way I've never experienced before." Andrew looked at Alexandr with surprise.

"I never believed that I would have really fallen in love with you. Oh. You must be very careful now. That pen I gave you, the sapphire? It is a camera and listening device. You must pretend that you still don't know this. In addition, you should know that we have been followed by two Russian agents since the beginning of our relationship. Not only that, there is a bug in my top pocket all the time. They are listening and recording everything."

"You mean we're followed even now?" Andrew was surprised. He was so shocked he hadn't stopped to consider this.

"Yes. In fact, I'm wondering what they are doing now on the shore. They can't hear our conversation with the listening device at such a distance. And the sound of the waves would also disturb their listening. We are safe talking here, but we must continue our act again when we get closer to shore." As Alexandr looked at Andrew, his eyes filled with tears again.

"But I don't know what to do now. Monday of last week when I reported to General Kupcov, the director of my department of KGB, he gave me all the photos and videotape to show you. He gave me an order to reveal my identity and begin to pressure and blackmail you. He knows almost everything about you. I now also know that there are two other workers in the American Embassy who have already been blackmailed and who are controlled by the KGB. They know you pretty well, Andrew. They know you are a CIA agent who is handling the data processing collected from the entire CIA network in Russia. To break down this network is their highest priority now. I just couldn't go through with my orders last weekend, but now I'm out of time. I wish I had never been born, Andrew. Please forgive me."

Andrew looked at Alexandr and reached his right hand out to Alexandr's head, pulling him closer and kissing him. He had already forgiven Alexandr. After all, he really hadn't had a choice.

"Last Monday, I was pressured again. I knew if I didn't tell you the truth, I could be charged with betrayal and executed. I told them that since you had undergone such strict training in America as a special agent, I suspected that using homosexual activities to blackmail you might not work. But I told them that you were deeply in love with me. I said that I might be able to convince you with the threat that if you don't cooperate with us, I would leave you permanently, and those photos and videotape would be sent to the American Embassy. I bought some time, but it was all I could think of, Andrew. Please help me!" Alexandr looked at Andrew eagerly and was begging for mercy. He was beginning to panic.

"Let me think, Alexandr, let's calm down. We can figure out something. Slow down your kicking. We don't want to reach the shore until we have figured out some solution."

Andrew and Alexandr allowed the lifesaver to float on the water for some time while Andrew thought through possible ways out of this impossible situation. After 15 minutes or so, he said, "This is what you'll do. Tell them that I agree to cooperate with you. However, since the information is so important to them, I have two conditions. First, I want two million dollars. Tell them that I will need that money once my betrayal of my country has been discovered. I will need that money to hide somewhere in the world. Tell them I want them to send one million dollars to my Swiss bank account at the beginning, and another million dollars when I finish handing over the information. Second, tell them they cannot remove you from your current duty. I won't deal with any other Russian secret agent. Tell them that I will deal only with you until my departure from Russia."

"You really want to betray your country for me?" Alexandr was shocked at what he heard.

"No. This is just to buy us more time to figure out the next step. This is very serious. We only have one chance to get this right. For your sake, we need to buy you some time. Time is our enemy now." Andrew looked at Alexandr solemnly.

"Tell them that there are three levels of secret codes to access the classified data. These codes are changed every two weeks at different times. I will receive the first level of codes next Tuesday. Tell them that by then they should have deposited one million dollars into my account. I will check my account with the computer to see if the money is there. If it is, I will tell you the first level of codes next Tuesday night. Once they have all of the information, I mean, all three levels of secret codes, they should deposit the other million dollars into my account immediately. You should also tell them that this is a one-time deal for these three levels of code. After two weeks, when the codes are changed, if they want them again, they must pay another two million dollars," Andrew said.

"Then what?" Alexandr asked urgently.

"I don't know yet. We must have a secret way to pass messages between us. Since both of us are bugged and watched, we must find a safe way. We cannot speak and if I write with your pen, the camera will reveal what I've written. By the way, do you know how many bugs are in the American Embassy?" Andrew asked.

"Many, most likely. Remember, two of your people have been blackmailed to work for the KGB."

"Do you know their names?" Andrew asked.

"That's impossible. Everything like this is classified as the highest secret in KGB. There are only a few top Communist officers who know their identities."

"It doesn't matter. We will have to pass messages by writing. Since the pen you gave me is in my jacket's pocket at all times, I will find excuses to keep my jacket someplace out of their sight. Remember, once you read any message I give you, immediately destroy it by burning it or flush it down the toilet. You cannot make any mistake. Any mistake could mean our funerals." Andrew stared at Alexandr gravely for a moment before continuing.

"Remember now, this is the access code for my National Swiss Bank account. 'EagleAmerica1776.' This code can be used only for deposits, not for withdrawals."

With a plan of action ready, Andrew and Alexandr once again headed towards the shore. By the time they reached it, it was nearly 5:30. The weather had become colder as the sun set and they shivered as they came up out of the water and stumbled toward the car. They changed quickly. Andrew switched on the car's ignition and turned the car's heater to full blast to warm them up. Alexandr got the sandwiches and drinks out of the trunk and climbed into the car. Their ordeal had left them very hungry. This had been a long, terrible day, and it wasn't over yet. Andrew scanned his surroundings, and in the far distance spotted a car. He knew this was the car of the KGB agents and felt his temper rise again. How dare they put him in this position! How dare they use Alexandr this way! After his initial burst of anger Andrew calmed down a bit and sat thinking about the events of the afternoon. He suddenly realized that if Michael hadn't put the lifesaver in the trunk, he would have drowned. And, if Alexandr hadn't thought to retrieve it before chasing after him, they both would have drowned. He felt a deep appreciation in his heart for Michael's friendship and thoughtful consideration.

"This is the second time he has saved my life," Andrew thought.

Once they had eaten a bit and were warmed up, Andrew and Alexandr headed back to Leningrad. They stayed in the rest of the evening, ordering and eating dinner in their hotel room. Now, they just wanted to enjoy what could be their last night together.

The next morning they didn't get up until almost noon. They had been awake most of the night, loving and enjoying each other until sometime after three in the morning. In the mid-afternoon, Andrew returned the car and walked back to the hotel. They called a taxi to take them to the airport. It was a quiet flight back. Now that Andrew knew that they were both bugged, and under constant surveillance, he didn't feel like talking very much. It was a disturbing feeling to know someone was watching you all the time. Furthermore, he had to find a way to solve this problem. He had to try and stay calm and ponder every detail. After he dropped Alexandr off at his apartment, he went home and meditated. In the last couple months, he had started to realize how much meditation helped him concentrate, see clearly, and make informed decisions.

3rd Meeting with General Kupcov

As usual, Alexandr came to the KGB office to meet General Kupcov on Monday morning. Since the General had not received much information from the agents' surveillance last weekend, he was anxious and eager to hear Alexandr's recounting of the result of the bargaining. When Alexandr knocked on the door and entered the room, he was surprised to see General Kupcov standing up and waiting for him. He could see the general's anxiety reflected in how he stood there waiting for his results.

Alexandr looked directly into General Kupcov's eyes and saluted with a smile that implied that everything had gone smoothly as planned. When General Kupcov saw Alexandr's smiling face, he knew that they had subdued another American agent, one of the most important ones this time. He suppressed a relieved sigh and sat down.

"Доброе утро Генерал Капков." ("Good morning, General Kupcov,") Alexandr said.

"Хорошо. расскажите мне подробно с начала." ("Well? Tell me in detail everything that happened from the beginning.") General Kupcov commanded impatiently. He scrutinized Alexandr's eyes intently.

Alexandr knew that his eyes had to keep contact with the general's. If they didn't, the general would easily see through his lying. He had to appear honest and sincere. This had been part of his training, a facade that could fool honest people as well as the most suspicious people. With the general, he had to put on his best act ever, since the general was well aware that his agents were good at putting these masks on their faces.

"Чтобы избегать прослушания американского секретного агента, я пригласил Эндрю к берегу в Санкт-Петербурге в прошлую пятницу. Мы были там однажды и хорошо провели время. Я надеялся, что это напомнит ему о нашей любви и стало искренним в наших отношениях." ("To avoid the American secret agents following or listening I invited Andrew, the CIA agent, to the beach in Leningrad last Friday. We had been there once before and had had a good time. I was hoping this would reassure him of our love and the sincerity of our relationship,") Alexandr said.

"Я знал это из сообщения других агентов. Продолжить." ("I knew this from the other agents' reports. Continue.")

"Когда мы были там, я нашел оправдание и взял его к воде к расстоянию, которое было безопасно от шпионящих слушающих устройств. Я боялся, что мы могли бы сопровождаться американскими агентами. Когда мы были в воде, я сказал ему, что я был российским секретным агентом, и все действия любви в прошлом были все заранее спланированы. Когда я сказал ему, он был столь потрясен и уставился на меня некоторое время. Я продолжал и сказал, что у нас есть все фотографии гомосексуальных действий. Российское правительство желает сотрудныхать с ним. Когда он услышал об этом, его глаза стали красными, и и он заплакал. Он был настолько расстроен что отплыл в глубоководье ." ("When we were there, I found an excuse to take him to the deep water at a distance which would be safe from long-distance listening devices. I was afraid that we might be followed by American agents. When we were in the water, I told him I was a Russian secret agent and all of the love actions in the past were pre-arranged. When I told him, he was shocked and stared at me for a while. I continued and said we had all the photos of our homosexual actions. The Russian government wished him to cooperate with them. When he heard of this, his eyes turned red with tears. He was so upset he turned and swam away into the deep water.")

"Да, я видел это сообщение от других двух агентов." ("Yes, I had this report from the other two agents too.") The General looked at him and nodded his head.

"После того, как он плавал некоторое время, я понял, что он забывает, насколько пасно отплывать далеко от берега. Я немедленно возвратился к берегу и взял спасательный круг из автомобиля, и возвратился к воде и пробовал найти его. Не было легко, так как я терял из виду его. Я продолжал плавать в течение чем одного часа и не мог найти его. Я начал запаниковать и бояться, что он, возможно, утонул. Я думал об усилие, которое я вложил в эту миссию, напрасно. Когда я думал, возвввращаться к берегу, я увидел, что он машет мне руками приблизительно на расстоянии в 80 метров." ("After he had swum for a while, I realized that he must have forgotten how dangerous it could be if he swam too far from the shore. I immediately went back to the shore and retrieved a life-saving tube from the car, then returned to the water to try to find him. It was not easy since I had lost sight of him. I kept swimming for more than an hour and couldn't find him. I began to panic and fear that he might have drowned. I thought of all the effort I had put into this mission. I worried it would all be for nothing. Just as I was thinking of returning to the shore, I saw him waving his arm at me from about 80 meters away.")

General Kupcov listened intently to Alexandr's narration of the event since he didn't know about all of this. "Почему Вы пытались его спасти? Вы его любите?" ("Why did you go after him and try to save him? Do you love him?")

"Нет. Генерал Капков. Вы шутите? Я могу любить его, но я никогда не влюблялся из него. На мой взгляд, Коммунистическое будущее более важно чем что - нибудь, особенно личное сострадание. Это всегда было образованием, которое я получил от моего отца. Я боялся, что, если он умер, тогда мы потеряли наш шанс сломать чистую работу ЦРУ в России." ("No, General Kupcov, you must be joking. I may like him, but I could never fall in love with him. To my mind, the Communist future is far more important than anything, especially personal compassion. That is what my father has always taught me. But I was afraid that if he died, then we would have lost our chance to break down the CIA's network in Russia.")

"Он любит Вас?" ("Does he love you?")

"Я действительно верю так. Я мог сказать по его эмоцийям. Я полагаю, что он в меня влюбился." ("I really believe so. From his emotional responses to me, I believe he has fallen in love with me deeply.") Alexandr looked at General Kupcov with a firm expression on his face.

"Продолжить." ("Continue,") General Kupcov said.

"Мы плыли друг к другу. Он так устал что умер бы через 30 минут. Он смотрел на меня со смесью восхищения и гнева. Его глаза были заполнены слезами и смешались с морской водой. После нескольких минут, он начал успокаиваться. Он тогда спросил меня, что хочет российская сторона. Он сказал мне, что при использовании фотография гомосексуальных или видеозапись, чтобы шантажировать его не будут работать, так как он не был женат, и гомосексуальные действия были очень обычны в Америке. Он не чувствовал бы слишком много позора, даже если бы это было показано. худшее, с которым он мог столкнуться, это увольнение с правительственной работы." ("I swam toward him until I finally reached him. He was extremely tired and probably would have sunk into the water and drowned in another 30 minutes. He looked at me with a mixture of appreciation and anger. His eyes were filled with tears, mixed with the seawater. After a few minutes, he began to calm down. He then asked me what the Russian side wants. He told me that using those homosexual photos or videotape to blackmail him would not work since he was not married, and homosexual activities were very common in America. He said he wouldn't feel ashamed even if they were revealed. The worst he would probably encounter was being removed from his government job.")

This was as Alexandr had predicted in his last meeting with the general. General Kupcov began to appreciate Alexandr's wisdom in foreseeing the possibilities. When Alexandr saw General Kupcov had quietly accepted his story without questioning him any further, he believed the general was convinced.

Alexandr continued, "Тогда я сказал ему, что я действительно люблю его. Если он не будет сотрудничать, то я буду удален немедленно. Естественно, все фотографии и видеозаписи пошлют американскому Посольству. Я смотрел на его лицо с просьбой и искренним выражением. Я знаю, что он глубоко любит меня. Он сохранял спокойствие в течение приблизительно 10 минут, и я мог видеть, что он был в эмоциональной борьбе в это время." ("I then told him that I hated to do this to him because I really do love him. I also told him that if he does not cooperate, I will be removed immediately. Naturally, all photos and videotapes will be sent to the American Embassy as well. I looked into his face with a begging and sincere expression. I could see his love for me on his face. He kept quiet for a while and I could see he was struggling emotionally at the time.") Alexandr looked at General Kupcov and could feel how much the story appealed to him and how anxious he was to hear the rest. Alexandr intentionally paused.

"Я очень хочу пить. Можно немного воды?" ("May I have some water, sir? I am very thirsty.")

General Kupcov looked at him irritably, saying, "Вперед. вода в том углу." ("Go ahead. There is some water in the corner.")

Alexandr went to the corner of the room where there was a pitcher of water, some coffee cookware, and a few glasses. He picked up a glass and poured some water for himself. Still intentionally drawing his story out, he asked, "Хотели бы Вы немного кофе или воды? Генерал Капков." ("Would you like some coffee or water, General Kupcov?")

"Лейте мне немного кофе и быстрые..." ("Pour me some coffee and continue. Quickly!") the general said as he began to lose his patience.

Alexandr brought a cup of coffee, sugar, and cream and placed them on the desk in front of General Kupcov, then returned to the precise spot where he had been standing before. He waited until General Kupcov had taken a sip of coffee and turned his eyes back to him before continuing.

"Он сказал мне, что он будет сотрудничать с нами только при двух условиях. Если мы не соглашаемся ни с одним из этих условий, он предпочитает пожертвовать его личной репутацией и карьерой." ("Andrew told me that he would cooperate with us only under two conditions. If we don't agree with any of these conditions, he would rather sacrifice his personal reputation and career.")

In a way, General Kupcov was very happy to hear this and was hopeful that Andrew would cooperate with them. But he was also anxious to hear about the two conditions Andrew had. He did not appreciate Alexandr's slow pace of talking and urged him on, "Каковы условия?" ("What are the conditions?")

"Сначала, российская власть не может удалить меня. Он не повел бы никакого дела с любым другим российским агентом. Кроме того, я должен держать с ним хорошие отношения, до его отъезда из России. Я полагал, что это условие состояло в том, потому что он меня глубоко любил." ("First, I am not to be removed from my duty with him. He will not conduct any deal with any other Russian agent. In addition, I must maintain my good relationship with him as I have been until his departure from Russia. I believe that this condition is because he loves me and wants to be with me as much as possible.")

General Kupcov nodded his head and motioned for Alexandr to continue.

"Второе условие - он хочет два миллиона долларов. Он сказал, было три уровня секретных кодексов, которые позволили нам получать доступ к американцу, высоко классифицировал секретную информацию. Первый уровень кодексов получит доступ к некоторым низким секретным данным уровня, средний уровень должен получить доступ к секретной информации соглашений между американским правительством и другими западными странами. Наконец самый высокий должен получить доступ к работе сети ЦРУ в России. Эти кодексы изменены каждые две недели, и все три уровня кодексов выпущены к нему в три различных раза." ("The second condition is that he wants two million dollars for the deal. He said there are three levels of secret codes which will allow us to access the American highly-classified secret information. The first level of codes will access some low-level classified information, the middle level is to access the secret information of agreements between the American government and other western countries. Finally, the highest one is to access the CIA network in Russia. These codes are changed every two weeks and all three levels of codes are released to him at three different times.")

All of this information confirmed what the Russians had already discovered from the other two turned American Embassy workers. What the Russian government needed now were the three levels of secret codes. The general knew that they were on the right track and that he would receive high praise and a reward from the party if he was able to break down the CIA network in Russia. Alexandr sipped some water from the glass in his right hand and continued,

"Он сказал он хотел бы, чтобы мы внесли один миллион долларов на его личный счет в швейцарском Национальном Банке немедленно. Первый уровень кодексов достиг бы его рук в следующий вторник утром. Если он проверит его счет и найдет депозит, то он даст мне кодексы в следующий вторник ночью. Второй уровень кодексов будет в следующую пятницу, и третий уровень будет в следующий понедельник. Он сказал, как только весь три уровня кодексов был показан к нам, он хочет, чтобы мы внесли один миллион долларов." ("He said he would like us to deposit one million dollars into his personal account in the Swiss National Bank immediately. The first level of codes will reach his hands next Tuesday morning. If he checks his account and finds the money there, he will give me the codes next Tuesday evening. The second level of codes will come out next Friday and the third level will come out the following Monday. He said once all three levels of codes were revealed to us, he wants us to deposit another million dollars immediately into his account. If we don't do this, he won't cooperate with us anymore. That means if we want to know more secret codes in the future, he won't give them to us. Naturally, if we deposit the money this time, the next time he would keep the same deal, two million dollars each time.")

"Это означает, что он был продажным американским секретным агентом." ("That means he was a corruptible American secret agent.") General Kupcov laughed with pride since he believed it would be very hard to corrupt any Russian secret agent. "Каков пароль его швейцарского Счета в банке?" ("What is the password of his Swiss Bank account?")

"'EagleAmerica1776.' Это - за депозит только и не может использоваться, чтобы снять." ("'EagleAmerica1776.' It's for deposit only and cannot be used to withdraw.")

When General Kupcov heard the password he scoffed inside. "EagleAmerica1776. Ha! Such a patriotic password."

"Он также спросил меня, если я убегу с ним к другую страну, если все это будет выставлено на показ. Если ЦРУ узнает все это, он может быть обвинен в предательстве." ("He also asked me if I would run away with him to another country if the whole thing is exposed. If the CIA knew the whole thing, he can be charged with betrayal of his country.")

The General sat up and looked at Alexandr curiously. "Каков был ваш ответ?" ("What was your answer?")

"Я сказал ему, что я пойду с ним без любого колебания, так как я так.любил его." ("I told him I would go with him without any hesitation since I loved him so much,") Alexandr said dispassionately.

General Kupcov laughed out loud. He was proud of Alexandr that he was able to play this American agent so skillfully. He asked Alexandr to wait in the office and told him he would return in a few minutes. Alexandr knew that the general would go report to his boss and set up a plan. Since he knew it would be a while - for this big of an event they would take at least half an hour - he found a chair and sat down. He had stood for nearly an hour and his legs were tired. Relief coursed through Alexandr as he felt he had escaped from today's possible danger, but his relief was short-lived. As Andrew had said this would buy him some time, but now what were they going to do? He began to worry again and didn't know what further plan Andrew could have. He thought about his mother and his future, and he felt very sorry for himself.

About twenty-five minutes later General Kupcov returned and Alexandr promptly stood up, but General Kupcov invited him to sit down again. This was very rare: that a high-ranking officer would ask an underling to sit. It was especially rare for this general. Alexandr now knew for sure everything would be okay, at least for the moment.

"Мы согласны. Он получит один миллион долларов ко вторнику 5:00 Премьер-министр. Мы хотим его первый уровень секретных кодексов во вторник ночью." ("Tell the American that we agree with the deal. He will receive one million dollars by Tuesday at 5:00 p.m. We want his first level of secret codes Tuesday night.")

6
DEFECTION

Confession

Andrew, meanwhile, had returned to his office Monday morning still trying to figure out what to do next. After thinking it over for a couple of hours he decided to tell his boss the whole truth of what had happened. The Russian tactic of using sexual encounters to blackmail workers could be a huge problem for all of the western embassies. Though he knew telling his story would bring him some serious embarrassment because of the homosexual activity he was involved in, he also knew he had to face it. He just could not let this relationship destroy his faithfulness to his country.

Settling on this course of action, Andrew first took out the pen from Alexandr to write something non-important. Then he placed the pen on the desk and after a moment covered it with some papers, making the covering of the pen seem unintentional. This would stop the pen from recording his actions.

"How many other cameras and bugs are in this building?" Andrew wondered.

Andrew took some paper out and used another pen to write a few sentences on it. Then, going to his boss's office, he knocked on the door and waited for a response.

"Come in." It was Mr. Buckley's voice.

Andrew entered quickly and handed Mr. Buckley the note by shaking his hand, while at the same time saying, "Good morning, Mr. Buckley. The briefing for the advisors is almost done. Could I get you to take a look at it before I send it along to the final editors?"

Mr. Buckley opened the note, which said, "Extremely important. Need to talk to you in a secure place."

It was obvious from Andrew's note and the way he delivered it that there was something seriously wrong that could not be discussed in his office.

"Well, I was just about to go for a cup of coffee. Why don't we go over the briefing while I drink it?" he smiled at Andrew and started walking. He led Andrew to the kitchen to get some coffee, then walked toward the secure room in the basement where Andrew had met with the security director, Colonel Powell. The secure room was completely isolated and was checked for all manner of surveillance devices daily. Mr. Buckley sealed the door behind him.

"Mr. Buckley, I have made a terrible mistake and am in a compromising position with the KGB," Andrew began, somewhat abashed.

When Mr. Buckley heard this, he was very surprised and shocked. He was also very disappointed by Andrew's behavior. But being the experienced CIA agent and director that he was, he knew this was not a time to respond with emotion. It was the time to remain calm and handle this event wisely. He looked at Andrew intently and told him to sit down.

"Why don't you start at the beginning and tell me exactly what happened," Mr. Buckley ordered sternly, pushing a button on the meeting table. The button turned on the room's surveillance system to record any conversation and event happening in the room. This recording could only be seen or reviewed by a couple of high-ranking officers in the embassy.

Andrew related to Mr. Buckley how he had become acquainted with Alexandr and how he had in truth fallen in love with him, explaining that this was the first time anything like this had ever happened to him. He continued to explain everything in detail up through the events of the past weekend at the beach and outlined his proposed plan for moving forward. Mr. Buckley took in Andrew's serious demeanor, his willingness to come forward with this story that cast him in a very bad light, and the intelligent way he had thought of a possible means to remediate matters. He knew Andrew was not a traitor; but instead was willing to risk revealing his embarrassing sexual entrapment rather than betray his country.

"Does Alexandr know who the two embassy workers are who have betrayed our government?" Mr. Buckley asked.

"I am sorry, sir. Alexandr said it is kept top secret, and only very high-level KGB agents know."

"We must be careful about anything we say in this embassy until we find a solution. We must find out who these traitors are. I appreciate your honesty, Andrew. You're doing the right thing in coming forward with this information." Mr. Buckley paused thoughtfully. "Perhaps we can even find a way to use this situation to our advantage. We'll have to make the best of it," he added.

"I gave Alexandr a non-existent secret deposit code to a Swiss National Bank account. If one million dollars is deposited into the account, that means the KGB has agreed to the deal and I must provide them the first level of codes."

"What is the secret deposit code you gave him?"

"It is EagleAmerica1776, sir."

"Andrew, based on what you've told me it sounds like Alexandr truly loves you. Otherwise, why would he risk his life to tell you the truth of how he had trapped you? I trust your instincts on this. Now you tell me the truth. Do you love him?"

Though Mr. Buckley believed Andrew, he still had a duty to be absolutely certain that Andrew was not now acting as a double agent. He had to be very careful in his handling of this situation.

Andrew lowered his head and said, "Yes. If necessary, I would risk my life to help him."

Mr. Buckley heard the gravity in Andrew's voice and sensed the importance of the matter weighing on him. If everything Andrew said was true, both Andrew and Alexandr were in serious danger. He didn't know how many embassy employees had also entered into similar traps and had betrayed their country. Though he had been told of at least two, he assumed there could be more. He also didn't know how many places in his embassy had been bugged. In addition, this kind of KGB trapping strategy might not have only happened in the American Embassy. It might have happened to all the embassies in the western world.

"Andrew, see me here this afternoon at 3 o'clock. I need to meet with my superiors and figure out a plan. I will talk with you this afternoon."

A Plan

That afternoon Andrew was once again in the secure office, anxiously awaiting Mr. Buckley. He was very worried and eager to know if his boss had devised a solution. A couple of minutes after 3, Mr. Buckley entered the room with a smile. Andrew respectfully stood up and looked at his boss with an expression that was both hopeful and hesitant.

"Please sit down, Andrew, we are going to make this work. I have contacted the relevant departments and we now have a plan." Mr. Buckley looked at Andrew with a smile and continued, "We have re-classified all levels of the government data sectors. The KGB will not get any important intelligence from the first level of classification, except regarding one particular event. That is that there is a possible defection of a famous Russian physicist, possibly taking place this coming Thursday in Latvia. No further details about this event will be available at this level. Therefore, when you reveal this first level of codes, the KGB will only receive intelligence we want them to see, so no problem there. As a matter of fact, I believe they may already have some information about this possible defection. Providing them codes to information that confirms what they have heard from another source does not harm us, and it helps you earn their trust. We have also opened an account at the Swiss National Bank with the deposit code you gave them, EagleAmerica1776."

Having reassured Andrew that his first step in cooperating with the KGB would not harm his country in any way, Mr. Buckley proceeded to fill him in on the remaining details of the plan. The operation had been named "Soaring Eagle." They talked for hours and, at the end of their meeting, Andrew grasped Mr. Buckley's hand with both of his. He could not help the tears that filled his eyes. He left the room with deep appreciation.

Operation – Soaring Eagle

Tuesday afternoon at 4:50, when Andrew checked it, he saw that one million dollars had been deposited into the Swiss National Bank account. He thought to himself, "the eagle is ready to take off." He went to Mr. Buckley's office and gave him a signal that meant everything was going according to plan.

That evening, he went to Alexandr's apartment, where Alexandr had been waiting for him anxiously. They embraced in the doorway, and he could feel that Alexandr was trembling. They rested in this moment, feeling their hearts beating together. When they sat down, Alexandr looked at him with a worried expression.

Andrew did not say a word but simply kissed Alexandr, putting his whole heart into it as before. Then he took his jacket off and led Alexandr to the bathroom as they used to do, to take a shower together before having sex. Once they entered the bathroom, Andrew's face turned very serious. There was no surveillance system in the bathroom and the bug Andrew carried with him was in his jacket in the living room. He handed Alexandr a paper with written instructions on it. Turning on the shower faucet, he quietly said, "Alexandr, you must study these instructions carefully. After you have them memorized you must burn them. I have another sheet of paper with the secret code that I will give you later in front of the KGB's surveillance camera."

Alexandr quickly placed the paper in a drawer in the bathroom cabinet. During their shower Andrew briefly outlined the plan and then answered Alexandr's many questions. Once Andrew was satisfied that Alexandr understood what was going to happen, they finished their shower and went to bed.

Since this might be their last time together for a long time, they made the most of it, enjoying each other's bodies with an almost desperate passion. After sex, Andrew dressed and went out to stand in front of the two-way mirror. Alexandr followed him and stood facing him. Andrew removed a sheet of paper from his pocket and gave it to Alexandr.

"I have received the deposit from your side. Here is the first level of secret codes. After you have read it, please destroy it immediately."

Alexandr opened the paper, reading the one line of secret code, "G0T0H3AV3N." It was very easy to remember, simply 'go to heaven' with the Os replaced with zeros and the Es replaced with 3s. He put his arms around Andrew and gave him a deep kiss. His eyes were red.

Andrew pulled away slightly and said, "Alexandr, remember you told me that you would go away with me if I have to run? You know, the CIA will not be fooled forever."

Alexandr knew that Andrew was acting for the KGB observers, but his own response was sincere. He held Andrew closer and kissed him again. "Of course. I will keep my promise. You know I love you."

Alexandr released Andrew and went to fix some dinner. They kept their conversation light while they ate, drinking vodka and speaking of nothing important until Andrew mentioned in an off-hand manner, "Oh yeah. I almost forgot. I must fly to Latvia this Thursday morning and return that evening. There is some embassy business that I need to take care of. I was just wondering if you could come and keep me company. We would have a good time there. And I'm sure you could help me get around in that new place. You know my Russian is not that good. I often misunderstand what people say."

"How about the second level of secret codes?" Alexandr asked.

"Why do you ask about the second level codes?" Andrew responded. "I told you I won't have them till Friday morning. I'll give them to you Friday night." Andrew looked at Alexandr with irritation. Of course, they both knew it was only a show.

They were quiet for a couple of minutes. Then Andrew adopted a conciliatory tone and asked, "Will you go to your martial arts practice again this Friday? My ankle has recovered completely. It's time to show you that I can also fight."

"Okay. We'll do it."

"How about Thursday, then. Will you go to Latvia with me?"

"I must ask my director for permission to go. You know he is not easy to deal with. Can I call you at the embassy?"

"No, no. Please don't! They will know about us. The CIA records and listens to all of our telephone conversations at the embassy. How about if I come see you tomorrow night?"

"Okay. I'll see you at 7:00 p.m. here. I don't know when my rehearsal will be finished. It could be early or late. I have another key to this apartment. Please wait for me if I am late," Alexandr said as he picked up a key from a drawer in the kitchen area and gave it to Andrew.

"Please try to make it. It will mean a lot to me if we can travel together to another republic of the Soviet Union."

"I can't promise, but I will try," Alexandr replied.

Right after Andrew left, Alexandr received a phone call from General Kupcov. He had been listening to their conversation through the monitoring system in Alexandr's apartment.

"Александр, Вы сделали хорошую работу. Теперь, скажите мне, что является кодом." ("Alexandr, you have done a fine job.

Now, tell me the code.")

Alexandr told General Kupcov the code and continued, "Генерал Капков, пожалуйста скажите мне, если я должен пойти в Латвию с Эндрю или нет? Я должен дать ему ответ завтра ночью." ("General Kupcov, should I go to Latvia with Andrew or not? I need to give him an answer tomorrow night.")

"Ожидай моей дальнейшей инструкции." ("Wait for further instruction.") General Kupcov hung up the phone.

Alexandr went to the bathroom and took out the paper that Andrew had given him earlier. It contained the plans for Soaring Eagle, which he studied very carefully. As he read the plan, he could not help the tears that came to his eyes. Knowing that he could not stay in the bathroom too long or the KGB would suspect him immediately, he lit a match and burned the paper in the sink, rinsing the ashes down the drain. When he came out of the bathroom ten minutes later, his eyes were still red.

At 2 o'clock in the morning, Alexandr's telephone rang.

"Номер 21. Это - Генерал Капков. Вы инструкции. Из того, что мы узнали в их первой классификации уровня, это казалось, что есть известный российский Физик, и его жена перейдет на сторону западного мира в этот четверг в Латвии. Нет никакой информации о том, кто они, когда, и где. Я подозреваю, что миссия Эндрю в Латвии имеет к этому некоторое отношение." ("Number 21. This is General Kupcov. You have an instruction. From what we have found out in their first level classification, it seems there is a well-known Russian physicist and his wife who will defect to the western world this Thursday in Latvia. There is no information about who they are, when, or where. I suspect that Andrew's mission in Latvia has something to do with it.") He paused for a moment.

Ваш приказ - идти с ним и узнать кто этот физик и его жена, когда, и где предательство могло бы иметь место. Помните, притворитесь, что Вы не знаете ничто об этом. Если они будут знать, что мы знали об этом, то они немедленно изменят план." ("Your order is to go with him and try to find out who this physicist and his wife are, and when and where the defection might take place. Remember, pretend that you don't know anything about this. If they know that we know about this, they will change their plan immediately.")

"Да. Генерал. Я приложу все усилия." ("Yes, General. I will do my best.")

The other side hung up the phone. Alexandr felt tired but when he tried to sleep again, he could not. He lay there worrying all night.

Farewell to Mom

Early Wednesday morning, Alexandr took a train to his hometown, Vladimir, to see his mother. He arrived in town around mid-morning and headed directly to his family home. When he walked in the house, he immediately took off his jacket with the KGB bug in the pocket and placed it in the closet. He expected that nobody would be home except his mother. His father was on a special training mission and his two eldest brothers were with their respective units. His third eldest brother was still in Moscow for his graduate school and seldom came home.

Alexandr went into the living room and saw his mother there, sewing clothes to make some extra income. He knew that he would not be seeing her for a long, long time or maybe ever again. When he thought of this, his eyes turned red and he could not keep his tears from falling as he called out to her. She looked up at the sound of his voice and stood up right away, so happy for the surprise visit. Alexandr had never come home to visit during weekdays because he was always busy in rehearsal. He only came home on Saturday and Sunday. Furthermore, if he came home on the weekdays he could not see his father or brothers.

Alexandr threw his arms around his mother in a tight hug.

Alexandr had always been more demonstrative than his three elder brothers, but his mother knew that there was something strange today about Alexandr's sudden visit and emotional behavior. She could feel something would or had already happened to him.

"Все хорошо? Александр. Вы плачите?" ("Are you okay Alexandr? You are crying,") she said tenderly.

It took a few moments for Alexandr to calm down. Though he had undergone serious training in controlling his emotions as a secret agent, he could not help it right now. When he saw and held his mother he simply couldn't hold back. There was only one other person in the whole world who could also break his emotional control, and that was Andrew. He understood now how very much in love with Andrew he really was.

Alexandr released his mother and took her hands in his.

"Мама. Я ухожу в четверг. Моя команда приняла контракт для кругосветного путешествия, и я - один из актеров. Я должен пойти с ними, займет много месяцев или даже год." ("Mom, I am going away this coming Thursday. My show team has accepted a contract for a world tour and I must go with them. It will take many months or even a year,") Alexandr said.

"Это уже завтра! Но это очень хорошая новость! Хотя мне нравится видеть, что ты рядом со мной, я думаю, что твоя карьера важнее. Это редкая возможность увидеть мир. Будете ли ты в Америке?" ("That's tomorrow already! But that is very good news! Though I like to see that you are near me, I think your career is more important for you. This is a rare opportunity for you to see the world. Will you be in America?")

"насколько я знаю, мы будем там через месяц." ("As I understand it, we will be there in a month,") Alexandr answered.

Alexandr's Mom lowered her voice and said, "Александр. Когда ты в Америке, если будет шанс, сбегай из команды и проси защиту." ("Alexandr. When you are in America, if you find a chance, escape from the team and ask for protection.") She looked at Alexandr with a serious expression on her face.

Alexandr was shocked to hear this. He paused for a while, then said, "Тогда я вероятно никогда Вас не увижу. Мама." ("But then I will probably never see you again, Mom.")

"Нет. Нет. Александр. Слушай меня. Твоя жизнь и будущее более важны чем я. Если я буду знать, что ты в Америке, то я буду очень очень счастлива." ("No. No, Alexandr, listen to me. Your life and future are more important than seeing me. If I know you have your freedom in America, I will be very, very happy.")

"Но что скажет отец и мои братья? Они преданные коммунисты и будут против моего бегства." ("But, what are Dad and my brothers going to say? They are loyal Communists and would be against my defection.")

"Не волнуйтесь о них. Я знаю, что глубоко в их сердцах, они не любят Коммунизм. Они в западне или неволе этой действительности." ("Do not worry about them. I know that deep in their hearts, they don't like Communism. They are just bound by tradition to serve their country, under threat of harm.")

"Мама." ("Mom.") Alexandr's tears spilled down his cheeks.

His mom used her hand to caress Alexandr's hair back gently, just like when he was a child. "Все, что я хочу видеть, - ваша свобода. Я хочу, чтобы Вы были счастливыми." ("All I want to see is your freedom. I want you to be happy.")

No one in Alexandr's family knew he was actually a Russian secret agent, or that his body had been used as a sexual tool to acquire information. When Alexandr thought about this, he was even sadder and felt the true depth of his mother's love.

"It is true that a mother's love is the greatest love in the whole world," he thought.

Alexandr knew if he defected, his family would be interrogated and possibly tortured by the KGB for a long time. He worried about the harm that might come to them because of his actions, however, he was very confident that they would not be killed due to their loyal records in serving the country.

His mother prepared a few of Alexandr's favorite dishes for lunch. They had been able to afford better food since Alexandr had started sending good money home. While they were eating, Alexandr brought up the issue of their income.

"Мама. Я не знаю, как послать Вам больше денег, если я нахожусь в Америке? Я не знаю то, что случится?" ("Mom, I don't know how I can send you more money if I am in America. I don't know what will be happening.")

"Не волнуйтес я о нас. Даже если ты вообще не пошлете никаких денег вообще, мы все выживем." ("Don't worry about us. Even if you don't send any money at all, we can still survive easily.") She looked at Alexandr's face and smiled a smile of true love.

Alexandr left his home to return to Moscow with a mixture of feelings, of love and sadness, and of loss. "I hope I can see my mom again someday." He knew that his future was risky and uncertain.

When Alexandr arrived back at the Moscow train station, it was only 4 p.m. Since his appointment with Andrew wasn't until 7, he decided to go see his brother at Moscow University. Upon entering the lab where his brother worked, he again took his jacket off, replacing it with lab clothes. This was standard procedure in any high-tech lab since the environment must be kept sterile and had the added benefit to Alexandr of preventing the KGB from being able to listen to his conversation with his brother. Since the KGB would know he was seeing his brother, they wouldn't suspect anything.

Alexandr and his brother went to a small office in the lab to talk and, as soon as they entered, Alexandr's eyes teared up. His brother asked, "Что не так? Александр. Вы очень эмоциональны." ("What is wrong? Alexandr, you look very sad.")

"Завтра, моя группа отбудет в кругосветное путешествие. Я не увижу вас в течение долгого времени." ("Tomorrow, my performing group will depart to have a world tour show. I might not see you for a long time.")

"Как долго?" ("How long?")

"Может быть один год." ("Maybe a year or so.")

"Заботься о себе." ("Take care of yourself,") his brother said sadly.

Since Alexandr and his brother's ages were closer to each other, they had had a closer relationship with each other than with the other brothers. They had played together and talked to each other since they were very small.

"Пожалуйста, позаботьтесь о Маме. Я не буду в состоянии наблюдать за ней некоторое время." ("Please take care of mom for me. I won't be able to watch her for a while,") Alexandr said.

"Я буду стараться изо всех сил. Только заботься о себе." ("I will try my best. Just take care of yourself.") His brother stepped forward and hugged Alexandr tightly to his chest. Then a student came in, and they separated and said goodbye.

Before Defection

Alexandr arrived at his apartment around 5:30 p.m.. While he waited for Andrew, he began to cook dinner. Actually, he had brought back some traditional food from his home. His mother had insisted he take it with him back to Moscow. He turned his sound system on and played some of the Chopin that he and Andrew both liked. He again worried that tonight would be the last night they would be able to be together for a long, long time. The thought made him sad, but at the same time he was excited for what might happen next. He just hoped that everything would turn out as they had planned.

Andrew opened the door a little before 7. He thought Alexandr would not be home yet and was surprised to see him there with dinner ready. They hugged and Alexandr kissed Andrew fiercely.

"I didn't go to rehearsal today," Alexandr explained. "I just went to see my director and got his permission for the absence today and tomorrow. I can go with you tomorrow morning now. Actually, I went home to visit my mom this morning. I returned only a couple of hours ago."

"How is your mom?" Andrew had suspected that Alexandr would go home to say goodbye to his mother. Alexandr's love for her had always been obvious.

"She is fine. Actually, a lot of food on the table is her cooking."

Andrew saw there was enough food on the dinner table to feed four people. He sat down, smiling. Alexandr looked at him warmly and poured some vodka into his glass. Andrew also knew that if everything went according to plan they might not see each other for a long time, or even forever. He raised his glass in a toast, "To our future..." He had been about to add "... and to your freedom," but caught himself at the last moment. He knew that the KGB were watching and listening to everything. Any hint that there was an alternate plan in motion would be a big disaster for everyone.

"Your mom's cooking is excellent. It's better than the Russian food we've had in any restaurant," Andrew said.

Alexandr looked at him with a smile. In the background Chopin's music was soft and a perfect accompaniment to their tender feelings. After dinner, Alexandr pulled on Andrew's hand and tugged him into the bathroom so they could shower together. They washed each other, hugging and kissing passionately until the warm water ran out. They just enjoyed being together so much. After the shower, they went to bed to continue their loving as long as possible.

A little after 10 that night, Andrew rose. "Alexandr, I must go now," he said, getting dressed. "There are a few things I still need to prepare. I haven't packed for tomorrow's trip yet. As a matter of fact, you should also pack, as simply as possible. You won't need much as we'll be returning tomorrow night. I'll meet you at the airport Sheremetevo-2 at 7:00 a.m. The flight leaves at 8:38 a.m., so don't be late. We won't have much time."

"I don't have a ticket yet," Alexandr pointed out.

"Don't worry. I'll arrive early and take care of it before you get there. You know, as an embassy worker, I get special treatment from your government."

Andrew left to return to his apartment thinking, "So far, so good." But he needed to be more careful. He had almost revealed a hint of their secret to the KGB that night.

Thursday morning, Andrew was at the airport by 6:30 a.m. In spite of his early arrival, Alexandr was already there waiting for him.

"Alexandr, you're early again."

"I couldn't sleep all night. I am just so excited. This is the first time I will go to Latvia. This will be another vacation just like going to Leningrad the last two times."

"Hmm, well, not quite like that. Let's go purchase your ticket first. I already have mine."

At the ticket counter they were able to get Alexandr a seat on the plane next to Andrew. There was no problem getting him a ticket since he was accompanying a diplomatic officer working in the America Embassy. Andrew made sure to purchase a round trip ticket for Alexandr, knowing that the KGB would check what they had purchased within just a few minutes.

After they checked in, they went to a cafeteria for a quick and simple breakfast. They did not talk much. It seemed that silence was more precious than talking now. They simply wanted to enjoy every second of being together today. They both knew if the plan failed, though Andrew may not have too much trouble, to Alexandr this would be life and death.

During take-off on the airplane, Alexandr wanted desperately to hold Andrew's hand, but he couldn't do this in public. They must hide their true relationship whenever they were in a public place. "Why is it so difficult to set feelings free from the bondage of tradition?" he wondered.

The flight from Moscow to Latvia was not long, the distance from Moscow to Riga being about 550 miles. Still, Alexandr was so tired he fell asleep shortly into the hour and a half flight. When the flight attendants came to serve drinks and breakfast, Andrew did not wake him but just let him sleep. He knew that it would be a big day for Alexandr, the day of changing his destiny and future.

When the airplane landed, the bumpy landing woke Alexandr up. "What's happening?" he said, startled and still on edge.

"Shh, you slept. You feel better?"

"Yes. Much better," Alexandr replied.

They went by taxi from the airport to the Konventa Seta, a nice hotel which the American Embassy had reserved for Andrew. The hotel was located on the street, Kaleju iela 9/11, which was only about half a mile from the American Embassy. Though they would not be staying overnight, the embassy had booked it so that Andrew would have a place to rest or to hold a private meeting, whatever might be necessary to conduct his business.

When they had checked in to the hotel, Andrew called the American Embassy in Latvia immediately to report his arrival. He talked with them about a few things, especially arrangements for the evening. Tonight's meeting would be at 7:30 p.m. and their flight would leave at 11:20 p.m. That meant they must leave for the airport immediately after the meeting.

Finished with his phone call, Andrew considered their options for the rest of the day.

"Let's go out and do some short sight-seeing and then have lunch. I need to rest for a while this afternoon. Later tonight I have an important meeting at the embassy."

"Tonight! Will we have time to catch our flight back to Moscow?" Alexandr pretended to be surprised.

"Don't worry. The meeting is at 7:30 and should last only an hour. We should have enough time to get to the airport, but you should be here ready to go and waiting for me when I return around 9. We will have to leave for the airport immediately."

They went out and took a walk in the downtown area. Though the culture in Latvia is similar to Russian culture, it still had its own traditions unique to the region and its people. Their wanderings brought them to a nice restaurant where they sat down and ate a typical Latvian meal, along with some good vodka. They enjoyed a nice lunch but with little conversation. They knew if they talked too much now, it could be dangerous since they might unintentionally reveal some secrets to the KGB. Both of them were still bugged, and most likely were being watched. The risk of exposure was especially true right now as they were both feeling very anxious and emotional and were having difficulty hiding it.

It was already 2:35 in the afternoon by the time they returned to the hotel from their outing. They lay down on the bed, not talking, just holding each other, and eventually both of them drifted off to sleep. They would need to be well rested for tonight. When Andrew's watch alarm went off at 6:15 he was already up and prepared to leave. He gently shook Alexandr awake.

"Alexandr, I must go now. Remember to be here ready to go when I return. We won't have much time to catch the airplane." Andrew kissed Alexandr on the cheek and left with his briefcase.

Decoy

About five minutes after Andrew's departure, Alexandr received a phone call on the hotel phone,

"Номер 21. Это - Лейтенант Смирнов. Я отвечаю за операцию КГБ здесь в Латвии. Я только говорил с Генералом Капковым, и он хотел, чтобы Вы сообщили мне немедленно." ("Number 21, this is Lieutenant Smirnov. I am in charge of KGB's operation here in Latvia. I just talked to General Kupcov and he wanted you to report to me immediately.")

"Понятно, Лейтенант Смирнов. Я еду. Пожалуйста, дайте мне адрес." ("Understood, Lieutenant Smirnov. If you tell me where to meet you, I will come immediately.")

Actually, from the listening devices in Andrew's pen and

Alexandr's pocket, General Kupcov was wondering why Alexandr hadn't yet put any pressure on Andrew to reveal the secret plan of the Russian physicist's defection tonight. Now Andrew had left for the embassy. It seemed that Alexandr had failed his mission. The General had become upset, and immediately ordered six agents in two cars to follow Andrew en route to the embassy. He instructed these six agents to intercept the defection when they had the right opportunity. He had then contacted Lieutenant Smirnov, the chief of local KGB headquarters, to get in touch with Alexandr and question him about this. He even instructed Lieutenant Smirnov that, if necessary, he should arrest Alexandr when he reported, and he immediately gave an order to activate Alexandr's bug tracking network. From this tracking network, he would know where Alexandr was exactly within a minute or two.

Right after Alexandr hung up the phone, he got dressed for a long trip. Taking his gun out of his luggage and checking it again to make sure it was loaded, he put the gun into his jacket pocket. Once he had reassured himself that everything was ready, he called a taxi and left the hotel. He asked the taxi driver to take him to downtown Riga where there would be a lot of traffic at this hour. He expected that General Kupcov would soon activate his bug-tracking network, if he hadn't already, and would be able to locate him in a very short time. The bug had to be gotten rid of as soon as possible.

Once the taxi arrived on the busiest downtown street, Alexandr started speaking in the back seat of the cab, addressing his remarks to General Kupcov, who he knew would be listening on the other end of the bug's transmitter,

"Генерал Капков, я застрял по пути. На дороге был несчастный случай. Пожалуйста, передайте сообщение Лейтенанту Смирнову." ("General Kupcov, I am stuck in heavy traffic. There was an accident on the road. Please pass this message to Lieutenant Smirnov.") He hoped that this message would buy him extra time and perhaps even confuse General Kupcov for a while.

Before the taxi arrived at the next traffic light, Alexandr quickly took the bug out of his top pocket and tucked it in the car under the seat. While the taxi driver was wondering to whom Alexandr had been talking, the taxi had reached the next intersection and stopped at a traffic light. Alexandr gave a signal to the driver to pull to the curb, where he paid the fare, giving the driver double the amount that the meter showed. The taxi driver was shocked at the amount of money in his hand, and thanked Alexandr profusely as he stepped out of the car. Naturally, the driver wasn't aware that his cab would be stopped by the KGB in just a short while.

Alexandr suspected that, in addition to the tracking device he carried, there would also be agents assigned to follow him once he left the hotel. As soon as he stepped out of the car, he entered a shopping center and mingled with the big crowd of people there. He drifted with the crowd until he reached the other side of the center, then hopped into another taxi and quickly left the place. After about ten minutes of checking anxiously out the cab windows, he was sure that he was not being followed. Feeling somewhat safe once again, he asked the taxi to turn around and drive back toward the American Embassy.

At the same time, General Kupcov was able to see with the tracking system that Alexandr was heading in the wrong direction for his meeting with Lieutenant Smirnov. There was no way for the General to know that he was tracking the wrong taxi to a different location. He contacted Lieutenant Smirnov and asked him to send people out to search for Alexandr and arrest him immediately.

Just 15 minutes later, while driving toward the American Embassy, Alexandr saw that the taxi he had taken earlier had been stopped and was being searched by two KGB agents at the corner of a street. Another agent was questioning the driver. Alexandr quickly hid his face down and behind his jacket until his taxi passed the area. A cold sweat broke out on his body. The speed with which the KGB had located the bug took him by surprise. If he still carried it, he would have been arrested already.

When Alexandr saw the American flag a couple blocks ahead, he yelled to the driver, "Pull over right here. In the dark...." He again overpaid the driver, then stepped out of the cab and into the shadows.

In Riga, Latvia, the American Embassy was located at Raina bulvans. Just across the street, there was a large national park called Bastion Hill (Bastejkalns). In the center of the park, there was an arched bridge over the city canal, Pilsetas Kanals. The park was very beautiful and had always been a popular place for people to take walks and relax. Beyond the park toward the Daugava River, on the street, Kalku Str., was the famous Riga Polytechnical Institute. The distance from the national park to this institute was only about three tenths of a mile. That meant the distance from Riga Polytechnical Institute to the American Embassy was only about four tenths of a mile. In the other direction, about three tenths of a mile to the east of Riga Polytechnical Institute, was Hotel Riga. That placed these four important sites – the American Embassy, Bastion Hill National Park, Riga Polytechnical Institute, and Hotel Riga - all within a circle of about four tenths of a mile from each other in Riga's central area.

When General Kupcov received the report from Lieutenant Smirnov that they had found the bug but no Alexandr, he was furious. He contacted the two KGB agents assigned to follow Alexandr and was told they had lost him in a crowd.

Contemplating where Alexandr could have gone, he thought, "There are two possibilities. One, Alexandr has a contact in downtown Riga for his defection, or, two, he is planning to meet Andrew somewhere to escape with him."

Having come to this conclusion, General Kupcov immediately instructed Lieutenant Smirnov to have all his agents focus on the Riga downtown area in their search for Alexandr. He also contacted those KGB agents who were following Andrew and told them to be on the alert for Alexandr's possible appearance.

By now it was almost 6:45. Though there was still some light from the sky, it grew darker every minute. Alexandr peered out from the shadows of his hiding place to see if he could spot any KGB agents who might be keeping an eye on Andrew while he was at the embassy. He knew that Andrew would have been followed when he left the hotel. He also knew that these KGB agents might have already received an instruction to arrest him from General Kupcov. He must be very cautious and alert now. If he were caught, it would be death to him. He looked around carefully but couldn't see anybody near the embassy. In fact, the street was almost empty. Since there were many western embassies located in this area, there were not usually too many people on the street after 6 p.m.

Suddenly Alexandr saw some movement in the shadows on the next block. He quickly relocated himself and climbed a tree nearby. In just a minute or so, two KGB agents reached his original hiding place and came to stand directly under the tree in which he was hiding. He could see them much more clearly now. Holding himself motionless and breathing as quietly as possible, he eavesdropped on their conversation, discovering that four KGB agents had been ordered by General Kupcov to search for him around the embassy area. Two drivers remained in the cars. While they were searching for him, the agents kept watch on the main entrance to the embassy. A few minutes later they moved on. Now, Alexandr believed that the safest place to hide was probably in this tree.

When it was nearly 7, Alexandr knew it was time to act. He descended from the tree quietly and cautiously, his heartbeat getting faster and faster and his palms starting to sweat. Every step must be taken carefully now. He looked around and relocated himself to another dark place near where three taxis were parked waiting for potential passengers. There were always a few taxis in this area since almost all embassy employees took taxis home once they finished their work. Often some employees would work late. These taxi drivers were happy to wait for them since they always paid with handsome tips.

Alexandr stayed silently in the darkness and waited for any further development. Suddenly, he saw Andrew come out of the embassy with another person. The embassy's car immediately picked the two of them up and drove them away. The four KGB agents who had been searching for Alexandr just as quickly went running toward their cars on the other side of embassy and, within 15 seconds, he saw them come speeding out of the darkness in two cars following Andrew's car. Cold sweat ran down from his forehead. He knew that if he had been in a taxi coming from that direction, he would have been spotted in the headlights by these KGB. That would be a big disaster.

Alexandr hopped in the taxi parked nearest him and asked the driver to follow the cars that had just sped away but to also keep back a safe distance. He needed to keep watch to see if everything would go according to plan. He knew if anything were to go wrong, they would need to change the plan quickly.

Within ten minutes, Andrew's car arrived at Bastion Hill Park and came to a stop. Andrew and his partner from the embassy left their car and walked into the park. The two KGB cars also stopped at the park, opening their doors to expel four KGB agents who immediately hurried after Andrew. Alexandr asked his taxi, which had stopped a short distance away, to wait for him while he also entered the park, intent on following the followers. Alexandr had undertaken surveillance training when he was in training camp, and was able to tail them expertly, without being detected. He knew exactly how to deal with the situation.

In this way – Andrew and his partner, the KGB following them, and Alexandr following the KGB – all came to the center of the park where the arched bridge, Pilsetas Kanals, was located over the city canal. Standing on the bridge a man and a woman stood waiting for Andrew and his partner. The four exchanged just a few words before immediately turning to walk out of the park together, getting into the embassy car and driving away. The KGB agents rushed to both stay hidden from their quarry and also return to their cars where they quickly resumed following the embassy car and its occupants while

Alexandr, back in his taxi, again followed the KGB.

Andrew's car drove at top speed toward the A9 highway. The KGB cars followed behind, trying to find a location in which to stop them. Nearly 20 minutes into the car chase Andrew's partner from the embassy turned to Andrew, who was faithfully wearing in his top coat pocket the sapphire pen Alexandr had given him and introduced the man and the woman that they had collected at Pilsetas Kanals.

"Mr. Steinberg, I would like to introduce you to our guests, Mr. Brown and Ms. Whidden. Both of them work for the British Embassy."

When General Kupcov heard this and saw the faces from Andrew's pen's spy camera and listening device, he was shocked and frozen for a moment. Suddenly, he realized that they had entered into a CIA trap. This was a decoy. The real defection was happening somewhere else. He immediately gave an order to check the airport in Latvia. He also ordered one of the cars carrying two KGB officers to return to the downtown center immediately and ordered the other car with two KGB officers to continue following Andrew's car.

Andrew and his partner, Erik Taylor, the officer working at the American Embassy in Latvia, knew that they would be followed. They had kept on the A9 highway and, once they were sure they had provided enough time for their plan, they purposely revealed the identities of the British workers.

Defection

In Riga Polytechnical Institute, an all-day conference was being held. There were hundreds of scientists that had come from all of the eastern Communist countries and also some from western countries. There were also five scientists from Moscow University and six from other known Russian universities participating in the conference. All of the participating Russian scientists were being followed and watched by the KGB. General Kupcov was aware that one of them would be trying to defect but didn't know which one. The first level of information he obtained from the American Embassy was not clear. Therefore, he ordered eleven KGB agents to follow these eleven professors.

Professor Olenin, after he finished his speech, stayed at the conference for about an hour before walking back to his hotel, Hotel Riga, a little before 7 o'clock. He believed that he had done a good job in today's speech. Though he was nervous, outwardly he remained calm and confident. He knew that tonight would be the most important night of his and his wife's entire life. When he arrived at their hotel room his wife, Alena, was ready and waiting for him. From her facial expression, it was easy to see that she was very nervous. Her legs were trembling. When she saw her husband, she immediately stood up and gathered her things. Professor Olenin and his wife went down to the check-in counter area where a man with a jacket was waiting for them. The professor shook his hand and then this gentleman bowed to the lady.

As they moved to leave the hotel, many people were just stepping in, forcing Professor Olenin and his wife to squeeze their way through. In the process, the professor felt someone bump into him, but he didn't pay much attention to it. Finally, they were able to get out of the hotel and get into a car that had been waiting for them. Immediately, they drove away. The agent who had just bumped into Professor Olenin also quickly jumped into a car, and he and his partner set out to follow Professor Olenin's car. While they were driving, the signal of the tracking device that had been planted in the professor's pocket appeared on the tracking screen in the car. This signal was also being transmitted to General Kupcov's desk. By this time, they were still not sure if Professor Olenin was the one going to defect.

Once they left the city, the car that the KGB officers were following picked up speed. Naturally, the KGB car picked up speed as well. The two cars drove very quickly toward the west of Riga on highway A9. Just a few minutes later, the KGB agents realized that they, too, were being followed by another car that did not belong to the KGB. They reported this to General Kupcov. It was obvious to them that the car following them was either American CIA or British MI6, and that it was escorting the professor's car. This situation had General Kupcov pretty convinced that Professor Olenin was the one going to defect tonight. From the direction they were heading in, he figured out their possible methods of escape. He knew that there were only two possibilities. One was by boat from the small city of Ventspils located on the west coast of Latvia. The other was to escape by air from the small city Liepaja that was about 60 miles to the south of Ventspils. Liepaja had a small airport that they could fly out of. Knowing that he could not ask just those two agents to intercept the professor's car and arrest him since only two could not defeat a group of CIA or MI6, the general immediately notified two of the four KGB agents following Andrew's car to change their route and join the KGB who were following Professor Olenin's car. Unfortunately, it would take at least 30 minutes for the agents from Andrew's detail to catch up with the professor's detail. Then, since he didn't know how many CIA or MI6 agents were helping the professor, the general also ordered any other available KGB agents to cease whatever they were doing and join the chase of the professor's car as backup.

All cars were now running very fast on the A9 highway. Before the professor's car reached the town of Saldus, half way to the west coast of Latvia, the escort who met Professor Olenin at the hotel said, "I've just been notified that we are being followed."

The professor's and his wife's faces immediately tensed up with anxiety. The professor's wife, Alena, began trembling again. Professor Olenin suddenly realized that he might have been bugged when he stepped out of the hotel. He remembered he had been bumped by some rude guy as he stepped out of the door. Immediately, he checked his pockets and found a tracking bug in his right-hand wind-coat pocket. His face turned pale as he held it out and looked at the escort agent.

"Give it to me, Professor Olenin," the escort said.

When the car reached to the town of Saldus the road split in two directions, one going to the town of Ventspils, near the west coast of Latvia, and the other going to Liepaja, which was also on the west coast of Latvia about 60 miles south of Ventspils. Right before they reached the split, the escort threw the tracking bug out the window.

Meanwhile, after a little over an hour of driving, Andrew's car finally arrived at a port in Cape Kolka, next to the Baltic Sea. This town was located northwest of Riga, about 75 miles (120 km) from Riga center. Once they arrived, they drove straight to a dock near the beach, exiting the car and entering a small house. Alexandr, who had known their intended destination and had had his taxi speed ahead, was already there and waiting in his taxi when he saw the two KGB agents park their car some distance away from where he was. One of the agents stepped out and followed Andrew's group to the house while the other one remained in the car, presumably reporting in to KGB headquarters. Alexandr paid his taxi driver, giving him a handsome amount of money for his efforts. Alexandr was confident now that everything was going according to plan and he would no longer need the taxi. The driver was shocked by the amount of money he received, but to Alexandr, all of the rubles would not be useful anyway.

As his taxi drove away, Alexandr approached the KGB's car carefully and swiftly. When he was near, he overheard the KGB officer receiving his instructions from headquarters. The agents were to just keep an eye on developments and not to arrest anyone since there were no Russians or Latvians inside the little house, only American and British Embassy employees.

When the KGB agent stepped out of his car and put his hat on, he found a gun was pointed at his head. Before he could realize what was happening, he had been knocked out by the handle of the gun. Alexandr put both the agent's hands behind him and handcuffed them together. Then he took the agent's hat, putting it on his own head, and stealthily approached the second KGB agent in the darkness. When the other KGB officer saw him, he mistakenly thought he was his partner. By the time he realized that this approaching person was not his partner, Alexandr already had a gun pressed to the man's forehead. The agent was shocked motionless in surprise. He was ordered to turn around and face away from his captor. Just as the agent realized that his captor was Alexandr, the Russian secret agent they had been searching for, Alexandr knocked him out cold with the butt of the gun and again handcuffed his hands behind him.

Alexandr went to the door of the house and knocked: Knock, Knock-knock, Knock-knock, the secret code agreed upon between him and Andrew. Andrew opened the door and was overjoyed to see Alexandr standing in front of him, smiling and safe.

"Thank God you're here! I have been so worried about you."

"Everything is okay," Alexandr reassured Andrew. "Two KGB officers are down outside, handcuffed."

They did not waste any time, but immediately everyone left the house and ran out onto the dock, where they took a fast speedboat and headed for the West German coast. Andrew took the sapphire pen out of his pocket and threw it into the sea. He knew if he kept it, they could be tracked. Although, given the super-fast speedboat they were in, even if the Latvian coast guard found them and chased them they would have little chance of being caught. Furthermore, they would be in international sea territory in just half an hour.

A Surprise

When General Kupcov realized what had happened, his face turned red and his body shook with his anger.

"If I catch this betrayer, I will take care of him by myself," the general swore.

General Kupcov contacted the coast guard in Latvia, but it was too late. The speedboat was already well on its way toward international waters and there were hundreds of boats in the sea. It was not possible to catch them.

Farther south along the western coast, the two KGB officers who were following the professor's car finally came to the small airport LPX in Liepaja. The driver could see the professor's car heading toward a small jet which already had its engine running. The officers didn't know what to do. One jumped out of the car and ran to the control room. When he saw two workers were tied up on the floor there, he was shocked. Before he knew it, he was knocked out from behind. The KGB agent who had remained in the car was also subdued in a couple minutes.

Actually, four CIA agents had arrived at the airport just a half hour earlier. Since it was a small airport and there were no planes going out or coming in at that time, there were only two employees in the control room. The CIA agents had easily disarmed them and handcuffed their hands behind them. Five minutes later, a private jet landed and parked on the runway. When the four agents saw the embassy car approach about 25 minutes later, they knew "Eagle" was ready to take off. Once the airplane had taken off safely, they left immediately. They knew a big group of enemies would arrive soon.

Within 12 minutes, a group of four KGB agents arrived, followed only five minutes later by Lieutenant Smirnov's people. But it was too late. Once the newly arrived agents saw one KGB agent knocked out on the ground, another handcuffed in a car, and the two control tower officers on the floor inside, they knew that they were too late. They contacted General Kupcov in Moscow to let him know about the situation. The general knew that even if he requested an interception by air, it would be too late. The small private jet had already entered international air space. General Kupcov sat completely frozen in his chair. This mission was a complete failure. He did not know how he was going to report this to the top Communist officer. Now it would be hard for him to defend himself.

Freedom

On the airplane, a British secret agent was trying to help Professor Olenin, and his wife adjust to the situation. The tension on the professor's face reflected just how nervous he was. His wife, next to him, had not ceased trembling since the beginning of the action. The couple sat there stiffly while the British agent tried to ease their tension, but he failed. About half an hour later, their pilot saw three American fighter jets take up positions in front of them, and he established communication with them. These fighter jets were based in West Germany and had been ordered to escort this small jet safely to their base.

The pilot told the passengers over the telecom, "Lady and gentlemen, we are now under the escort of American fighter jets. Everything is safe."

Professor Olenin smiled as his tension disappeared. Because the pilot had spoken in English, the professor translated the announcement for his wife. She could not help the tears that flowed from her eyes. Now they knew they could expect to see their 16-year-old son, an exchange student in London, within just a day or so.

Back on the speedboat traveling quickly away from the coast of Latvia, Andrew introduced Alexandr to everyone: three British agents including the captain, and Erik Taylor, the American Embassy employee. The captain brought out a bottle of champagne and gave it to a British agent, who opened it and poured it into six cups.

"Congratulations everyone. To a successful mission and to your futures," he toasted.

Alexandr looked first at Andrew and then at everyone else with a smile, "Thank you all so very much. I don't know how to pay you back." When he said this, his eyes turned red.

"Alexandr, you're in the free world now." Andrew looked at him with so much joy. Definitely, this was the best champagne they had ever had.

"What will happen to me?" Alexandr asked Andrew.

Actually, Andrew did not know. He looked at the British agent, expecting him to answer the question.

"From what I understand, when we arrive in West Germany you will be immediately transferred to England. There you will be questioned by both the British and American sides. When you have answered all of their questions, you will be placed in a protection program. You will remain in this program until all disturbances with regard to you cease. Usually, that takes a couple of years."

"Where will I be in the future?" Alexandr asked.

"I don't know. Normally, they will ask you where you would like to go and, if possible, respect your request. But your choices will be limited to England or the U.S."

Alexandr looked at Andrew. He knew where he wanted to go. "I want to go to America, Andrew. I want to be where you will be," he thought.

"How can I ever try to find you in America, if I ever become free to do so?" Alexandr asked Andrew.

"Contact my dad. He always knows where I am," Andrew replied and quickly found a piece of paper to write down his father's telephone number for Alexandr.

When they arrived in West Germany, authorities were waiting to quickly whisk Alexandr away. Alexandr and Andrew gazed at each other for as long as possible, looking intently into each other's eyes to express wordlessly what they could not say in public. This would be their last memory of each other for some time.

Within only a day or so, Alexandr had been transferred to England to be questioned. Andrew didn't have another chance to see him before he was gone.

Once in England, Alexandr was questioned by both British MI6 and American CIA. Now these intelligence agencies began to realize how many secrets in the western countries were being revealed to the Russian KGB through the western embassies. They immediately notified all the friendly western countries about this. All American Embassy employees had their backgrounds thoroughly re-reviewed, some were even secretly tailed by CIA agents for a while, and all of their Russian friends were investigated. The search for the two American Embassy workers in Moscow who had betrayed the United States unexpectedly turned up not two but three, while the embassy building itself was remodeled and swept for bugs, turning up five.

As for the Russian side of things, Alexandr's defection had caused the KGB authorities a serious headache. The network they had worked hard to establish for more than ten years was broken down. Now they would have to change their strategies and start from the beginning.

Andrew stayed at the air force base in West Germany for two days of questioning and was then ordered to return to America immediately.

7
FREEDOM

Andrew returned to the United States on August 12th of 1984 and was transferred to another department for a less classified job in Washington, DC. What had happened in Moscow had made the CIA lose their trust in him. He was assigned to a less important job that was not crucial to the government's security. The lateral transfer was not a demotion *per se*, but it still had the effect of Andrew losing his enthusiasm and motivation at work. He was very disappointed and became increasingly depressed. Within a month or so, his personal belongings from his Moscow apartment and office were shipped back to him by the American Embassy.

A couple of days after his arrival, Andrew found out that only two months after his departure to Moscow, his girlfriend Judy had already begun to go out with another guy named Ben. Now Andrew understood why he hadn't received an answer from her whenever he tried to contact her. He was very upset to learn about it, but the knowledge didn't take him completely off guard as he had already entertained thoughts that she might have done something like this.

Judy, for her part, was surprised when she heard that Andrew had returned from Moscow so soon. After she found out that he was back, she tracked him down in his new office, arriving unannounced one afternoon. She apologized to Andrew and expressed her regret. She was not happy in her relationship with Ben, and it had recently fallen apart. She said that she wished to come back and be with Andrew again. They talked for a long time.

Though he was willing to talk to her and politely heard what she had to say, due to his past experience with Judy, Andrew turned down her offer. He felt that he couldn't trust her anymore. He opted instead to just keep himself busy with work and with visiting his family and friends more often and tried in this way to reduce his feelings of depression and loneliness. In reality, he was just biding his time, waiting to hear from Alexandr. But a lot of time went by and he never did.

Day by day, Andrew's depression got deeper and deeper. He could not forget the time he had spent with Alexandr and the rare connection they had shared. Though they had known each other for less than two months in Moscow, the memories would stay with him forever.

A year passed and it was time for the annual party offered by the CIA in a public garden on Labor Day weekend. More than 500 people were there, including participants working for the government and the families and friends they brought with them. The weather was beautiful, and the temperature was just right for a perfect cookout. Good food and drinks were abundant, as well as some entertainments sponsored by the government. The party grounds were alive with the sounds of children running around and being happy.

Andrew, after thinking about it for a while, had come to the party with the express purpose of finding a new girlfriend. It was hard to move on, after the wonderful relationship he had had with Alexandr, but he could not continue living this way. When he arrived at the party, he was surprised to see that Judy was also there standing on the other side of the garden. He was thinking of leaving to avoid any face-to-face contact with her when she saw him and walked toward him.

"Andrew, long time no see. I hope you're doing well," she greeted him.

"Uh, hi Judy. It's a surprise to see you here. I wouldn't have thought you'd want to join this kind of party."

"Well, my boss invited me personally. He wanted to introduce me to his family. So, I came just to be social for a while. Actually, I am very happy to see you here."

Though it had been more than a year since Judy talked to Andrew after his return from Moscow, she still had not found a lover she really liked. To her, the important part of any relationship was the sex, and Andrew was still the best sex partner she had ever had. She had tried calling Andrew several times but had never received a call back from him. Meeting him at the party offered her a new opportunity to persuade him to get back together again. She tried assuming a more polite and humble demeanor that would hopefully demonstrate to Andrew that she had changed and matured.

"I miss you a lot, you know," she said with a little smile.

Andrew just looked at her smiling at him. He took his time, seeing how he felt about her now, and it seemed that the anger he had had was no longer as strong as when he was freshly returned from Moscow, especially after more than a year of loneliness and depression. He really needed some companionship and he began to recall what it had been like to have sex with Judy.

"She is awfully good looking, and really very skillful in bed," Andrew thought.

Judy could sense that Andrew was wavering. He seemed to not be as angry as the last time they met and that encouraged her. "Let's just talk for a while like old friends," she suggested. "No hard feelings, okay? Let's go get some food and drink and chat for a while."

Andrew looked into her eyes with a smile. After they got something to eat, they found a spot in the shade to sit down and talk for a while. They avoided talking about unhappy things. Judy was respectful of almost everything Andrew said, and for a couple hours they had a good time together. Then it was time for Andrew to leave since he had an appointment to get together with Paul and Jeff, the old friends he used to swim with. Occasionally, since Andrew returned, they met and had drinks in a club.

"I must go. I have to meet my friends in an hour," Andrew said.

"Please give me a call, Andrew," Judy implored as she gave him her business card.

A few days later, Judy called Andrew to invite him out for dinner. Since Andrew had had a fairly good time with her at the government party, he thought perhaps she had changed, and so, he accepted her invitation. Surprisingly, she took him to a Japanese restaurant for sushi. During dinner, Judy apologized again for her previous behavior and expressed her wish to get together with Andrew. The conversation went well, and they had a good evening.

After a few days of consideration, and in spite of the fact that he didn't feel completely comfortable about it, Andrew still decided to take Judy back. He was lonely, and desperate to regain some feeling of companionship. So, they started going out together again. However, Andrew soon realized he didn't have the same feeling with Judy that he used to. There was no getting around the chasm between them. He knew this was for two reasons. One, she had dumped him. It was just like a broken mirror - even though it had been glued back together, it did not matter because the crack would always be seen. Two, he just really missed the time he had spent with Alexandr, and the honest and sincere relationship between them. Andrew just could not forget him. Their relationship was a rare experience, and he knew that he might never find another person that he could connect with so deeply. He resigned himself to living life in this way, a pale comparison to the love he had experienced.

Time passed in a bit of a haze. Andrew buried himself in his work and fought against bouts of depression that sometimes lasted for weeks. Alexandr had now been in the government's safety protection program for more than two years and Andrew still had not heard from him. There was no way that Andrew could contact him. And no one, except a few highly classified personnel, would ever know where he was. He missed Alexandr so very much, especially whenever he had a fight with Judy.

After about 11 months of going out together, Judy's personality shifted back into its original pattern: aggressive and dominating. The way she treated him once again made Andrew very uneasy. On October 11, 1986, a Saturday, Andrew had a huge fight with her during dinner in a restaurant. It was her birthday and a week previously, Judy had given him a hint of what she wanted from him, a diamond ring. She implied, strongly, that she was ready to marry Andrew. Andrew, however, had no desire to marry her. When Andrew offered her a gold bracelet for her birthday instead of the diamond she was expecting, her disappointment quickly turned to anger. They had a huge fight right in the restaurant, and she again made an embarrassing scene. Judy could feel that Andrew just didn't love her.

Andrew returned home from the restaurant still upset and unable to figure out how to handle the situation. He turned on the TV to watch the 10 o'clock evening news and saw a report that the General Secretary of the Communist Party of the Soviet Union, Mikhail Gorbachev, and the American President, Ronald Reagan, had met together in Reykjavik, Iceland to discuss reducing intermediate-range nuclear weapons in Europe. As he watched the report, he began to realize that the Communist system was collapsing, and the cold war was over. He was numb with shock and almost stopped breathing for a moment. "Gorbachev will be the greatest Communist leader in human history," he thought. While he was still absorbing this sudden news and its potential effects, the telephone rang.

"Andrew! This is Alexandr. I got your number from your dad only five minutes ago. I have a new name, Tony Rones."

Andrew immediately recognized the much-loved voice he heard on the phone. He sat frozen for a moment, and then burst into tears.

"Alexandr! I am so glad to hear your voice. I have been waiting for this call for more than two years! How are you doing? Are you well?"

"I'm very good. I stay in a small town, Tucson, Arizona now. They told me that I should keep away from big cities for a few years. I bought a small parcel of land here in the countryside. I am very happy here in America, I just miss you so very much," Alexandr said.

"What are you doing now?"

"Actually, both the British and American governments gave me some money to help me settle down here. I set up a small gym and have been teaching martial arts in this town for a year already."

"Why didn't you call me earlier?"

"I couldn't. They told me that I must keep myself out of reach from anyone I have known until it was safe. You know I must listen to their advice. They tried to protect me. But now I have just received a phone call from them and they told me that I am completely safe, and I can contact anyone I like! You know, the Russian Communist Party is collapsing. The Cold War is almost over. I don't have to worry about them anymore!" Alexandr said with a trembling voice.

Andrew could feel how much excitement and joy Alexandr had when he heard the news.

"You are the first one I called. No, the second. The first one was your dad. I am so glad you gave me your dad's phone number on the boat, otherwise I wouldn't have known how to find you!" Alexandr was very emotional. Andrew could tell that he was tearing up as he talked.

"Can we meet sometime? I want to see you. I miss you so much," Andrew said.

"Actually, I was hoping you would move here and stay with me. You know, I have a house and about ten acres of land. I would love for you to come and stay with me. Would you?"

"Really? You want me there? I will find a way! Don't worry. If I come, I believe I can easily find a job there. Give me your phone number and address."

Alexandr told him his telephone number and address which Andrew carefully wrote down. They talked about the past and their imagined future together until nearly midnight. When they were too tired to talk anymore, they hung up.

The Secrecy

On the following Monday, Andrew went to his boss's office and handed in his resignation with the standard two weeks' notice, which his boss approved. He could barely contain his excitement. His new life would begin in two weeks. Andrew went back to his office and immediately called his travel agent for a ticket to Tucson.

Two weeks later, Andrew was on the airplane. He closed his eyes and recalled all that had happened over the last three years. He knew clearly what he really wanted in his life – to step off the path of traditional expectation that he had been on and be true to his own spirit. There was nothing else now but his freedom of feeling and action. He was very confident that he had made the right choice. He knew that he was on the right path toward finding his freedom of expression. He felt that he was like an eagle flying in the sky. Free.

ABOUT THE AUTHOR

Dr. Yang, Jwing-Ming was born on August 11, 1946, in Xinzhu Xian (新竹縣), Taiwan (台灣), Republic of China (中華民國). He started his wushu (武術) (gongfu or kung fu, 功夫) training at the age of fifteen under Shaolin White Crane (Shaolin Bai He, 少林白鶴) Master Cheng, Gin-Gsao (曾金灶). Master Cheng originally learned taizuquan (太祖拳) from his grandfather when he was a child. When Master Cheng was fifteen years old, he started learning White Crane from Master Jin, Shao-Feng (金紹峰) and followed him for twenty-three years until Master Jin's death.

In thirteen years of study (1961–1974) under Master Cheng, Dr. Yang became an expert in the White Crane style of Chinese martial arts, which includes both the use of bare hands and various weapons, such as saber, staff, spear, trident, two short rods, and many others. With the same master, he also studied White Crane qigong (白鶴氣功), qin na or chin na (擒拿), tui na (推拿), and dian xue massages (點穴按摩) and herbal treatment.

At sixteen, Dr. Yang began the study of Yang-style taijiquan (楊氏太極拳) under Master Kao Tao (高濤). He later continued his study of taijiquan under Master Li, Mao- Ching (李茂清). Master Li learned his taijiquan from the well-known Master Han, Ching-Tang (韓慶堂). From this further practice, Dr. Yang was able to master the taiji bare-hand sequence, pushing hands, the two-man fighting sequence, taiji sword, taiji saber, and taiji qigong.

When Dr. Yang was eighteen years old, he entered Tamkang College (淡江學院) in Taipei Xian to study physics. In college, he began the study of traditional Shaolin Long Fist (Changquan or Chang

Chuan, 長拳) with Master Li, Mao-Ching at the Tamkang College Guoshu Club (淡江國術社), 1964–1968, and eventually became an assistant instructor under Master Li. In 1971 he completed his MS degree in physics at the National Taiwan University (台灣大學) and then served in the Chinese Air Force from 1971 to 1972. In the service, Dr. Yang taught physics at the Junior Academy of the Chinese Air Force (空軍幼校) while also teaching wushu. After being honorably discharged in 1972, he returned to Tamkang College to teach physics and resumed study under Master Li, Mao-Ching. From Master Li, Dr. Yang learned Northern-style Wushu, which includes bare-hand and kicking techniques as well as numerous weapons.

In 1974 Dr. Yang came to the United States to study mechanical engineering at Purdue University. At the request of a few students, Dr. Yang began to teach gongfu (kung fu), which resulted in the establishment of the Purdue University Chinese Kung Fu Research Club in the spring of 1975. While at Purdue, Dr. Yang also taught college-credit courses in taijiquan. In May 1978, he was awarded a PhD in mechanical engineering by Purdue.

In 1980 Dr. Yang moved to Houston to work for Texas Instruments. While in Houston, he founded Yang's Shaolin Kung Fu Academy, which was eventually taken over by his disciple, Mr. Jeffery Bolt, after Dr. Yang moved to Boston in 1982. Dr. Yang founded Yang's Martial Arts Academy in Boston on October 1, 1982.

In January 1984, he gave up his engineering career to devote more time to research, writing, and teaching. In March 1986, he purchased property in the Jamaica Plain area of Boston to be used as the headquarters of the new organization, Yang's Martial Arts Association (YMAA). The organization expanded to become a division of Yang's Oriental Arts Association, Inc. (YOAA).

In 2008 Dr. Yang began the nonprofit YMAA California Retreat Center. This training facility in rural California is where selected students enroll in a five-year to ten-year residency to learn Chinese martial arts.

Dr. Yang has been involved in traditional Chinese wushu since 1961, studying Shaolin White Crane (Bai He), Shaolin Long Fist (Changquan), and taijiquan under several different masters. He has taught for more than forty-six years: seven years in Taiwan, five years at Purdue University, two years in Houston, twenty-six years in Boston, and more than eight years at the YMAA California Retreat Center. He has taught seminars all over the world, sharing his knowledge of Chinese martial arts and qigong in Argentina, Austria, Barbados, Botswana, Belgium, Bermuda, Brazil, Canada, China, Chile, England, Egypt, France, Germany, Hungary, Iceland, Ireland, Italy, Latvia, Mexico, the Netherlands, New Zealand, Poland, Portugal, Saudi Arabia, South Africa, Spain, Switzerland, and Venezuela.

Since 1986 YMAA has become an international organization, which currently includes more than fifty schools located in Argentina, Belgium, Canada, Chile, France, Hungary, Iran, Ireland, Italy, New Zealand, Poland, Portugal, South Africa, Sweden, the United Kingdom, the United States, and Venezuela.

Many of Dr. Yang's books and videos have been translated into other languages, such as French, Italian, Spanish, Polish, Czech, Bulgarian, Russian, German, and Hungarian

For more books by Dr. Yang, Jwing-Ming please go to the YMAA Publishing website.

https://ymaa.com/publishing

Dr. Yang, Jwing-Ming